By Ronald Ady Crouch

ISBN: 978-1-77145-353-0

BWL
Books We Love, Ltd.
Chestermere, Alberta
Canada

Ronald Ady Crouch Copyright 2015

Cover art by Michelle Lee Copyright 2015

All rights reserved. Without limiting the rights under copyright reserved above, no part of this publication may be reproduced, stored in or introduced into a retrieval system, or transmitted, in any form, or by any means (electronic, mechanical, photocopying, recording, or otherwise) without the prior written permission of both the copyright owner and the above publisher of this book.

This is a work of fiction. Names, characters, places and events in the story are either a product of the author's imagination or have been used fictitiously. Any resemblance to actual people, living or dead is entirely coincidental.

Dedication

To the good guys on the front line

If without laws there is anarchy, what is there when there are no consequences?
Ronald Ady Crouch. 1998.

Acknowledgment

For me, writing a novel is the easy part, a solitary endeavour, but never lonely. As the story unfolds my characters come to life and together we craft the story. The challenging part is getting published. Without my agent, my best friend, my wife Catherine my characters and I would remain unknown. Thanks to her, this is my third novel with Books We Love. A special thank you to Judith Pittman of BWL for her support, advice and patience. My thanks also to David Goldenberg who has seen action in Afghanistan and very kindly provided advice. Thanks to my stepson Chris Salewski for providing technical computer support. Thanks to my Special Forces contact for his expertise. To Bob; still waters run deep my friend. To my good friend Sean, your contribution had me in fits. To my three children, Oliver, Melanie and Alaister. Without realizing it, you were the inspiration for my storytelling.

Prologue

In September 1985, four Russian diplomats were kidnapped in Beirut by Moslem fundamentalists. They murdered one of their hostages. Russia sent over a team of their elite Special Forces units, Spetsznas. They in turn, abducted twelve fundamentalists, decapitated one of them, and sent the head back to the group's leader in a box. With a message. *Release our three hostages or we will shoot yours, one by one.* The three hostages were released. Years later, one of the original members of that Spetsznas team made a very poignant statement, *The British and the Americans don't have the stomach for such things, they play by the rules. We Russians don't play by the rules.*

I've lived my life outside the rules of accepted conformity. It's served me well. I'm not constricted by modern-day niceties. In fact, I don't play by the rules at all. Exodus Chapters 21-23. An eye for an eye. I hope that's going to be inscribed on my headstone, assuming I have one. As for turning the other cheek, I've never been an advocate of that biblical philosophy. Why let your adversary break your jaw on both sides of your face. In the real world, that's just plain stupid.

* * *

The heat was oppressive. The Humvee's ac had long since packed up, the least of our worries at the moment, as we made our way along the excuse-for-a-road in southern Kandahar. Like warm rain gathering on a hot windshield, the sweat began to pool between my shoulder blades before running down my back in tiny rivulets. I could feel the uncomfortable wetness at the back of my skivvies and longed for a shower when we got back to base camp. It would be at least another two hours of driving across the Red Desert before we got back there. A desolate landscape of hard packed sand and rock, stretching for miles. Like my three fellow buddies from Special Forces Two Squadron, we never stopped scanning the horizon for signs of the enemy as our small convoy rolled and pitched over the sand.

"Sam, I do believe it's your turn to buy the beers when we get back to Canada. My noon day prediction of Afghanistan's scorching heat was right on the money. Again. Forty-nine degrees Celsius."

I turned to look at the big smiling face of my best friend, doing his best to keep us on the road, his huge hands gripping the wheel like he was driving an eighteen-wheeler. "Leroy, I think you've got inside information on this. Goddamn it, you always nail it. I guess that's why they call you, *The Weatherman.*"

"Come by that name honestly, too. And, that's because, unlike you Mr. Stephens, I'm a good Catholic boy. Got me a direct line to the Almighty hisself."

We all began laughing. Me, the Weatherman, and our two rear passengers, Pete and Andy, on their first tour of duty, and not yet given a nickname.

The flash of intense white and yellow light, and the simultaneous massive explosion, lifted our Humvee clear off the ground. It caught the third vehicle in the convoy. There was nothing recognizable left of the vehicle and nothing left of its occupants to bury with full military honours. Their DNA scattered across the desert.

We were the fifth vehicle from the front, but even so, the Weatherman was decapitated by flying shrapnel, his huge black head spinning across my lap and out through the passenger window. It was Pete and Andy's first, and last tour of duty. As the Humvee went through another somersault, I was ejected from the vehicle, landing hard on the edge of a huge sand dune. When the Humvee finally came back down to earth on its roof, Pete's neck was broken. Andy lay trapped under the roof, with only his head and mangled torso visible. He was screaming. There was smoke, and dust, and flames; all around the convoy, the sound of men crying out for help.

The uninformed believe that if they were sitting in a restaurant and heard an explosion across the street, they would have time to dive to the floor for cover. Think again. The explosive forces would reach you far quicker than a speeding bullet. Everything I witnessed that afternoon happened within the blink of an eye, if not faster.

I was up and running back toward the convoy, to my squadron, to my friends. Andy was still alive when I reached him. The decision still haunts me to this day. With herculean strength, I managed to raise the Humvee's crumpled roof off his body. He bled out immediately. The weight of the vehicle was keeping his arteries and blood vessels closed. I didn't know how severe the gash was across his abdomen. Looking up from his sightless blue eyes, I saw the pick-up trucks racing across the desert toward us. The *Haggis* weren't finished with us yet. And I wasn't done with them either. I raced back down the line of mangled vehicles.

"Contact! Right, five-hundred metres. Dismounted insurgents in open!" Then I saw it.

"In coming!"

The RPG whistled just overhead. No time to help the injured and dying. Pulling back a dead soldier, who moments ago had been manning a machine gun atop one of the undamaged Humvees, I opened up on our approaching killers. There must have been fifty of them. It wouldn't be long before the fight got close and personal.

"Allahu Akbar!" I sent my bearded attacker to meet all those virgins he thought were waiting for him with a bullet through the head. I took his head off with my knife and pushed it into the sand to face his friends.

"That one's for the Weatherman you assholes!" They were, by now, retreating. They knew there'd be some heavy airstrikes coming their way if they stuck around too long.

"Jesus Christ, Sam! What is wrong with you?"

"Sir, you always drilled into us the importance of keeping our heads in the heat of battle. I guess their commanding officer didn't give them the same speech."

"He thinks he's still fighting General Custer."

"Shut up, Malloy, when I need your input, I'll ask for it. I'm gonna have to report this."

"Hang on, sir, I'll make it right." I could feel his eyes on me as I hurried across the hot sand to my handiwork. Quickly I reunited body and head, it wasn't perfect, but I was pleased. I turned toward my lieutenant, a big grin on my face. "There you are sir, good as new. Anyway sir, it was all done in the heat of battle. You know, part of my heritage."

"That's why they call him *The Warrior.*" Lieutenant Reynolds rolled his eyes in frustration.

"Where's the Weatherman?" Malloy took one look at my face and knew. "That's the best bit of news I've heard all day. I owe that asshole ten bucks, guess I won't need to pay him now."

We all loved the Weatherman. I thought for a

moment Malloy was going to lose it and shoot the lieutenant. If it had just been Malloy and me, no-one would have been the wiser.

"Okay," said the lieutenant. "Air support's on the way. Where's our comms guy?"

"Right here Lieutenant."

"Get on the TAC SAT and call in the 9 Line Medevac."

"Yes sir."

"Let's prioritize the injured and have the most severe casualties ready to go first. Des, Jamie, Nick, setup the casualty collection point. Let's get the injured triaged as quickly as possible. Ray, Jack, consolidate the ammo. Stephens, Malloy. Look for the dead and ... You know what I mean. Did anyone take any pictures of anything that went on here?"

"This is a solid bunch, Lieutenant. We take care of our own. What happens in Vegas, stays in Vegas."

"I hope for your sake, Stephens, you're right. At least you didn't scalp him."

"There's still time sir."

Lieutenant Reynolds grimaced.

"Stephens?"

"Yes, sir?"

"You did well. If it hadn't been for you, it might not have turned out so well. But I've still got to report this. You understand?"

"No, sir, I don't. In battle I understand only one thing."

"And what's that?"

"OIV, sir. OIV."

Chapter One

"So you want to join Toronto, Mr. Stephens? Why should we choose you, as opposed to another candidate? Say one who has a degree or two. Don't get me wrong, your resume is excellent. Joint Task Force in the Canadian military, honourably discharged, numerous citations for bravery in the field of battle. Served overseas in Afghanistan, Iraq. Worked on peacekeeping missions with the UN. All very impressive, very impressive indeed."

"I think my resume speaks for itself, gentlemen. As for choosing to become a police officer with this service, I'd like to give back to the community. There are a lot of First Nations people living in Toronto who have a lot of problems. They are unlikely to trust the predominantly white police officers. No disrespect, gentlemen. Being Native, I understand my people. My home is on the reserve. I can help forge a better understanding between my people and the white people, and others who have come to make their home on, Native land."

The Superintendent began reading through a stack of papers, and then looked up at me over the top of his gold-rimmed spectacles. "You're a member of the Cheyrone."

"Yes, sir."

"I know where you are, my wife and I have dined at the casino a few times. You're just outside Port Albert. That's quite a commute into Toronto for you."

"It won't be, sir. I have a small condo down on Harbourfront." My interview panel all looked up at me in unison. It was obvious what they were all thinking. *Indian casino money.*

"Not married?"

"No, sir."

"Living with someone, a significant other, I mean?"

"No, sir. I don't like to be tied down. I couldn't do with all that stress of a wife, or *a significant other,* as you put it, being emotionally upset every time I deployed overseas, worried whether I'd ever come home. It meant I could focus on staying alive better that way. But then, that's just me."

"According to my sources, there have been some rumblings about your soldiering methods. I was advised that you get the job done. It was put something like this. *Stephens would be a great asset in the Russian military.* Would you care to elaborate on that, Mr. Stephens?"

"No, sir. As you know, Superintendent, I worked in Special Forces. Much of my work was Top Secret. I can't talk about what I did in the military. Your police service has an intelligence branch. I'm sure you wouldn't want any of those officers talking about their work."

"There's a rumour that you decapitated some

of the enemy. Is that true?" This from an inspector.

"Gentlemen, as you know, rumours are just that. Rumours. They are fictitious accounts of events that took place, but at which the rumour mongers were never present. Add to that, the nickname I was given by my brothers-in-arms, because I am Aboriginal, and you can see how the rumour got started in the first place."

"And what was your nickname," asked the Superintendent.

"They called me, *The Warrior.*"

"Well, we can't have that sort of nickname being used in this service, that's downright racist if you ask me."

"Superintendent, we all had nicknames on my platoon. My best friend was called, *The Weatherman.*"

"And what's he doing now?"

"Well, Inspector, he's not doing a whole lot. After an improvised explosive device was detonated, he and I went flying out of the Humvee we were in. For a moment I cradled his head in my lap. It was a shame the rest of his body wasn't attached at the time. He looked pretty upset."

The room was silent. A hair falling from anyone's head and hitting the floor would have echoed. "He wasn't upset about losing his body, he was mad that I'd lost the bet that day and it was my turn to buy the beers. When we got back to Canada I drank his beer, in fact I drank a whole lotta beers that night. In fact, gentlemen, I got roaring drunk."

The Superintendent smiled. "My son was in the Airborne. You remind me of him. Such a waste. Good to keep a sense of humour in a crisis like that. Good for you, Stephens. He'd have liked you."

The Inspector again. "Give an example of when you felt prejudice toward someone and how you dealt with that feeling."

"The only example that comes to mind, sir, was in Afghanistan. Part of my military training was as a sniper. My spotter and I were on a high cliff overlooking a huge ravine. On the other side of the ravine was another cliff face, way off in the distance. There were two Haggis, I mean, Taliban tribesmen peeking out from the rocks, high up on the opposite cliff. They didn't know we were watching them. They were waiting for our soldiers to head up through the ravine and ambush them. I confess, at that moment I felt extreme prejudice toward these two men whom I had never met. I overcame that prejudicial feeling by shooting both of them in the head as they looked over the rock."

Judging by the facial expressions around the table, they didn't like my example. The Inspector tried another question. "Give an example of a racial incident and how you dealt with it. Try not to use any military examples."

"I can't give you an example of that, because I don't have a racist bone in my body. I served with men and women from all over the world, all nationalities, creeds, religions, all colours. I never had a problem with anyone. Other than assholes. I guess I'm prejudiced toward assholes."

"Mr. Stephens," said the Superintendent. "You're going to be dealing with *assholes* everyday of your policing career. How are you going to handle them on the streets of Toronto? You can't shoot them all, or beat them all up."

"Befriend them, cultivate them, turn them, and forward all that intel to the specialist units. Like my mother always said, *Be charming to your enemies.* Where necessary, arrest and charge those for breaking the law, using only as much force as necessary to effect the arrest."

The Inspector liked that answer. The Superintendent smiled. He knew it was bullshit.

* * *

"Right then, here's your key. Don't forget to put the parking pass in your windshield. Your pod's here on the map." The night officer pointed to a map of the Alderson Police College.

"Pod?"

"Yes, Mr. Stephens. Pod. Don't ask me why they call it a pod. There's a central room, like a small lounge and four rooms run off from there. Plus the washroom and showers. You in the military?"

"Why do you ask?"

"I was a soldier myself once. Infantry. Long retired now, of course. This job helps with my pension. Can spot a military man a mile off."

"Special Forces. Need to know basis. Don't ask any more questions or I'll have to kill you."

"Judging by the size of you, that wouldn't be too difficult. What's your first name?"

"Sam."

"Well listen, Sam, a word of advice. It says here you're with Toronto."

"That's right."

"Well, we have some aboriginal officers from fly-in reserves on this intake. Not many, mind you. They tend to keep themselves to themselves. It's not uncommon for some of the new, freshly minted, white recruits to think they're the bee's knees. Watch your back, I'd hate to see you kicked-out for, how shall I put it, excessive use of force, if you get my meaning."

I glanced at the man's nametag. "Thanks for the heads-up, Tom. I promise not to hurt anyone, too badly."

"You'll do just fine here, son. You need any advice or help with anything, you let me know. Oh, one other thing, kiss the Director's ass a lot. He likes that, but somehow I don't see you doing that. You're more likely to kick it, I think."

I smiled. I liked Tom. He'd been around the block I could tell, and knew a thing or two. I thanked him and made my way along the maze of long narrow corridors to my *pod.*

My room, though small, was clean. There

was a window looking out over acres of freshly cut grass. Sprinkled around the whole complex were an assortment of trees, conifers and deciduous. It gave the whole place a park like appearance. Pleasant. Not intimidating. The window was screwed shut. Some geek's idea of regulating the air system. Knowing students would remove the screws, they installed screw heads that didn't conform to your everyday hardware store screws. I opened my hockey bag and took out a small tool kit. I removed the screws, opened the window and let in some fresh air. This was obviously going to be a regular routine.

The desk was adequate. I would have liked a larger and more comfortable chair. I'd put that on my shopping list. Might as well be comfortable as I was going to be here a while. The sink plug was going to have to go. Designed so it didn't actually stop the water draining out from the sink, to avoid flooding I guess. I worked on the plug, interrupted by the sound of swearing and laughter as my neighbours arrived. They sounded young and boisterous, not like soldiers. Like schoolboys. I didn't like them already. Then my door flew open and three young men began to breech my privacy. They didn't look like they were old enough to shave.

"You boys should head on home, it's getting dark. Your mothers will be worried sick about you."

"Who are you, the plumber?" This from the

big one. The weight lifter. Broad shoulders and all muscle. I was still coiled under the sink.

"I think he's the course comedian. Don't give up your day job Tonto."

"You, my friend, are too little to be awkward. I would appreciate it, for your own safety, if you didn't call me Tonto."

The third one squeezed in past the other two, all steroids.

"Tonto, hurry up with the plumbing, I'm taking this room."

"I guess the guy from Toronto isn't here yet," said the small guy.

"It don't matter, Russell, he can have the other room. I like the view from here." He looked down at me contemptuously. "Come on, buddy, I need to get my shit put away, I don't have all day."

I rolled out from under the sink, brushing my long black braid back behind me, and stood up.

"Did you guys drive here," I asked pleasantly.

"What do you think, dumbass?" replied Steroid.

"Do your cars have airbags?"

"What are you, straight off the reserve?" said the one with the broad shoulders, picking up my bag and tossing it out into the hallway.

"Think of me like your car's airbag. When you follow the rules, it's there to protect you. When you don't, it can cause serious injury or death. Now. Pick up my bag and gently place it back on my bed, then leave my room.

Otherwise, I'm going to deploy without warning, and who knows what's going to happen."

Steroid came in fast. I was impressed. The sink was to my right. My right hand still holding the long plumber's wrench. The handle was smooth, round and silver, with black jaws at the end. As I expected, Steroid grabbed me by my collar with his right hand. It was a powerful grip. A worthy opponent. I fought the urge to smash the wrench into the left side of his skull. I'd only been here an hour and I really wanted to complete my constable training. A manslaughter investigation was going to be very inconvenient. Second degree murder would really put a damper on things. Instead, I swung the wrench underneath his wrist and then over on top, grabbing the other end with my left hand, with my own wrists crossed underneath his. I bent low dragging him down and into me. He was already in a lot of pain. That pain was soon forgotten when my head slammed into his nose. Blood, lots of blood. Very inconvenient. The bloodstained carpet was going to take some explaining. Shoulders came in with a swift punch to the left side of my head, I raised my shoulder and the blow glanced harmlessly away. Left knee to Steroid's balls and he was out the door, right elbow to Shoulders head, and he was down, too. The little guy's contribution to the disturbance was to wet himself. I slapped him hard across the face, bringing tears to his eyes.

I locked the door behind them and closed the

window. There was going to be some fallout, I didn't need a citation for opening a window without lawful excuse. I didn't like the new pattern on the plain blue industrial carpet. Too red for my liking. I didn't bother unpacking, I wasn't sure I was going to be staying the night anyway, at least not in this facility. I made my way back down the labyrinth of hallways to reception. Tom was still at his post, ramrod straight, boots gleaming.

As soon as he saw me he began shaking his head slowly, like a teacher disappointed with a student.

"Sam, I knew when I met your roommates it was going to end badly. Mr. Carter is on his way to Emerg, with probably a broken nose. Mr. Turner is accompanying him. Apparently, he has a very bad headache. As neither of them is in any fit state to drive, Mr. Avery will be driving them."

"There's blood on my carpet. A lot of blood. I don't think the Director is going to like it."

Tom sighed. A long sigh. "Apparently, according to Mr. Carter, he entered, I'm guessing, your room by mistake. There was no one in there, but then he saw a bag on the bed. Realizing his mistake he spun around quickly, caught his foot on the chair and fell, smashing his face on the desk as he went down. Hence the blood on the carpet. Mr. Turner gave no explanation for the huge red bruise to the side of his face. However, the red handprint across Mr. Avery's face was rather telling."

I was very impressed, but said nothing. *I might get to like these guys after all.*

"Is there video, Tom, to substantiate Mr. Carter's story?"

"Fortunately for you, Sam, there is not. I'll have to report it, exactly as explained to me by Mr. Carter, of course. You haven't unpacked yet have you?" I shook my head. "Good. I'll have to find you another room while I get hold of the cleaning staff."

"No need, Tom. Being around blood is nothing new to me, but I guess you have to follow protocol. A room with a similar view would be appreciated. I like trees."

"There'll be an internal investigation, Sam. Protocol, that sort of thing. Nothing to worry about. Wouldn't do for anyone to change their story now."

"I guess not," I said. "I don't have a story to tell. Apparently."

Tom gave me another room. I liked it. More trees, better view. I could see young women coming and going on the far side of the building. Recruits, like me, but prettier. Well, some of them. Replacing the screws in the window in my old room was no problem, but the sink stopper was hell to put back the way the establishment had it. I locked the door to my new room and set about removing the window screws and making the sink just the way Mr. Stephens liked it. Same blue carpet, but no pattern this time. I made a mental note to try and keep it that way.

I lay on my bed with my boots propped on my bag so as not to dirty the bedspread. I didn't want to push my luck with the cleaning staff. I don't know why, but I thought of *the Weatherman.* It felt like he was in the room with me. I could see him sitting in the chair facing me, a huge grin on his face. *Sam, I won another bet. I said you wouldn't last an hour before you was in the shit, and true to form, you didn't let me down. No siree. I be watching over you, Sam.* And he was gone. "Leroy, I still got that ten bucks I owe you in my pocket. When we meet again in the spirit world, I'll give it to you. I carry it with me all the time. Same two five dollar bills."

I sat up, surprised. I could hear voices. They were speaking in my native tongue, Ojibwa. They were now in the small central lounge. I left my room, climbed the short flight of stairs to the lounge. Three very stocky men were seated around the television, watching the hockey game.

"Turtle Lake?" I said. They all nodded, not taking their eyes off the game. To them, I was an apple. Red on the outside, white on the inside. I nodded. The oldest of the three cast his eyes toward the empty chair. I sat and watched the game with them. There was very little conversation, as is our custom, unlike the white man, who can't seem to stop talking.

It was one nil for the Penguins. When they scored their second goal against the Bruins, they all leapt off the couch, dancing and hugging one another. I remained seated, my face in my hands. By the end of the game it was three-two for the Penguins.

Billy Big Canoe handed me a Bud. “Sam Eagle Eyes. Drown your sorrows. Next time you come to Turtle Lake, we gonna kick your ass again on the ice. You are a legend, Sam. We hear many stories about you, and now you’re gonna be a cop. Not any cop, a Toronto cop. Good for you, man. Oh, Tom asked us to keep an eye on you. He said you have a way of getting into trouble. We told him we already knew that.”

I got up, slapped Billy on the shoulder, and returned to my room. Hopefully I’d make it through a second night at the Academy.

Chapter Two

Breakfast was good. I piled one plate with bacon, eggs and toast, the other with pancakes and butter. I brought my own mug for coffee. There wouldn't have been room for the six small canteen cups on my tray. Not being a morning person, I found an empty table and sat down. My three brothers entered, nodded in my direction, and respectfully left me alone. I picked up my mug, a picture of the Weatherman smiling back at me. A nerdy-looking sergeant was making his way purposefully toward my table. He had a runner's build. By the look of him, he wasn't likely to stick around in a bar room brawl. Running away quickly was obviously his best course of action.

"Stephens. The Director wants to see you in his office, immediately," he squeaked.

"As soon as I've finished with the Weatherman, I'll be right there, sergeant." By the perplexed look on the man's face he must have thought it was some kind of aboriginal thing. He'd be worried about a human rights issue. Wouldn't be good for promotion prospects. I knew he'd be looking it up on his *smartphone* as soon as he turned his back on me. He hadn't walked ten feet before his hand came out of his pocket with his phone.

Predictable. I made a mental note of that.

I stood to attention. "Sit down, Stephens. You know why you're here. It was all captured on video last night," lied the Director.

"That's good, sir, but I have no idea why I'm here. I can't think of any monumental incident I've been involved in, not since I left the military that would warrant me being summoned to your office."

He scowled at me from behind his desk, his Adam's apple sticking out like a golf ball lodged in his throat. I found his Hitler moustache offensive. I didn't like the man, and I knew the feeling was mutual.

"Mr. Williams, the duty officer last night gave me a complete statement on what took place. It's all here." He jabbed a finger on a manila envelope to emphasize the point.

"You mean Tom?"

"I mean Mr. Williams. Tom Williams."

"In that case, I don't know what I can say to further assist you with whatever you need my cooperation with, sir."

"You and Carter got into it last night, which sent him to hospitable with a broken nose and as a result, your carpet will have to be replaced and not at the taxpayers' expense!"

"With respect, sir. You have me at a disadvantage. As I'm sure you are aware, I reported finding fresh blood on my carpet to the duty officer, with the name tag, Tom Williams over his breast pocket. I told him about it immediately I discovered it. At the time it happened I was in the washroom sitting on the toilet. When I came out, I found the blood."

"And what did Mr. Williams tell you?"

"That he would have to report it that was all."

"Did he offer any explanation as to how it happened?"

"No, sir. As you said, it's all on video. You'll no doubt have watched me leaving my room for the washroom, and not that I time my bowel movements, seen me returning to my room. I'm guessing, maybe ten minutes later. Sir."

"Was there anything out of the ordinary, Stephens?"

"With regard to my bowels, sir?"

"Don't play games with me, Stephens. From now on, you are a marked man. The first opportunity I have to get rid of you, believe me, I will. Now get out."

I saluted crisply, turned swiftly and marched out of his office, noting the photograph on his desk. Bible-thumper wife and two spoilt looking brats. The Director didn't wear the pants at home. I passed Tom in the busy hallway. He winked as he passed, a mischievous grin creasing his face.

* * *

Our instructor was ex-military. Short, stocky, and with a pug nose. "This morning, my recruits, we're going to discuss interview techniques, but not in too much detail. We use the Reid's Nine Step rules of interviewing. We don't use the word, *interrogation.* The liars, I mean lawyers, don't like that word. If you're that interested in it, you can do some research on your own time, when you get back to your divisions. Those of you who make it that far, Mr. Stephens. You'll eventually discover in time whether you're traffic oriented or crime. Particularly in the criminal field, you'll need good interview techniques. Remember one thing if nothing else. No one is going to talk to you if they don't like you, so try not to hurt them too badly when making an arrest. It might be you interviewing them later on."

Sergeant Dipper continued with the lecture, glossing over each of the nine points. "Am I keeping you awake, Mr. Stephens? Perhaps you would like to remind us of the various points?"

"In the military I never went past point one, only point one wasn't the same as yours. Very rarely did I have to go to point two or point three. There was no point four. Corpses don't answer questions, though they can still pass wind." This caused an outburst of laughter.

"Go on, Mr. Stephens, this is fascinating stuff."

"Well, it was virtually impossible to get the Taliban to like you, unless perhaps you were willing to convert to Sharia law and become a Muslim. I found point one, dangling your subject out of a high window by his ankles, produced very quick results. The other points are classified if that didn't work. If we had used the Reid's Nine Step rules there, I'd still be talking to my first prisoner fifteen years later."

"Thank you, Mr. Stephens. We are not in the military and having been there myself, point one is not in the manual. People. You can listen to Mr. Stephens for entertainment value, but do not, I repeat, do not, under any circumstances follow anything he tells you while serving as police officers. In due course, we will all be reading about our friend here, Mr. Stephens, as he spends some quality time in our beloved prison system."

* * *

Somehow I got through week one and was well into my second week. I couldn't wait for Friday afternoon. Load up the old Chevy Caprice Classic and head back to Harbourfront for the weekend. My car was old, but the geezer I bought it from had kept it in mint condition since driving it out of the showroom and back home into his garage. With the low kilometers on it, the engine was hardly broken in. The transmission was as tough as a tractor's. Even the sand and sable paint work had kept its shine. They don't make them like that anymore. Probably a good thing. Gas mileage was not one of its selling features. On the Peninsular reserve,

I got my gas at discount prices. One of the perks given us aboriginals by those that took our land away from us, centuries ago.

Thursday after lunch, a three mile run followed by DT. Defensive Tactics. Fresh out of the military this was going to be a breeze. As I expected, Sergeant Swift led the pack all the way and finished well ahead of all of us. As I said, no good in a bar brawl, but good at running away. I came in third. I was happy with that. Not out of breath, and ready to fight if I had to. Everyone else was exhausted and sucking wind. Not good. Swift was breathing hard, too. He looked over at me contemptuously, head down, hands on his knees, sweat dripping off his face, T-shirt soaked. I'd hardly broken into a sweat. I needed another few miles for that. Avery, Turner, and Carter, had come in together somewhere in the middle of the pack. Avery threw up on the grass. My brothers from Turtle Lake came in ahead of them, laughing and joking. But out of breath. We made our way over to the drill hall for DT.

As I expected, two instructors, dressed all in black, like Ninjas. *Instructor*, boldly printed in white lettering across their chests. As I expected. One big, mean looking guy, and the other, thinner build, but all muscle. They were here to show us how it's done. To separate the weak ones. I thought of Avery. In a few minutes he was going to be in a world of hurt. They would pick on him, bully him, and eventually break him.

As expected, knuckle push-ups. Lots of them. Carter and Turner were in their glory. They looked at me and began doing them one armed. Mistake. The big instructor saw them.

"You two! Carter and Turner. Too easy for you?" he bellowed in a broad Scottish accent. We each wore white T-shirts with our names in black lettering across the front. "When I give you an order, you will carry it out as given. Not your version of it!"

Now, we were all going to suffer. The two instructors, who didn't have their names on their T-shirts, were going to make this into a competition. We were going to do push-ups until the last one of us dropped and they were going to join in because they knew they were going to beat us all.

If I'd had any sense, I'd have just quit and let them win. But I was too stubborn for that. Now it was just the three of us pumping up and down. Them and me. Then it was just the two of us. The big one and me. Up and down, up and down. Everyone else was standing in a semi-circle watching. I heard him grunting, his face turning from red to purple. Then a cry of anger, driving himself onward. Up and down and ... There was no up for him. I continued. Up and down, rubbing salt into the wound. Not smart. But necessary. At least, I thought it was necessary.

He was angry. I was still pumping away rhythmically, no huffing and puffing, no grunting. No anger. I knew what was coming.

He kicked up into my stomach. I rolled away quickly, swinging my hands around with lightning speed, grabbing his foot. My foot came up quickly between his legs and made contact, but it was a glancing blow. He spun out of my grip and came down on top of me. He was a ground fighter and a good one. His fist caught me hard in the face, bringing tears to my eyes as he went for the choke hold, slamming my neck in a vice-like grip. He was now on his back, choking me from behind. Instantly, I slammed my head back and heard the crunch as it made contact with the bridge of his nose. At least the blood wouldn't stain the highly polished concrete floor. I felt his grip loosen. Now I was the one choking him out. It didn't take long. I counted eight seconds. His body went limp. I jumped up quickly, expecting his buddy to jump me. He didn't. You can strike a punching bag a thousand times, but other than catching you off guard on the return swing, a punching bag will never strike you back, no matter how big it is, or what colour it is. There is no substitute for real unarmed combat. OIV.

"Stephens!"

"Yes, sir."

"Help me get Mr. Mackenzie to the washroom."

"Yes, sir."

Together the other instructor and I helped Mackenzie up, one arm each over our shoulder.

"You're good, sonny," he said. "Bloody good." Then he turned to the younger man. "I'm all right, Keith. I'll clean myself up. I deserved that. Give me five minutes and I'll be out. Get the rest of 'em back to work."

It was nearer ten minutes when Mackenzie came back, looking bruised and battered, but smiling.

"Right, you miserable looking lot! That was a practical demonstration of a good hands-on street fight. You'll not get training any more real than that. Never before in my life have I received such a thrashing. On the street, down a dark alley, if I'd have jumped this man, I'd be dead now. Ask yourselves this. If someone as mean as me had jumped you, where would you be? Or worse still. Say you met the likes of Stephens here, who hates the police. There you are out on the street in your nice new police uniform, still looking at your reflection in the shop windows, your parents still proudly showing everyone your graduation pictures in your number ones. Then along comes Stephens who has a hard on for the police. Now you know what will happen to you. You'll be hospitalized or dead. For all of you, it won't be about winning, because you won't beat a man like Stephens. It'll be about holding on until the cavalry gets there. At least in the big towns and cities, that won't be long. But in the rural areas, that could be a *long* time. A minute of fighting on the street wearing a police uniform will seem like an eternity. And don't think because you're a woman, it won't happen to you. You'll be seeing some video footage as the course progresses that'll make you wonder what you've got yourselves into. It's not too late to quit. Remember this, if nothing else. If you quit in here, you're gonna quit out there. Right, Mr. Wilson. Let's start them off with two minutes of continuous attack on the punch bags."

I had a lot of respect for a man like Mackenzie. He knew he'd screwed up, lost his temper with a recruit and got his ass-kicked. He licked his wounds and got right back at it. Like a true soldier. Both of us knew that some big mouth would talk about it and both he and I would be back in the Director's office. And I was right.

* * *

I stood to attention and saluted. The Director ignored me. He was pretending to read through a file folder on his desk in front of him. Tactics. Put your subordinate under stress. Pile on the anxiety, only I wasn't feeling under stress, and neither was I anxious. I could always return to the military, or I could take that security job at the casino. I had options.

"Sergeant Mackenzie is currently under suspension pending an investigation. Every single person present at that outrageous excuse for a defensive tactics exercise has provided a statement. You, Stephens, should pack your bags today and prepare for dismissal from this training facility."

Sergeant Swift smiled from the corner of the room. Under different circumstances, he would need to be running fast in the opposite direction. I remained professional. Still standing to attention. I wasn't going to be invited to sit down today. The Director finally raised his head and glared at me. I wanted to rip that moustache off him so badly.

"Because of your discreditable behavior, coupled with that of Sergeant Mackenzie's, regrettably two of our recruits have resigned. You however, will not have the luxury of resigning. You will be fired."

My mind said, *Options. Military or casino? Military.* Breathe in. Breathe out. Control the rising rage.

"Permission to speak; sir."

"Go ahead, Stephens. Be mindful, your statement will be recorded." He nodded toward Swift, who dutifully pressed the record button on the tape recorder, clearly visible on his desk. The Director sat back in his chair, steepled his fingers, placing the tips of them against his lips, and waited.

"Sergeant Mackenzie approached me in the cafeteria at lunchtime. Together we came up with the idea of making the DT session as realistic as we could. He wanted to give the recruits a taste of what the real street can be like on a bad day. He knew I was ex-military with a lot of unarmed combat experience. I thought it was a great idea and readily agreed. It was all consensual. With respect, sir, Sergeant Mackenzie is a first class instructor. His heart is in the right place, though in hindsight, and I'm sure he'd agree, our actions, though well intentioned, were misguided." It was all bullshit. The only part that was true was about Mackenzie bumping into me in the cafeteria. Plenty of recruits and staff would have seen it, but likely didn't hear the verbal exchange. It was short, brief, and unpleasant. There always had to be a semblance of truth in a lie, something that could be checked and corroborated. I'd already given Mackenzie the cover story, so we were golden. They'd check it out, looking for holes, and end up frustrated when they came up empty handed. Give it a week and Mackenzie would be back at work, with a black mark in his file. I doubted, if his file was anything like mine, it wouldn't be the only one. In my case, I knew that for every black mark I earned, I had a commendation to match it.

"I'm putting you on notice, Stephens, that if I have to speak to you again regarding another discipline matter, you can forget a career in policing in any service throughout Canada. Sergeant Swift will be my eyes and ears and will report directly to me regarding your behaviour. Mark my words, there had better be a vast improvement in your conduct. As you can see, I have quite the file on you already."

"With regard to my overall performance, sir, such as academic work, tests, physical effort, do you have any complaints?"

"You're dismissed, Stephens. Get back to your next class and close the door behind you."

"Yes, sir." I duly saluted and left him alone with Swift. I was going to have to watch my back from now on. Swift was a coward. He would never deal with me head on. The first chance he got to run to his master with some made-up dirt he would.

Chapter Three

Week three. I was in early again for breakfast. I liked to sit alone and drink my coffee, uninterrupted. By now people got to know that I liked to be left alone in the mornings. Lunch and dinner were different. I was more sociable.

"Good morning, Sam. Mind if I join you?"

"Yes." She sat down anyway. Right opposite me. I hoped this wasn't going to be a regular thing.

"You're not exactly the friendliest man I've ever met. You're not gay are you?"

Breathe in. Breathe out. Suppress the rising anger. She knew she'd hit a raw nerve. I could see it in her eyes.

"What do you want, Annie? I see you already have a following of males sniffing around you everywhere you go like little puppies."

"I don't date anyone other than from my own race. Our people are already weakened by intermarriage."

"Sounds racist, but I can respect that. Are you asking me to marry you, Annie? I don't even know you. I'll admit you're cute. In fact, I'd say you were too beautiful. Being with you would worry the life out of me. Everywhere we went men would be ogling you. I'd be fighting every day."

"You're funny. Much as I like you, this is not a marriage proposal."

I looked long and hard into her steel grey eyes. Her light brown skin was unblemished. Chiseled features, high cheekbones. Slim, tall, raven-black hair tied in a long ponytail. Delicate, but strong.

"Like what you see?"

"Annie, you're like a deep river running through the mountains. Breathtakingly beautiful, but too deep to know what lies below the surface."

Her eyes locked on mine. "Unless you dive in, you'll never find out."

"Again. What do you want, Annie?"

"Help. I want you to teach me how to fight, not the way they teach us here. I want to survive on the street, not get my ass kicked. I want to learn your kind of self-defence."

"That's your first mistake, Annie."

"What is?"

"Don't use the words, *self-defence.* You might defend against the first blow, but after that, Annie, it will be an all-out attack on your attacker. The most important part of any fight is your mental state. You can be as strong as an ox, Annie, but if you don't have it up here, *the warrior spirit*, you won't make a very good fighter. All you need to know is OIV. Overwhelming, Incapacitating Violence. Give me your hands."

Annie slid her hands across the table toward

me. I enveloped them in my own and held them firmly. We sat staring into each other's eyes. "Think back to our ancestors, Annie, how brave those warriors were. When you leave my table, from now on throughout the rest of your life, you will be a warrior. You will fight like a warrior, to the death if necessary. Should you die in battle, let those that search for your killer, know that they will be severely injured. What Band are you?"

"Ojibwa. Bear Clan."

"Great warriors, Annie. Make your ancestors proud of you. There is only one problem, though?"

"What's that?" she whispered.

"I don't know why I should help you. You're with the Dalton Regional Police." She laughed.

"Toronto wouldn't take me."

"Their loss. Meet me tonight in the drill hall, say seven o'clock." She came around the table smiling like a little girl and gave me a peck on the cheek.

"Can I get you another coffee?"

"Sure," I replied. "Black, no sugar."

"I know," she said. "I've been watching you for weeks."

"I know you have, Annie," I lied.

I watched her walk away, as did all the hot-blooded males, and even a few of the female recruits. I didn't like the way Swift continued to stare after her. He looked angry, pissed off about something. I continued to stare at him. He glanced in my direction, obviously uncomfortable, embarrassed even, as though I had caught him playing with himself under the table. Briefly, he tried to give me a tough guy look, but couldn't pull it off. Finally, he looked away. Within minutes he got up and skulked away, not before a sideways look in my direction.

* * *

Dead on seven o'clock I walked into the drill hall. Annie was already waiting for me, dressed in black sweat pants and T-shirt with a magnificent eagle printed on the front.

"I've already warmed up, so we can get started."

"Fine by me, Annie." I dropped my kit bag on the floor and pulled out two pairs of sparring gloves and some pads. I tossed her a pair of gloves "Put these on. Our first exercise is one of meditation. Stand relaxed, take some deep breaths and close your eyes. Imagine that you are all that stands between saving your village and the enemy at the gate. The fate of the children and the elderly left behind rests with you. Make it real. I am the enemy. I am going to slaughter you all, one by one. Be the warrior, Annie. Remember, overwhelming, incapacitating violence, but don't make it a free-for-all. Make each and every strike count by only targeting vulnerable areas of the body.

We'll go more in depth as the sessions progress." We stood silently for a few minutes. "Open your eyes and let's get started."

When she opened her eyes I was taken aback by the ferocity that shone within them. She was unbelievably fast as she struck at the hand pads I was holding. Periodically I would give her a glancing blow against the side of the head. She didn't tear up or lose control in temper. She was focused and fought back hard, but forgot to control her breathing. It wasn't long before she was winded.

"Annie, that was outstanding, in fact, unbelievable. Now, control your breathing. Don't hold your breath, keep breathing in and out. This time we're going to spar. Pretend you're terrified of me, plead for me not to hurt you, look vulnerable. That will throw your attacker off, then explode into a violent fury, and give it everything you've got. Sometimes, the better option is to temporarily disable your attacker and then run as fast as you can to safety."

I was impressed. I pulled my punches, but one caught her on the lip, enough to make it bleed. She kept going. "Breathe Annie, watch your breathing!" She was relentless. Despite my best efforts, one got through, catching me on the nose. More blood.

"I'm sorry, I'm sorry."

"Keep going! You don't quit until I say so!"

At the end, we were both breathing hard and sweating, our arms bruised from warding off punches, hammers strikes, and vicious slaps.

"I need some water," she said, picking up a water bottle.

"No water, Annie. Get used to it. You won't have that luxury on the street. There's no *time out* in the real world. Survival in a combat situation is also opportunity. From now on, everywhere you go, assess your surroundings. Look for possible weapons of opportunity. For instance, shopping in the supermarket. Supermarkets have knives for sale. Know where they are. Just about anything can be a weapon of opportunity if you use your imagination. The orbital bone that holds the eyeball has a small hole at the end where the optical nerve enters. Strike your attacker hard enough in the eye with a pen or even a pencil and it will end up stuck in their brain, assuming it doesn't snap of course. It's important to remember, Annie, we live in Canada. Using such force without justifiable reason will be hard to explain to the courts, assuming you get caught. Some of what I will teach you will end up with you doing time if you're not justified in using it. Look at it this way. You're out jogging on a quiet path when you get attacked by a rapist. Kill him. Run away, tell no one. You get attacked on a busy street. Disable him. We'll finish off with how to defend against a knife attack and how to attack with a knife." I removed a commando knife from my pack.

"Sam, that's a real knife. Shouldn't we use a rubber one?"

"We'll practice with the real thing. Go slow, of course. Psychologically, using a real knife here will make the appearance of a real knife on the street not so daunting. If we use a rubber one all the time, when that real one comes out it'll be such a shock, valuable seconds will be lost. If you can create distance and you have a gun, use the gun every time, firing continually until the threat has been stopped."

At first, Annie attacked me, hard and fast as I wanted her to. I had to work quickly to disarm her and counter attack, sometimes disarming her and using the knife against her. Then it was my turn to attack her. Slowly at first, until she fell into the rhythm and we increased the speed. She was a natural.

"In a knife attack, Annie, expect to be cut or stabbed, work through the shock of seeing your own blood and keep fighting. In the majority of cases, people don't even know they've been stabbed, their adrenaline is pumping so hard. Sometimes they bleed out, go unconscious and die."

I showed Annie all the places to strike with the knife, a knowledge of the human body was essential. A knife in the hands of a trained knife fighter was like watching a graceful, but lethal dance, as the fighter sliced at one artery and then the next, working around his victim's body until it collapsed.

"That's enough for tonight, Annie. I've taught you more in one session tonight than in years of belonging to a martial arts club. Now it's up to you to practice it, even in your sleep. We'll work on some ground fighting techniques next session."

"Thanks, Sam." Rising up on her toes she gave me a peck on the cheek. "Can I ask your advice on something?"

"Sure, go ahead."

"I'm having trouble with one of the instructors. He keeps coming on to me and won't take no for an answer. He obviously knows I'm struggling with some of the work, especially the HTA. He's says he can give me private tuition and to remember he has a big say in whether or not I get through this course."

"The Highway Traffic Act is not my strong point, either. You and I can work on that together. The guys in my pod are having a hard time with it, too, so let's get together and help each other out. As for Sergeant Swift."

"How did you know it was him, you're the only person I've confided in about this?"

"I think the peck on the cheek in the canteen this morning wasn't for my benefit, but to send him a signal. I was watching him afterwards. He was pissed. Now, we're both going to be in his sights."

"I'm sorry to drag you into this. I was going to go to the Director's office and report it."

"I'd advise against that at the moment, Annie. The two of them are inseparable."

"What do you suggest?"

"Come with me. I've got something in my car that might just help resolve the problem."

"Now?"

"Now. You can be sure he's already making his own plans and we need to be ready."

We hurried out of the building to the recruits' parking lot, well away from the facility. Staff parking was, of course, much closer.

"This is not what I expected you'd be driving, I figured you for a muscle car. This is an old man's car."

"Annie, sit in the passenger seat and don't get out until I tell you. You will not discuss any of this with anyone. I need your word on this. If you ever betray me, our friendship is over, permanently."

"What have you got in there, a rocket launcher?"

"Something far more useful for this operation. If all else fails, I'll activate the rocket launcher." Annie looked horrified. "I'm joking, Annie. Are you solid?"

"Yes of course. You can trust me. I give you my word, I won't tell anyone."

While Annie sat in the front passenger seat of my car, I opened the trunk, removed the carpet and spare wheel cover, revealing a full-size spare tire, not one of those donuts. Without very close scrutiny, the tire looked normal, except this one was in two longitudinal halves. Using a concealed electronic keypad, the tire opened. To the untrained eye the inside contained electronic gadgetry. To a surveillance trained operative, it contained some very sophisticated listening devices.

"Annie, this Canadian pin contains a minute microphone. Start wearing it all the time. It's linked to my computer and smartphone. We don't need hours and hours of unnecessary and useless communication. I'll set it up to be activated by your voice with a command signal. To activate it, all you need to say is, *Sergeant Swift.*" I handed Annie the small pin with the Canadian flag. I got out my phone and opened my surveillance portal. "Okay, say your command signal, as though you were in conversation with him."

"Sergeant Swift."

"Okay, Annie, we're good to go. To deactivate say, *I love Sam Stephens.*"

"Are you kidding?"

"All right, *Are you kidding,* will do."

"Is this legal, I mean, are we okay to do this?"

"Well, it could be argued that were you a sworn police officer, which at the moment you are not, you might need a judge's order to do this. Seeing as, technically you and I are still civilians, I don't see a problem. In any case, we're not looking for a lawsuit here, are we, Annie?"

"No, I just want him to back off."

"Legal or not legal, once he gets to hear what will inevitably be on record, you can be sure he won't be teaching anymore."

I made my way back to my pod for a long hot shower, after escorting Annie back to her building.

* * *

"Annie."

"Sergeant Swift."

"I'm just doing my rounds. Been working out?"

"Yes. Is there a problem?"

"No, not at all. I was wondering if you'd like to take me up on my offer to help you with your Highway Traffic Act. I know you're having some trouble with it. I could take you out for dinner, and we'd go through it in a less stressful environment. But don't worry, I've got your back. I guarantee, if you let me help you, you will pass this course."

"I don't think that would be appropriate, Sergeant. In any case, Sam Stephens has offered to help me."

"You don't like being seen with white guys, is that it?"

"No, not at all. I only date my own people. I have lots of white friends."

"That sounds very racist to me, Annie. I'm sorry, but I may have to make a note of this in your personnel file. *Racist tendencies.* That will be the end of your police career. But it doesn't have to be. We don't have to make babies. There's contraception, you know. We could just practice. You be nice to me, Annie, and I give you my word, you are going to pass out from this academy with flying colours. Guaranteed. I would forget all about Stephens, if I were you."

"And why is that?"

"He's not going to be with us for much longer. You can take that to the bank. I'll give you to the end of the week to be, *nicer* to me, Annie, otherwise you can start thinking about another career."

"That's sexual harassment."

"It's your word against mine."

"I'll report this to the Director."

"Go ahead. I'm sure my father-in-law will be only too pleased to see you. I've already made a report to him about how you've been *coming on* to me, saying that you'll let me sleep with you if I get you through this course. No-one's going to believe a word you say. What's the matter, lost for words?"

"You make me sick."

"Good night, Annie. Sweet dreams."

Chapter Four

Sergeant Swift knocked on the Director's door.

"Good morning, Bob, come on in. Is everything okay, you look upset?"

"Sir, one of the handguns has gone missing from the armory."

"You're joking?"

"I wish I was."

"Have you double checked?"

"Triple checked. It's missing."

"We'll start with a search of the recruits' rooms, then their personal vehicles. We'll do the rooms while they're all in class this morning. If we don't find it, we'll drag them out, one by one, until we do. Got any suspects?"

"No, sir, none at all."

"Okay, assemble those members of staff not in class this morning and let's get this thing knocked on the head, quickly."

"Yes, sir."

* * *

Sergeant Matthews lifted the mattress, one of

dozens he'd done already that morning. There, at the foot of the bed was a Glock .40 calibre semi-automatic pistol. Loaded. He checked the serial number. AS 14378US, then radioed the Director.

"I've found it, sir."

"Where?"

"Under recruit Stephens' mattress."

"Who's with you to verify that?"

"Sergeant Collins, sir."

"Good work. I'll get hold of the police."

* * *

"Mr. Stephens. You are on patrol early one summer evening, when you come across a group of teenagers with backpacks. They tell you they are on their way to a friend's house. You hear the sound of what sounds like bottles clinking in one of their backpacks. What are you going to do? Listen up class, let's be mesmerized by Stephens' knowledge of the Liquor License Act, or lack thereof."

"Well, Sergeant Dipper. First of all, I want to establish if they are under nineteen years of age. If I have reasonable grounds to believe they are, I'm going to search the pack. If it contains an alcoholic beverage, my decision on what to do next, will depend on the brand of beer. If it's say, a premium beer, like Sleeman Honey Brown, I'm going to confiscate it under the powers of Her Majesty the Queen, and drink it later. If it's not a premium beer, my course of action will depend on two things. If I get *attitude*, then the beer will be confiscated and the said miscreant will be issued a ticket under the LLA. If no *attitude,* the said miscreant will pour each beer out onto the ground and no ticket will be issued."

"Mr. Stephens. Thank heavens I am never going to be your sergeant. I think the stress of having you on my platoon would give me ulcers if not a heart attack. Again, ladies and gentlemen. Do not do anything that our esteemed colleague, Mr. Stephens, would suggest. There's the right, that is, the lawful way, and as you've discovered, there's the other way, or *the Stephens way."*

There was a knock on the classroom door. Sergeant Swift hurried into the room. Annie looked over at me. She looked worried. I smiled. Dipper and Swift engaged in a short conversation about me. I knew it was about me by the way they kept glancing in my direction.

"Stephens, accompany Sergeant Swift to the Director's office." I got to my feet, edging out from behind my desk. "Take everything with you. You won't be coming back." I stole a glance at Annie. She looked horrified. I smiled again, leaving my books on my desk.

"I'll be back, Sergeant Dipper, meanwhile take care of my books."

"I said, take everything with you."

I didn't.

As we made our way along the maize of corridors, I decided to give Swift an opportunity to redeem himself. “Sergeant Swift, I estimate it will take us another one hundred and twenty seconds to reach the Director’s office. That’s how much time I’m going to give you to save yourself. To make right whatever it is you’ve done. After that, there will be no mercy.”

“Stephens, I’ll be adding *insubordination* to the list of charges against you. It pales into insignificance when compared with what you’re going to be charged with. I hope you’ve got a good lawyer.”

“She’s the best. I have two wishes. One, that your house is located in a picturesque setting, hopefully by the lake, and two, that it’s in your name because I’m soon going to be its new owner, once my lawyer’s sued your ass.”

The hallway was empty, just me and Swift. He stopped abruptly, did a quick about turn causing me to either stop or stomp all over him. I decided to stop. Less paperwork.

“You can forget about saying goodbye to Annie. Where you’re going, Stephens, you won’t be seeing the outside world for a long time. By then, she and I will be married with kids. You on the other hand will continue to be a loser.”

I smiled. “You’ve still got sixty seconds left, Sergeant. After that, all bets are off. If I’m such a loser, you must be a complete moron.” He poked me in the chest, hard. Well, hard for him. I let him.

"Don't you even want to know what you're going to be charged with? Are you that dumb?"

"Theft of a handgun from the armory, plus ammunition. Unsafe storage of a firearm, and that's just for starters. Insubordination. Threats to cause you bodily harm, so don't poke me in the chest again. I'm giving you something akin to a government health warning on the side of a cigarette packet. *Poking this man could cause serious injury or death.*" He looked stunned, the spiteful neurotransmitters in his brain firing frantically.

"Would you like to know what you're going to be charged with, Sergeant Swift?"

He attempted to poke me in the chest again. I was disappointed, I'd asked him politely, well as politely as I could, not to do it again. I grabbed his right hand, twisted it into a painful wristlock and forced him to his knees. "I guess you can add *assault* to that growing list."

"Your dreams of a career in policing are finished, you hear me, Stephens. Finished!"

He was just too stupid to figure it out.

The Director's door was open. He was seated behind his desk. Two men in suits stood in front of him. Not lawyers, or homicide detectives, the suits didn't look expensive enough. Probably general detectives. Like front line officers, jacks of all trades, but masters of none. Probably from the local police detachment. Not, Ontario Provincial Police.

Probably didn't want to be here either. That made three of us.

Swift knocked on the door, opening it wide. "I have Stephens with me, sir." That was obvious, I was now standing in the office. I wasn't exactly hard to miss.

I saw the Glock on the desk, directly in front of the Director. The two men in suits turned to look at me. They didn't look happy.

"Don't do it, sir. I know you've been under a lot of stress lately, but life really is worth living." The Director glared at me, his face turning red.

"You're not going to execute me, are you? Don't I get one final wish?"

"This is Detective Morrison and Detective Wilburn of the Alderson Police Service. This gentlemen, is Stephens."

"Mr. Stephens, I am arresting you for the theft of this handgun and ammunition from the Academy armory and for the unsafe storage of a loaded firearm, found this morning in your room, under your mattress."

Detective Morrison got out his note book. Swift had his back to the now closed door, as though he was going to prevent my escape from the room. I had no plans to escape. If I had, Swift and the door would have become one. The detective continued. "It is my duty to inform you that you have the right to retain and instruct counsel without delay. You have the right to telephone any lawyer you wish. You also have the right to free advice from a legal aid lawyer. If you are charged with an offence, you may apply to the Ontario Legal Aid Plan for assistance. I have some toll free numbers that will put you in contact with a legal aid duty counsel lawyer for free legal advice right now. Do you understand?"

"Could you say that again in my native tongue, Ojibwa?" No sense of humour.

"Do you wish to call a lawyer now?"

"No. I won't be needing a lawyer at this time, other than to sue Sergeant Swift when this matter is resolved."

Detective Wilburn produced a pair of handcuffs from a pouch on his belt.

"You won't be needing those, Detective."

"It's standard procedure. Every arrested person gets handcuffed for their safety and ours," he said.

"The only safety problem there's going to be here, is if you even attempt to put those things on me." Everyone bristled.

Detective Morrison took the lead. "We can do this the easy way or the hard way. Your choice."

"For your health and safety I'd like to do this the easy way by walking out to your car with you. There will be no problem. I give you my word. If you really insist on putting those on me, I would suggest the Director requests the presence of your Emergency Task Force."

Wilburn began to release a pouch clip on his belt. He was having difficulty being discreet because his jacket was in the way.

"Detective, as soon as I see that can of pepper spray, it will be in my hands and everyone in this room will get sprayed. If you pull a firearm on me, I'll take that, too. Now, let's do this the easy way. I am walking out of this room with you detectives. Sergeant Swift, get away from the door."

Wilburn went for the pepper spray, fingers fumbling. Before anyone knew what had happened, it was in my hand. I placed it on the desk.

"Are we going to keep playing this game? I won't tell you again, Sergeant Swift. Get away from the door."

He charged me. It was pandemonium in the room. Swift ended up across the desk in the Director's lap. Morrison went to grab me, now he was on his knees in a one-handed wrist lock. Wilburn panicked and went for his gun. Now I had the gun. It went very quiet then. I unclipped the magazine, emptied the bullets on the desk, racked the slide and out popped the bullet already engaged in the chamber.

"I'm not going to say this again. We're leaving together. Anymore nonsense and I'll handcuff the two of you and I'll drive us to the police station."

No blood. I was pleased. No bones broken, no black eyes. Ego's severely damaged. When we got outside I could hear the sirens wailing. Someone had pressed the emergency assistance button on their radio. To be expected. I figured the black Malibu for their car. As expected the rear passenger door was unlocked. I eased myself inside. And waited.

* * *

Cruiser after cruiser screamed up to the front of the Academy. Officers of all shapes and sizes leapt from their vehicles, some with guns drawn. A K9 unit arrived. A few ETF officers arrived brandishing C8 semi-automatic rifles. A young officer began screaming at me.

"Get out of the car! Do it now!" I was offended. Not because he was shouting at me, but because he had a military haircut. Buzzed short all round, except for a dark tuft of hair on the crown of his head. I'd have to remind him he was a police officer, not a soldier. Big difference. Unlike front line police officers, front line soldiers don't give out speeding tickets. It must have dawned on him, that I could not open the door from the inside. Finally, gun drawn he pulled open the door quickly, as though he was letting out a tiger.

"Get out of the car, do it now!" Taken down at gunpoint on Canadian soil. I was very disappointed. I eased myself out of the car, towering over the short, stocky officer.

"That's not how to treat a *real* soldier."

"Get on the ground! Do it now!"

"Stop shouting. I'll do it when I'm ready."

High voltage electricity jolted through my body. I was expecting to be Tasered. I could feel my muscles tightening, but in that split second before I was completely incapacitated, my arm dropped and tore out the two probes. Not by accident. Forward planning. Chances of success? Minimal. I got to my knees, glad I was wearing police pants and not my good jeans. Then I lay chest down on the ground, arms outstretched. And waited.

The sound of a German shepherd barking in my ear. Hands wrenching my arms back. My wrists finally handcuffed. They needed two pairs, my shoulders were so broad they couldn't get my wrists into one pair. Then Detective Morrison's voice as I was yanked to my feet, bits of gravel sticking to my cheek.

"I told you, Stephens. We could do this the easy way or the hard way."

"After what I've experienced in the military, believe me, this was the easy way."

"You're a hard man, Mr. Stephens. In the old days we'd soon have that beaten out of you. But this is a much more gentle society we're living in now."

"Lucky for you, Detective."

Chapter Five

The interview room was small, but clean. No windows, other than a small viewing hatch in the door. Walls, painted cinder block like most government buildings, only someone, probably a female facilities manager, had them painted a light yellow. No pictures, just a marker board on the wall with my name and an incident number and today's date in black marker. Very neatly written, either a woman or a neat-freak male detective. Probably Morrison. Two chairs, one in the corner, the ubiquitous uncomfortable grey hard plastic chair with metal frame and no arm rests. The accused's chair. At least it wasn't electric. The black soft plastic chair, with control knobs, up, down, recline, high-backed, and with arms. On wheels, too. Five of them. Like a used car salesman's chair. Cheap, but more or less comfortable. Only I wasn't about to be pressurized into buying a car I didn't want, besides, I already had a car. It was old, but I liked it. It started in all weathers and never once let me down. A chair on wheels, for moving in and out during an interrogation. They don't like that word in policing today. Not friendly enough. Smacks of water boarding. Sergeant

Dipper wanted us to remember, *It's an interview.* It's an interrogation, but without violence, not permitted anymore in modern day policing. I would have liked the old days, little paperwork, *Here's your confession, sign here.* Bad guys were bad guys and knew their place. Cops were cops and knew theirs. It was all cops and robbers, nothing personal. A bad guy got thumped, he deserved it. Accepted it. No point complaining, not unless you wanted to get thumped again. Social order, safer streets. Balance. Ying and Yang. Now, no respect, not even among criminals. Whiners, ready to complain at the first slap after being cautioned for their indiscretions. White shirts, just waiting to take that complaint and sewer another cop. Yes, I would have liked those days.

A small camera eye, trying to be something else, like some kind of light switch. No single light bulb dangling on a dirty electric wire. The ceiling light was bright, but not too bright. Nothing that could be regarded as torturous. Human Rights wouldn't like that. This one was encased in a metal frame, with glass cover. Industrial orange coloured carpet, a few stains, probably coffee. No blood stains, that was good. Between the two chairs, a cheap round table with grey melamine top and chrome plated column and feet. Very cozy, I could get used to this. Personally, I'd have the accused's chair chained to the floor. A useful weapon, not that I was going to need one. Steel door with steel frame, and no doubt, a reasonable lock.

The viewing hatch slid back. Morrison peered in. Then the sound of the lock turning and the door opening inwards as Morrison entered the room, alone. Foolish. Still wearing his gun. Stupid. Then I remembered, I was in Canada, not an overseas prisoner awaiting my chance to escape.

"It's Sam, isn't it?"

"Sure."

"Can I call you Sam?"

"That's my name, Detective. And how would you like me to address you?"

"Detective Morrison will be fine." He sat in the soft plastic chair with wheels. Every time he sat back, the chair squeaked. I wondered whether an expensive leather one would have done that. Probably not. The squeak seemed to annoy him, I could see it in his eyes and the way he frowned slightly. I'd have got another chair, myself.

"For the record, I am Detective Morrison of the Alderson Police Service currently stationed in Alderson. Also present in the room is Sam Stephens. Mr. Stephens, this interview is being recorded on video." He noted the time and date. "For the record, please state and spell your name." I did as he asked.

"I thought it was Sam, now it's Mr. Stephens."

Morrison looked annoyed. He placed a manila file folder on the table containing papers of various sizes.

"Do you know why you're here, Stephens?"

I didn't bother to address the new status of my name.

"I heard this police station makes the best coffee in Ontario and I wanted to find out whether it was true or not. You did bring coffee with you didn't you, Bruce?" He wasn't annoyed anymore. Now, he was pissed. The table remained between us. Not a good interrogator. I'd have removed the table from the room. Makes the subject very uncomfortable, especially when you sit close to them, knees almost touching.

"I want to advise you that you have been arrested for theft under five thousand dollars, unsafe storage of a firearm, and you are further arrested for possession of a restricted weapon, resisting arrest and two counts of assault police." He got out his notebook and read my rights to me again. "Do you wish to call a lawyer now?"

"You bet. Kelly Menzies." I gave him her Toronto office number and her personal cell phone number.

"I also have to advise you that if you have spoken to any other police officer or if anyone else in a position of authority has spoken to you in connection with this matter, I want it clearly understood that I do not want it to influence you in making a statement. Do you understand?"

"Of course."

"Until you have spoken to your lawyer, we can't discuss anything about the reasons for your arrest." He got up to leave the room.

"Bruce, I'd hardly say either you or your colleague got assaulted, not in a man's way. A couple of twelve-year old school girls wouldn't even regard it as an assault. As for resisting arrest. I was very compliant and quite willing to go with you to the police station. What happened was all dictated by your actions and that of Detective Wilburn."

"I'm sure the judge is going to love hearing that, Stephens."

"You've heard of the Supreme Court of Canada haven't you, Bruce?"

"I don't have time for this, you've requested to speak to your lawyer. I'm going to call her now."

"Well, consider this, Detective. According to the Supreme Court, a police officer should act with due diligence when conducting an investigation and obtain as much information as possible before effecting an arrest and charging an individual. So far, you've failed to do that. Ask yourself this. Why is this man I have under arrest not in the least bit concerned? Perhaps I should have given him an opportunity to tell his side of the story, albeit, under caution. Maybe he knows something I don't." Just for a split second, a flicker of panic crossed his face, and then was gone. But, it was there. He left the room, pulling the door shut firmly, but not quite slamming it. The lock, however, was turned in anger.

I sat in the comfortable chair, placing my legs on the hard plastic chair, my stockinged feet hanging well over the end. My boots were sitting outside the door together with the rest of my property, including my smartphone. I really wanted a cup of coffee. I put my hands behind my head and leant back against the wall. The chair squeaked again. I took myself to my favourite place by the waterfall, on a warm late fall morning. Granite rocks sloping over the landscape, forest all around me. Crimson, yellow, red and brown leaves fluttering in the trees. Purple, yellow, and white flowers growing everywhere the sun could penetrate. Lush green ferns on the tree line. Not a soul around for miles. The sacred tobacco carried in the breeze and down river, over the roiling crystal waters. I gave thanks to the Creator and thanked Sky Woman for this beautiful day and hoped for many more to come. The smell of wood smoke from my small campfire, started the traditional way. The smell of coffee brewing in the pot over the fire.

Morrison returned. "Your lawyer's on the phone. Come with me." I was escorted to a cell adjacent to a phone that hung on the wall. The phone was situated outside and in between two cells. Morrison ushered me into the left-hand cell and handed me the phone. The cord was long enough to stretch into the cell even with the door almost closed. I sat on the wooden bench, far too narrow for me to use as a bed.

"Your call is private. I won't be far away."

"Kelly, how are you?"

"You sound far too happy for a person under

arrest for some very serious charges. What's going on, Sam?"

I told her everything. Every single thing, down to the last detail.

"I'm leaving my office right now. Do not say anything until I get there. Do you understand?"

"I love you, Kelly."

"You're such an ass." The warmth and laughter in her voice as she said it, made me smile.

Morrison hung up the phone and escorted me back into the interview room. I sat down on the hard chair. His chair squeaked again.

"I don't know any lawyer worth their salt that would drive all the way here just to speak to you. Now you've spoken to her and no doubt she's told you the usual, *Don't answer any questions,* it doesn't stop me from asking them. Whether or not you choose to answer them is up to you."

I thought about the fundamentals of interrogation as taught to me in the military. The techniques involved depended on how much time there was before some catastrophic event or the risk to lives, civilian or military. Rule one. Nobody is going to willing talk to you if they don't like you. I didn't like Morrison. He didn't like me.

He placed a sealed plastic evidence bag on the table containing a .40 calibre Glock handgun. Matt black, luminous sites. The slide was back, a yellow plastic flag inserted into the chamber, the stem down the barrel. He stared across the table at me, waiting for me to break the silence.

"Tell me, Bruce, how can you afford to drive a brand new, shiny black BMW on your salary?"

He looked shocked. "Who told you that?"

"I guess your wife, Joan, drives the silver Equinox to her teaching job at the Catholic Elementary School. Tudor Street, now that's a lovely area to live and bring up kids. Very nice, Bruce. You've done well for yourself."

The veins in his neck were now standing out, his face red with rage. I remained seated as he leaped out of his chair. After all, it was all on camera. He couldn't compose himself and stormed out of the room, forgetting to lock the door. The gun was still on the table. Forgotten in the heat of the moment, but I knew Detective Wilburn would be monitoring the interview. He'd be in very shortly. Within seconds, I had the gun out of the bag and field-stripped on the table as he rushed into the room, snatching up the gun and hurrying back out again. My fingerprints now all over it. All on camera. I heard the door lock. I was glad I didn't have that coffee after all. It wouldn't be long before I needed to take a leak. Morrison was rattled, fearing I'd come after him and his family. I wouldn't of course. We were on the same team, more or less. He'd be in the Detective Office threatening to kill me if I so much as showed up within a mile of his home. He was probably already considering moving.

I sat back in the black chair again, feet over the hard plastic one and took myself back to my peaceful place by the waterfall. And waited. It was a long wait.

* * *

"I would like to speak to my client in a room that is not being recorded."

"I'll have the audio turned off, Ms Menzies." It was a different voice. Female, probably a higher rank than Morrison.

"I'd like to see my client's cell phone, please. Apparently, it contains information that will greatly assist your investigation. Of course, I'll hand it back to you after I have spoken to my client. Is that a problem?"

"I don't think so," replied the female officer.

"You understand the implications of listening in on our conversation, Inspector?"

"I assure you that will not happen. Of course, for safety, do you have any objection to my looking in your purse?"

"Yes, I do. But given the circumstances, I don't have time to argue about it."

The door opened. In walked my lawyer in a black suit jacket, over a white blouse with matching black skirt, above the knee and black Louis Vuitton high heels. Slim, trim, young and beautiful. She reminded me very much of Annie, down to her long black braided hair, only

Kelly's eyes were coal black. She wore a turquoise turtle brooch on her left lapel. The best Native criminal defense lawyer money could buy. I gave her a hug, and pulled out the black, squeaky chair to sit in. The short stocky officer with the military hair cut escorted me to the washroom across the hall. I made a mental note of his name. Constable Robbins. It was on a metal badge over his shirt pocket. According to his shoulder flashes he was with the Alderson Police Department.

"Don't try anything, Stephens. If you do, I'll have you tied up like a pretzel before you know what's happened to you."

"I'd like to see that, Constable Robbins." An unnecessary shove into the washroom. "You can do that here, Robbins, because you're relatively safe. Please, come into the washroom, close the door and do that again. After all, you're dying to tie me up into a pretzel."

"Now you sound like a queer. Hurry up."

"You're a wanna-be soldier, Robbins. I've met your type many times. You wouldn't last two minutes in my unit."

"Is there a problem here?" It was the Inspector.

"No, ma'am."

"Good. Remember Constable, Mr. Stephens' lawyer is sitting in the interview room awaiting her client."

Robbins escorted me back to the interview room, but not without one last word.

"We'll meet again, Stephens."

"I hope so. In fact, I'm going to go out of my way to make sure we do. As the Weatherman would say, *You can bet on it.*"

Not trusting the police, Kelly and I huddled in the corner whispering.

"Okay Samuel, let's see what you've got on that phone of yours."

Chapter Six

When Kelly returned, she was accompanied by Inspector Reynolds and a glum looking Detective Morrison.

The Inspector spoke first. "I wish you had brought this information to us sooner, Mr. Stephens. It would have saved us all a lot of time and trouble. I'm sure you have your reasons. Ms. Menzies and I have had a long conversation with the Crown's office. It has been agreed that all charges against you will be dropped. Personally, I would have preferred to see the assault police charges continued. However, as the Crown pointed out, given all the circumstances there would be no reasonable expectation of a conviction."

"Samuel, before we leave the police station, I've agreed that you will download the information from your phone to Inspector Reynolds. Naturally I would like you to send it to me, too. Just in case there's a problem."

"I'll do that, Kelly."

"Oh, one other thing."

"And what's that, Inspector?"

"I would like to know how you acquired information relating to Detective Morrison's private life."

"I can't tell you that, Inspector. Don't worry, Detective, you have nothing to fear from me, besides, we're both on the same team. What I'd like to know is, what are you going to do with the information I've provided you with?"

"I can't tell you that, Recruit Stephens," sneered Detective Morrison. "But I will tell you this, keep away from my personal business and my family, if you know what's good for you."

"I think that's enough," interjected Kelly. "For the record, Detective. My client is not intelligent. Don't ever make the mistake of thinking he is, because he's not. He's super intelligent. You'd all do well to remember that. Now let's get this business concluded, I have a busy schedule."

* * *

"You're speeding, Kelly."

"Samuel, what are you going to do, give me a friggin' ticket? Besides, I'm pissed with you." She brought the red Ferrari Berlinetta down to 90 km/h from 120. "How and why did you compromise your position, by upsetting Morrison with information about his car, his wife's car, where she worked, and where they lived, as well as the fact they had kids?"

"How? Can't tell you, but I used the time I had sitting in the back of his car waiting for the cavalry to arrive to activate my phone and make contact with contacts I still have, that will always remain nameless. Why? I wanted to rattle him, throw him off. Just head games, that's all. Thank you. You did a great job as always."

"When I drop you off at the Academy, Swift will already be under arrest. Do you think you might be able to stay out of trouble, at least until the end of the course?"

"I hadn't done anything wrong, Kelly. I was merely reacting to unfortunate circumstances. Besides, I wasn't going to let Annie be sexually harassed by that creep."

"I think you like Annie. Very chivalrous, Mr. Stephens."

"I'd have done the same thing for any woman, Kelly, you know that."

"I know you would, but every time the name *Annie* gets mentioned, your face betrays you, especially your eyes."

"Do I detect a hint of jealousy here, Ms. Menzies?"

"Samuel, my life is stressful enough without you being in it. I hope Annie knows what she's letting herself into, I really ought to have a long chat with her."

"Kelly, Annie and I are just friends."

"At the moment."

"Okay, that's the main entrance coming up on your left. Take the driveway down to the front of the building and drop me off there."

I gave my lawyer a hug and a peck on the cheek before exiting her vehicle. As I walked toward the door I could hear the powerful V12 engine, stuffed under the hood of the Ferrari letting go a few horses as it accelerated away.

* * *

"Good afternoon, Tom, how's your day going?" He began to shake his head in his usual disapproving manner.

"In the infantry, my commanding officer would have had you tied to a tree, he wouldn't have had a clue how to handle you. I don't think the Director has a clue either. Oh, he wants to see you in his office. He told me to tell you that the minute you stepped through the front doors. Make sure you've got your bullet proof vest on, and put two panels in the back. Good to see you again, Mr. Stephens, life is so dull without you on campus." He was trying not to smile, but the creases on each side of his eyes gave it away. "Sam, before I forget. A colonel was in to see the Director while you were out. He said his name was Colonel Wiggins, he said to tell you not to worry and he'd be in touch. Of course, I don't know what went on in that office, but I've never seen the Director look so pale. Is everything okay?"

"I guess it is now. It's good to see you too, Tom. You and me are going to have to sit down over a beer one evening, and put this world to rights."

"That we will, Mr. Stephens, that we will."

"Enter. Ah, Stephens come in and take a seat. I think you and I have got off on the wrong foot. What's happened to you since you've been here is quite unfortunate, especially in light of Sergeant Swift, who is currently no longer with us. I assure you, from this moment on there will be no need for your surveillance equipment to be installed inside the Academy."

"Have you spoken to Recruit Annie Greyeyes?"

"I have. Everything's fine. I can't tell you what was discussed of course, that wouldn't be ethical."

"I understand. Thank you, sir."

"We have an understanding, Stephens?"

"We certainly do, sir. If you'll excuse me, I have to catch up on lectures I've missed."

The canteen was still open and I was hungry and dying for a coffee. Catching up would have to wait. The canteen was packed when I entered, all conversation stopped as I made my way to the empty table at the far end on the right-hand side. Maybe they thought it was my last supper before packing up my gear and heading out, permanently. To my surprise, Sergeant Dipper and Mackenzie got up, leaving the other sergeants speechless. They walked over to me, and both slapped me on the back.

"Good for you, Stephens," whispered Mackenzie. "I just wish I'd been there to see it."

"Annie's got your notes," said Sergeant Dipper. "She was devastated when she found out you'd been arrested. She's probably still in her room, she's a mess."

I turned and left the canteen without saying a word. No coffee yet. I knocked gently on Annie's door.

"Annie."

"Sam?"

Even with that one simple word, I could tell she'd been crying. She unlocked the door and stood in front of me, bare feet, hair a mess, eyes red. She didn't stand for long, not even a second. She jumped up and threw her arms around my neck and squeezed so tight I had trouble breathing. The pressure eased as she began to sob. All the stress Swift had put her under came out. I eased her back into her room, wishing I'd taken another approach with Swift. Beaten him senseless.

"I think they'd frown upon wearing pyjamas in the canteen, Annie. Get dressed, I'll come back in a minute."

"What happened to the side of your face?"

"Road rash, don't worry about it. Everything's fine. You already know Swift's gone and all charges against me have been dropped."

"I was so worried about you. You risked your whole career for me and never asked for anything in return. I don't even know how to say thank you. No, don't leave. Sit on the bed, I'll change quickly."

I sat on the bed with my back turned as Annie slipped out of her pyjamas. In the small mirror I watched her dress. It was a beautiful thing. Her dark police shirt complemented her long legs. As she wriggled into her police pants our eyes met in the mirror. She smiled.

"Hope you weren't disappointed."

I stood up, held her in my arms. We stood there staring at each other. She let go of her police pants. As they slipped to the floor, we began kissing.

"Annie, there's a time and a place for everything. This is the time, but it's not the place. Not here."

"You're wrong. This is the time and to hell with the place."

We were late for dinner. The canteen was now closed.

"Well, looks like we're going out for dinner, Annie. Let's go change again and get the hell out of here."

We found a small restaurant, nothing too fancy. This was Alderson farm country, after all. London, though not that far away, was too far if we wanted to make it back at a decent hour. Missing the curfew would be another black mark. Not that it would be a problem if Tom was the night officer.

"Can I come back to your place for the weekend? I discovered a great way to show my appreciation."

"Just don't leave your toothbrush behind or clothes in my closet. I wouldn't want you getting any ideas."

"That's not very nice."

"Do you know where Dalton's sending you after graduation?"

"Pickering."

"Pickering. You might as well be in Scarborough. You're gonna be busy there, Annie. Lots of armed robberies, knife attacks, violent domestics, and drugs."

"I like busy. I've got to find myself an apartment as soon as I graduate."

"My place has a spare bedroom. You're welcome to use that, no charge to friends."

"Port Albert to Pickering, that seems a long drive. I was hoping to find one in town."

"I'm talking about my condo on Harbourfront. That's where we're staying for the weekend."

"You're kidding me, right?"

"No, I've had it a while now. I like Toronto. Well, some parts of it. I like the buzz there. It makes you feel alive. Everything is right there at my doorstep. Concerts, theatres, bistros, nightclubs, and beautiful parks. From my balcony I can watch the boats go by. Ocean going ships, lakers, sailboats."

"You really are a romantic at heart. Don't tell me you like classical music as well?"

"Mozart and Beethoven are my favourite composers. If you've never been to a live classical performance, I'll take you. Just don't ask me to go to the opera. I hate opera. Why are you smiling?"

"Who would have thought, the great and mighty Mr. Stephens likes classical music. I bet you even shed a tear when the cello gets played."

"Nothing wrong with showing your innermost feelings. Tell you what. Let's see what production is currently playing at the Ed Mirvish Theatre and I'll take you to the theatre this Friday evening. My treat." I took out my smartphone. "Would you like to see Phantom of the Opera? It's playing this Friday."

"I'd love to."

I scrolled through the phone menu. "Done. Mr. Samuel Stephens requests the pleasure of Ms. Annie Greyeyes at the Ed Mirvish Theatre. Did you pack a dress?"

"I did. Subconsciously, I must have been expecting this."

Chapter Seven

Billy Big Canoe, Joe Two Rivers, and Big Jim, were waiting for me in the pod after classes.

"Sam, we're having trouble understanding this sexual offences stuff. If I'd known the Criminal Code was going to be this complicated, I'd have studied for the Bar exam instead."

"Billy, you'd pass the bar exam no problem. I bet you could name every alcoholic drink in the world and have probably drunk most of 'em."

"Funny guy, Two Rivers. If anyone could pass that exam it would have to be Big Jim."

"I don't think so, Big Canoe."

"Gentlemen. Enough. Let's grab a bite to eat and head into town in my car. I'll bring a copy of the Criminal Code and we can discuss it over a pint of beer."

"You mean a couple of pints, Sam," said Joe.

"Sam don't drink more than one pint when he's out. He wants to *stay on guard for thee* twenty-four seven and sober."

"That's right, Billy. Never get so inebriated you can't defend yourself. Life has a funny way of coming at you when you least expect it. That attitude saved my life in the military more than once. Not to say I never got hammered, of course. Especially when I lost the Weatherman."

The room fell silent for a while. They all knew how much the Weatherman meant to me.

"The first beer is for Sam's friend the Weatherman."

"Thanks, Big Jim. The Weatherman would have liked you. All of you. Okay, be at my car in one hour and fifteen minutes. Bring paper and a pen for notes."

"Hell, we don't need no pen and paper to keep tabs on how many beers we drink. We just drink 'em."

"That's not what I meant, Joe."

An hour and thirty-five minutes later, the three of them showed up. As expected. No apology. Again, as expected."

"Annie not coming with us," asked Big Jim.

"No, she's got a girls' meeting in the library, going over some possible exam questions. Anyway, I need you guys to focus on the work, not on Annie."

"Don't worry, Annie wouldn't be a distraction. We're committed academics. You should know that Sam," joked Big Jim.

As we approached the bar, a line of Harley Davidson motorcycles were already parked out front, their chrome gleaming under the yellow glow of the outside lights. I counted. Twenty of them. A multitude of bugs circled the dirty bulbs overhead. I imagined a multitude of dirty bikers circling pool tables.

"You go on in, Sam. We're gonna have a smoke first. Don't wanna break any laws."

"Like you've never broken any before, Billy. Don't worry, all your secrets are safe with me."

"We hear any chairs being broken over heads, we'll be right in. Once we finish our smoke."

"Very reassuring, Big Jim."

The split second I walked through the door, all lively conversation ceased. There must have been thirty bikers in there, wearing their colours. Not good. Not good at all.

"Better circle the wagons boys," laughed one fat, but big, biker. He moved away from the pool table holding the cue like a club.

"Indians ain't welcome in here. Go back to the reservation where you belong," said a tall, skinny biker. He looked hard and probably was. The trouble with bikers is, they're bullies. You fight one, you have to fight them all. Individually, every one of them was a walking dead man, only most of them were too stupid to know it.

"You deaf, Indian?" said another. A small muscular guy. Safety in numbers. Had he been the only one in the bar, the same for all of them, not one of them would have spoken out of turn. They would have understood the immediate health hazard once they'd sized me up. I was disappointed. First they steal our land from our grandfathers. Then I go overseas to fight for the land they stole, only to return and be insulted. I could feel the *Warrior Spirit,* rising from deep within me, where I kept it locked away. Releasing it would turn a sparkling waterfall into a torrent of blood.

"Well, looks like we're gonna have to kick his dumb ass out of here," said the fat one.

They began to move toward me. In a flash, I bent my left knee, whipping out a large knife from my boot, the handle concealed by my pant leg. A more prudent man would have left. *Warrior, my money's on you,* said the Weatherman inside my head. *Kill every last one of them.*

The door opened behind me. Now there were four *warriors.* Each expertly holding a large hunting knife. The mob began to move in slowly, uncertainly. I began to rise to my toes at the point of springing to action. I would become a tree on a fast turning wheel, spinning, stabbing, and slicing. Each cut would be executed with perfection and accuracy. Five of them would die in the first few seconds, as the *Warrior* went into battle.

"Stop!" Shouted a voice from the far corner of the room. A tall well-built biker stood under the *washroom* sign. He was drying his hands on a brown paper towel. That one word was all it took for me to recognize my brother-in-arms.

"Malloy?"

"You know him?" said the fat biker.

"Know him? I fought with him. He saved my life more times than a cat's got nine. Good job I came out when I did. The *Warrior* and his friends would have killed every last one of you.

Welcome, boys, let me buy you a drink. No harm done. He turned to his biker friends. "It's cool." Like dogs dragged off a kill, the other bikers slunk away. "You won't be needing those swords now, we're all good."

I slipped my knife back into my boot.

"I figured you being a cop now, yes I heard, don't look so surprised. I figured you would know it's a criminal offense, carrying a concealed weapon. Not that I'd say anything, of course."

"I know you wouldn't, Malloy." We hugged and slapped each other on the back. "I heard too, that you had started your own outlaw motorcycle gang, *Malloy's Soldiers*. How's that working out for you?"

"Awesome, my friend. Friggin' awesome. Of course, we're only small at the moment. This is it." He waved his arm around the room to encompass his disciples. "Every last one of them is a former front line soldier. We'd have been a whole lot smaller if I hadn't come out of the washroom when I did. I know, I know, *you're disappointed.* Don't judge me too hard. After life in the military I couldn't settle back into civvy life. I needed action. I thought about the police, but knew I couldn't face all that paperwork and giving out speeding tickets to people just trying to get to work on time. It was close though. You and me would have made good partners, like the old days."

"It's not my place to judge you, my friend. That is for the Creator. No matter that we are on different sides of the fence, you will always be my friend and I will always have your back."

"As I will you, Sam. You can count on it." Malloy rose to his feet, beer glass held high. "A toast to the Weatherman!" The room erupted to the sound of glasses being chinked and the words, *To the Weatherman,* resonating around the room. The barman, pale with fright, replaced the phone. He had been too frozen in fear to punch in the numbers 9-1-1. Malloy and I moved away to another table to talk alone.

"You know, Malloy, you're unlikely to see old age."

"I know that, Sam. I'm at peace with that. You on the other hand, are a hard man to kill. The bigger clubs are a real threat at the moment. They want us to patch over to them, but I'm not willing to do that. I'm not ready for contract killings, international drug smuggling, and hard-core prostitution. Besides, their initiation ceremonies are too gross for even the likes of me, and that's saying something." We both laughed.

"Malloy, it's going to get ugly, you know that. If you don't dance to their tune, you and some of your members are going to die. Not only have you got to worry about them, the police are going to hound you. You won't be able to trust anyone. They'll be listening in on your conversations, surveillance teams are going to be targeting you. And just when you think you've got it made, a police tactical unit is going to take you down. You'll be looking down the barrel of an assault rifle all over again. You'll be broke before you know it with all the legal costs followed by maybe thirty-years in jail."

"You got any good news?"

"No. There isn't any. All I can give you is a parachute when it all goes to shit. You know my cabin, the one in the woods on the way to Bancroft?"

"Yeah. Spent some good times up there with the guys. Jesus, I miss the Weatherman, he was always so funny. Man, could he tell some great campfire stories."

"You still remember the code to get in?"

"Sure do."

"Pay attention. When it all goes wrong for you, and it will …"

"Ah, come on, Sam, lighten up."

"Listen to me. You go there, never in your own vehicle. Rent one if you have to. Tell no-one where you're going, not even your girlfriend, mother, or sister. Buy a throwaway cell phone and call me, then dump it, long before you get there. Pay attention to anyone following you. Never discuss our friendship with anyone. If things are that bad, I will arrange getting you out of the country. You can never come back, but I'll make sure it's somewhere warm."

"You don't sound like a police recruit in training to me, Sam. What the hell are you into, brother?"

"If I tell you, I'll have to kill you. I guess I

just can't shake the military training I was exposed to. Old habits, that's all. Don't read too much into it."

"I love you, man. You ever need help, you call me. Anytime."

The loudness of exuberant youth could be heard approaching the door. It swung open and in walked half a dozen recruits from the Academy, all full of piss and vinegar. I knew them by sight, but not to talk to. Not my type. All raring to go and stick it to the general public. Probably already got a ticket competition set up for the day their police services let them loose on their own. God help the public.

The bar went silent again. I could smell their fear when they saw all the bikers gathered together. You could see it in their eyes. The first two recruits stopped dead in their tracks, those following behind, bumped into the back of them. They were wearing police pants. Dressed in half blues. Incompetent. Half blues and unarmed. Stupid. No police radio. Foolish.

They looked across the room and saw me, recognition in their faces and shock, then disgust. I was sitting with the president of a motorcycle gang, all of them wearing colours.

"This place is full of low life. Let's go find another bar that doesn't stink so much," said the one nearest the door. He looked like a runner, had the build of a runner. In a second, he was going to need that skill.

I got up. "You!" My anger probably saved all

of them from a beating they would never forget. "If you want to mouth off, be prepared for the consequences. You best beat a hasty retreat before I pound you myself for insulting me and my brothers. Or, I can leave you to the bikers."

"Sorry, Stephens, I didn't see you there. I wasn't insulting you, just the scum you're with, I mean the bikers. No offence."

"You should choose your friends better," said the big guy among them. Probably a hockey player. Enforcer likely. Good at fighting on the ice. No ice here.

"You have a cell phone with you," I asked.

"Sure, what's it to you?"

"You have 9-1-1 speed dialed into it?"

"Yeah. Are you on something, buddy?"

"I'm not your buddy. Call 9-1-1 and ask for an ambulance. Have it start making its way here now. If you know your blood type, let them know that, too. It'll all save time."

No sooner the word than the blow. That's what my grandfather always told me. Good advice.

He wasn't backing down. I was disappointed. I seem to get disappointed a lot.

"I think you and me need to settle this outside," he said. "Maybe I'll call an ambulance, you'll be needing one. I'm gonna count to three and you better be back in your seat by then. One. Two."

There was no, *three.* A fast, sharp, but not too hard, brachial stun caused his knees to buckle. He hit the floor like a sack of potatoes.

Big Jim, Joe, and Billy, were already out of their chairs following on the heels of Malloy. As expected, the other five recruits did not want to play.

"Take your buddy outside for some fresh air. Keep an eye on him," I said. He was beginning to come to, disoriented. He didn't even know what hit him. "He'll be fine in a few minutes." I went back to enjoy my beer.

"Warrior, you haven't changed one bit," said Malloy. "You know they're gonna complain. That's probably the first bar fight they've ever been in, and the fastest."

"I never hit a man that didn't deserve it," I said. "I'm gonna have to wear one of those bicycle helmets with a mirror on the side from now on, so I can watch my back."

"That you will," agreed Malloy. "If nothing else, I'm sure you could win *the silly hat of the week award.*"

"Okay, I promised these guys I'd help them navigate through the Criminal Code. You might want to join us, Malloy. You might learn something useful."

All five of us sat down together and made a start on the *policeman's bible.* I finished my one pint of beer and nestled a mug of coffee.

"That ambulance sure took a long time to get here," said Billy. "He must have called for one after all."

I looked up. "That's not an ambulance. It's a cruiser and here comes some more. One of those greenhorns called it in. Their way of getting even."

"I'll join my men. Won't look so bad for you when they come in."

"Sit down, Malloy. Not once have we deserted each other in battle. We're not going to start now. It is what it is." He sat down again.

The door barged open. "Here we go," said Malloy.

I instantly recognized the first officer through the door. Constable Robbins.

"Hitler's arrived," I said, under my breath. "It'll be all downhill from here."

"You know him?"

"You could say that, Malloy. He arrested me recently."

Robbins stood in the centre of the room surrounded by eleven other uniform officers, as well as a sergeant and a K9 officer, minus his dog.

Robbins looked confident. "Have your ID ready for inspection! Every motorcycle out there will be checked, handlebars will be measured to ensure they conform to the Highway Traffic Act. Any violations found and the driver will ticketed."

"You don't *drive* a motorcycle, sonny. You *ride* one," said the fat biker. "Think of it like a beautiful woman. You don't *drive* a good looking woman, now do you? You *ride* her. Got the picture. I guess you're more a *driver* than a *rider.* Wife beater probably. Maybe even a closet pervert."

The whole bar erupted into howls of

laughter. I put my head in my hands and tried to stifle the erupting laughter. Big Jim, Joe, and Billy, were not so polite. They laughed so hard, tears ran down their cheeks. Robbins was so red with rage he looked like he was choking. Then he saw me.

"You! Outside. Now!"

I ignored him. I flipped through the Criminal Code table of contents until I found the *Canadian Charter of Rights and Freedoms.*

"Everyone has the right to life, liberty and justice and security of the person and the right not to be deprived thereof except in accordance with the principles of fundamental justice. Everyone has the right to be secure against unreasonable search or seizure. Everyone has the right not to be arbitrarily detained or imprisoned."

Robbins shot across the room, grabbed me by the shirt collar and tried to yank me out of my seat. Ordinarily, he would never have got that far, but I needed him to do that. Witnesses. Lots of them. Bikers, police officers, and police recruits. The police dog was still in the cruiser outside. Probably a good thing. I never really had a problem with dogs, any dog, big or small. Probably would have torn a chunk out of Robbins' ass.

Palm strike to the nose. *Bang*. No blood. Not hard enough. Distraction. Painful wristlock. *Slam*. Face down on the table.

"Sergeant, take your man out of here, before I file my own assault charge and call you as a witness. He's out of order. There's been no problems in here, not until the guys came in that phoned you, and now Robbins, who has a hard on for me. If you all want a fight for the sake of a good donnybrook, I'm all for that, but you are more than outnumbered. By the time my lawyer's finished with you on the stand, Sergeant, you'll wish you'd taken early retirement. Any breach of the peace inside this establishment has been caused by your man here."

"I've heard all about you, Mr. Stephens. Can't say I agree with your choice of company as a police recruit, but it's a free country. I'll have to file a report, of course. Now, perhaps you'd be so kind as to give me back my man. Undamaged."

I eased Robbins painfully to his feet and whispered in his ear. "The next time you lay a hand on me, reserve a hospital bed for yourself. You'll be needing it. Do it a third time and I'll have a plot already picked out for you." I escorted him back to his sergeant.

"Robbins, wait outside."

"You're not going to let him get away with that, are you, Sarge? He assaulted me. You saw him."

"I said. Wait outside! Don't make me repeat myself."

Robbins skulked away through the door. Ego severely damaged. I thought about that bicycle helmet with the rearview mirror and wondered what colour would suit me.

"I phoned my friend in the MP's. Knows you. Distinguished military career he tells me. All classified he said. Told me to make a friend of you, not an enemy. Better for my health, he said. Better for longevity, apparently. Are we good here, Mr. Stephens?"

I glanced again at his name tag. "We're golden, Sergeant Willoughby."

Chapter Eight

"Oh, my God. This is not what I expected. Sam. This place is incredible. Those paintings, they're massive. Who did your decorating? And your sculptures. They must have cost a fortune."

"I did my own decorating, Annie. Some of those carvings come from Curve Lake, they're very precious to me. The way they represent our Creator and Sky Woman fills me with joy and yet, their beauty wets my eyes."

Annie cast her eyes down. "The river inside you runs deep, Sam."

"Take a look around. Make yourself at home. If you decide you want to stay here instead of finding a place in Pickering, the spare bedroom is to your right down the hall. It has an en suite bathroom, so you won't have to share with me. I have my own."

Annie walked down the hallway and walked into the spare room. She squealed with delight, ran back down the hall, and leapt into my arms. I could feel her body heaving against mine and the wetness of her tears against my neck. I said nothing.

"No one has ever been so kind to me in my life without expecting something in return. You know what I mean."

"Annie, first, you are my friend. The only thing I expect from a friend is loyalty, honesty, and trust. I expect nothing more from you than these things. I try not to fall in love. It inevitably brings pain, especially in the business I was in. Sure, I have had women, but I always kept them at arm's length. I'm not the marrying kind, either. Think about it. They say two out of three marriages end in divorce. Realistically, out of the third that's left, how many of those marriages are truly happy? I bet, very few. If marriage was nothing more than a financial investment, nobody with any sense would risk their money investing with those odds."

An uncomfortable silence followed my monologue. Annie stood in the middle of the living room biting her bottom lip. I'd never said it before and a voice inside me kept telling me not to say it, and it wasn't the Weatherman. But I said it anyway. I couldn't help myself.

"I love you, Annie Greyeyes."

Her smile lit up the whole room. "I love you, too, Sam."

"No, you don't," I said, teasing. "Pleasure, before incredible pleasure. If we're going to take our clothes off, Annie, it's because we have a dinner and theatre date, remember? However, when we get home, I hope you won't be spending the night in the spare bedroom."

"Oh, I won't be, Sam."

As we walked along the downtown Toronto streets toward the Ed Mirvish Theatre, I was aware of men turning to look at Annie. Who could blame them? I'd have done the same. I didn't mind a casual glance, but ogling was a no, no. Oglers got shoulder checked or stared down.

"Easy, Sam. Are you okay?"

"A couple of Mississippi's is all right, more than that is disrespectful. Did you enjoy your dinner?"

"It was excellent. You really know Toronto, don't you. Who would have thought that down that dingy-looking side street was the most amazing bistro. The owner obviously likes you, finding a table for two without any reservation. The place was packed."

"It's always packed. Theo and I go back a long way."

"Got any spare change, mister?"

"Why?" I replied, staring at the disheveled looking man, panhandling.

"I'm hungry. I haven't eaten all day."

"You prefer tea or coffee?"

"Coffee. Why?"

I took Annie into a fast-food restaurant, bought a double cheeseburger and fries and a coffee, with sugar and cream on the side.

"Enjoy," I said, thrusting the coffee and brown paper bag into the man's dirty hands.

"Thank you, sir, you're a Christian."

"Actually, I'm not."

"Pretty lady, sir. All the best to you both."

"That was a nice thing to do, Sam."

"Not really. What would be nice is if I gave him our spare bedroom."

Annie squeezed my arm. "You can't. You already promised it to me."

* * *

"Thank you, Sam. That was a beautiful performance. The singing and dancing was incredible. I'm never going to forget this night. It's been wonderful."

"It has, hasn't it."

I saw them up ahead, on the other side of the street. Skinheads, but not quite. They had Mohican haircuts, shaved down both sides. Very insulting. Not cool. I didn't like them already. They crossed the street, heading toward us, as expected. Annie didn't seem to notice at first. Not street smart. Then she saw them. Her hand squeezed mine tightly. A tremor of fear. I squeezed her hand. A tremor of rage. One almost my size, big. Very big. The other two, not so big. One small. They formed a line across the sidewalk. The big one in the middle. The small one on the inside, nearest the stores. The third one nearest the road, nearest the traffic. A lot of cars, but moving slowly. Pity, I could have used that to my advantage. Still a possibility.

They were now ten yards away, eyes darting between me and the pretty young woman next to me, no longer holding my hand. No point wasting a second disengaging hands. The small guy made a grab for Annie. It all happened in the blink of an eye. Annie screamed and pleaded for the guy not to hurt her, then kicked him so hard in the balls I was sure her stiletto heel must have done some real damage. Then she was all over him. OIV. A beautiful thing. The street lighting wasn't bad, but not great. That was good. I brought up my small flashlight and turned it on. Its light was like a miniature sun, all bottled up in that tiny black metal casing. It was a weapon in itself. This was the real deal. Blinding light. Incapacitating light. The big guy couldn't see. I stepped past him, kicked the side of his knee, and broke it. Down he went, screaming in pain.

I saw the flash of silver from the knife blade, as the third skinhead thrust his right hand toward my torso. I was already moving fast and twisting my body away to the right, my left forearm making contact with his nose. Hard. Broken bone, cartilage and blood. Lots of blood. His blood, not mine.

Sirens, flashing lights, moving fast and close. The guy fell back into the road, his head bouncing off the metal push bar of the cruiser. Pity. I hadn't finished. Two cops jumped out of the cruiser, doors left open. The passenger ran around to the guy unconscious or dead on the road in front of the cruiser. No great loss to society anyway. The driver ran over to us.

Older seasoned cops. In good shape, too. I was impressed. No donut flour on these boys. The driver said, "It's okay, we saw what happened. Is the lady all right?" Annie was breathing hard, she wasn't crying, but the tears were in her eyes. Her first street fight. I was proud of her.

"Wow, young lady, you put up a good fight. Good for you. Whoever trained you deserves a medal."

Sirens in the distance, getting closer. Flashing emergency lights coming from both directions. Cruisers and two ambulances. Impressive. I couldn't find the opportunity I needed to do more damage to the big one. It would have to wait for another day. I put that thought into my mental notebook, compartmentalized, catalogued, with threat assessment level and level of corrective action required. It was a very small range. I normally only used two of the five levels. Bodily harm or death, depending on the severity of the transgression. All noted. Like an elephant, I never forgot and rarely forgave. I looked across at Annie and mentally noted my decision. It would be level one or two.

Annie's dress was torn, revealing her bra. I took off my jacket and wrapped it around her. She was shaking and in shock.

"Where are you guys from," asked the cop driving the first cruiser.

"We live together here in Toronto."

"Not much you really need to tell us here. My partner and I saw the whole thing. Would you mind if we took a couple of quick statements from you?"

“Let’s get it done,” I said. “Give me a minute with my girlfriend.”

“You were lucky, my friend,” he said as I turned away. “Look at your shirt. The blade cut clean through the fabric.”

I undid my shirt. There was a long thin red line of glistening blood. My blood. The wound was only superficial, but just deep enough to draw blood. No stitches needed. The paramedics placed a blanket over the guy lying on the road. They pulled it up over his head. I made another mental note. *Skinhead with knife. Dead. NFA required.*

Now, it was going to be a long night. They shut the road down. Yellow *Police Line Do Not Cross* tape was tied to road signs, lampposts, and the first cruiser, effectively securing the scene. Annie and I were driven to the police station in separate cruisers. Detectives were waiting for us. They weren’t pleased to see us, well maybe Annie. A female detective arrived and took Annie down the hallway, out of sight. She seemed compassionate, that made me feel better.

An older detective took me into an interview room. He looked like he should have retired ten years ago. Probably his second or third wife had left him and now he didn’t have a pot to piss in or a window to throw it out. He had a belly and a double chin. The exertion from walking from his desk, across the hall to the interview room caused him to wheeze. We both waited until he got his breath back. He was never going to retire. Couldn't afford to. I felt sorry for him.

"We ought to give you a medal and the freedom of the city, Mr. Stephens," he wheezed. "Let me shake your hand and thank you. Those three assholes are the scum of the earth. They'd have raped that girl of yours, you know, if you hadn't been there. Done it before. Haven't been able to prove it yet." He lent across the table awkwardly and extended his hand. We shook hands then waited for him to get his breath back. "Pity the other two didn't get run down by the cruiser and killed. I would have personally taken you and your girlfriend out for dinner. That is if ex number three hadn't fleeced me of my last penny. Bitch. I'm Detective Paul Johnson, the lead investigator on this case. Unfortunately because the asshole hit the cruiser and died, SIU have been notified. Very inconvenient, but nothing for you to worry about. As far as I'm concerned, you're nothing more than a witness in this case. Call me Johnny. Don't worry, I haven't started recording yet, so feel free to say anything you like. Now pay attention, I'm only going to say this once. The camera can't see my face, just the back of my head. So, if, when you're telling your story you see me making various facial expressions, pay close attention. Lots of smiles means, keep going, I love it. Exasperated look, change tack quickly before you sewer yourself. Got it?"

"Got it."

"Good. Can I get you a coffee?"

"Black, no sugar, thank you, Johnny."

"Give me a minute. While I'm gone I'll switch on the tape. If you pick your nose or fart, it'll all be recoded."

I liked Johnny. I got the impression everyone else did too, other than his ex-wives. One of the good guys. Old school, but not long for this earth.

He returned with two coffees and we got started. He was good. His facial expressions were a great help. I got lots of smiles and the odd exasperated look, which soon turned to smiles again. He carefully guided me through my statement to ensure I was always on safe ground.

Before leaving he gave me his card. Annie was sitting in the hallway waiting for me, my jacket still draped around her shoulders. She and the female detective, Jackie Collins, were laughing about something. She was good. I could see Annie liked her.

Jackie dropped us off at the front of the condo in the undercover grey Ford. "Good luck at the Academy," she said as she pulled away.

Annie and I sat at the kitchen table nestling a glass of Shiraz. I could see she wanted to speak, but hadn't yet formed the right words in her head. I let the silence linger. Just the sound of the fridge compressor kicking in and the *ticktock* of the kitchen clock. Life ticking away, one second at a time. Ordinarily, I never heard that clock, but in the early hours of this morning, it sounded loud …

"How do you do it?"

"Do what Annie?"

"It's like nothing fazes you. Like you don't have any feelings. That's not normal Sam."

I said nothing.

"Tell me. If I walked out on you now, would you even care? A man died tonight. A human being. Don't you care?"

"No."

"I don't understand you, Sam. You're like a machine."

"Well, Annie, know this much. It's not true that I don't have feelings. My feelings for you are incredibly strong. My feelings for the earth, the trees, the flowers, the sky, the lakes, the animals, birds, and insects, are strong. My belief in the Creator is strong. I have never in my entire life allowed myself to love a woman as much as I love you. If you decide to walk out I will be very hurt. I will not cry, or get angry, or get drunk. I will go for a long walk to clear my head. I will not come after you, and I will not let you back into my life to hurt me again. That is all I have to say about that. I will leave my wallet on the table, there is money for a taxi if you so choose."

"Where are you going?"

"For a long shower. You did very well tonight, Annie. You should be proud. I'm very proud of you. Sit a while. Don't make a decision in haste. Know this. I love you, Annie Greyeyes. You are like a bird to me, and always will be. You are free to come and go as you like, I will never clip your wings."

I resigned myself to being hurt and walked into my bedroom and into the en suite bathroom. I heard the kitchen chair move, then the sound of the apartment door opening and closing. With a heavy heart I entered the walk-in shower and let the water wash away the physical and emotional pain. Looking through the glass door, I saw Annie standing naked. Stepping into the shower she said, "Did you really think I had left you?" She was gently sobbing.

I said nothing and pulled her close to me.

"I'm sorry, Sam, I think I'm still in shock. I should be thanking you for saving me, not angry at you."

I placed my finger against her lips. "No need to say any more about it. When we get up I'm taking you out for brunch, and then I'm taking you to a little boutique and buying you a new dress."

"In that case, I'm going to be extra nice to you this morning." I inhaled sharply as I felt her body sliding down against my own.

Chapter Nine

Sergeant Dipper was in good form for a Monday morning. At least half the class looked hung over.

"I trust you all had a good weekend? Am I talking too loudly for you, Mr. Weeks? A little under the weather are we? Well, no apologies. All of you pay attention! This morning we're going to discuss the law relating to impaired operation of a motor vehicle, over eighty, and care and control of a motor vehicle as it relates to being impaired by alcohol or drugs. As I can see already, many of you look impaired, but fortunately for you there is no offence for being drunk in charge of a desk. Though there should be. This is the bread and butter of front line policing and one of the most complicated areas of front line policing there is. In short. It's a minefield. It is an area that will cause you the most headaches and heartaches. It will test your resolve and your belief in the judicial system. You will arrive at court with the most watertight case there is, that even Houdini himself couldn't get out of, only to find your case reduced to a careless or worse, dismissed all together. All on some bloody technicality. After you've gone through hell on the stand, you will wonder if

M.A.D.D. Mothers Against Drunk Drivers, is a figment of your imagination. Born out of the carnage on our roads, where our loved ones are killed by drunk drivers, you will be incredulous that our judges are letting these people off. But, fear not. The cost of hiring a lawyer to defend you in an impaired trial will bankrupt many. So, my friends. We win if we win, and we win if we lose. And don't let anybody tell you, *It's not about winning or losing, it's about justice.* That's nothing more than sanctimonious bullshit! You fresh faced little darlings, not you Stephens. You're in a category of your own. You fresh faced little darlings will soon find out that there is no justice. If you don't believe in fairyland, then you are sadly mistaken. The Canadian judicial system is really another name for *fairyland.* Don't look so crestfallen, Ms. Waters. Equate it to sport fishing. We catch them and they let them go again. It's nothing more than a game. You know, like Monopoly. Don't take it all too personal, otherwise you'll never get through five years, let alone thirty. "

At the end of another one of Dipper's memorable lectures he called Annie and I aside.

"No surprise, the Director wants to see the two of you in his office. But don't worry. He's actually concerned about you. I know all about it, not just what I read in the papers. My good friend, Detective Johnson, called me up and asked me to keep an eye on Annie. He said not to bother with you, Stephens. He's already asked his superintendent to get you into his

Division and to be personally assigned to him when the opportunity arises. Seems you made quite an impression. Anyway, are you doing okay, Annie?" Annie nodded. "Well, if you need to talk about it and it doesn't have to be me, I can put you in touch with the proper channels. In the old days, after being exposed to traumatic events like you two have, you were expected to *suck it up.* I know you're a tough military guy, Sam, but the same goes for you. I shouldn't say this, and don't let it go to your heads. The staff here are extremely proud of you both, especially you, Sam. You're a man's man in the true sense of the word. We'd all love to have officers like you on our platoons when we get back to real policing. Okay, don't just stand there. Chop, chop. The Director's waiting for you."

* * *

"Come in, come in. Sit down, the two of you. How are you both doing? What an unbelievable weekend for the pair of you. You know, Stephens, and please don't take this the wrong way, but I don't think I've been involved in as many skirmishes in my whole life as you have since you've been here. You seem to attract trouble. I just don't know what it is about you. You're like a magnet for it."

"The Creator gave me a good brain and a

strong body. Some use these gifts for evil purposes. I believe I have been given these things to help those who don't have the capability to stand up for themselves. That's why I became a police officer. I see myself as a big brother to those that don't have someone to stand up for them. Like a woman in an abusive relationship, beaten by her partner, enduring pain and suffering for years, but too scared to leave. Then I come into her life and make good the damage that has been done. I help restore her confidence and her self-esteem. The man, now has someone far more powerful to contend with, someone who won't back down. The difference between you and me, sir, is simply this. When a group of thugs blocks the sidewalk in front of you when you are walking with your wife, you will step aside for them, empowering them further. Unlike you, I will not step aside. I will beat the living daylights out of all of them. You think you don't attract trouble? Of course you do. You just don't recognize it and do nothing about it when it presents itself. Why is that? Because you are not, and never will be, a warrior. I, on the other hand, am a *warrior*."

"I think that's a little melodramatic, Stephens. I didn't get to this position by being a wimp, I can assure you. It took a lot of hard work to rise to this leadership position. Frankly, I think your comments are insulting."

"Sir, I've been at this Academy long enough to see that you are a manager, but never a leader. The word *leadership* is bandied around far too much in the police service. I'm sure there are a few managers that are leaders. There's no doubt in my mind I'll find precious few of them."

It was as though the air inside the room had become a gelatinous mass and we were all trapped inside, the Director and I just staring at each other. I think Annie had stopped breathing. The only visible thing that changed inside the room was the colour of the Director's face. It had gone through various colour changes from pale to crimson.

The Weatherman spoke to me. *Warrior, you're right. It's not that what you say is wrong, they just don't like to be told the truth. You don't have a filter, that's your trouble. Don't even think of getting promoted. Your card's already stamped ... Insubordinate.*

"I'll let your insolence go this time, Stephens. I'll put it down to the weekend's events. Now, leave my office. Ms. Greyeyes, I'd like you to remain."

I left the office and made my way to the canteen. I needed coffee. Ten minutes later, Annie sat down across from me.

"Sam, you are your own worst enemy. There is no way you could ever get a job in the diplomatic core. What were you thinking?"

"Did you know Annie, according to my old physics teacher, a cup of coffee with milk, or cream I guess, will retain its heat longer than a cup of black coffee of equal size?"

"With or without sugar?"

"Do you know, I can't remember."

"Stop smiling, Sam, you're exasperating, do you know that? Don't you even want to know what he said to me?"

"Predictable. He told you that being involved with me was going to hurt your promising career. *I can see young lady that you have the potential to go places in the police service and rise all the way to the top. I'm sorry to tell you this, but I feel it is my duty to do so. If you hang around with a man like Stephens, he'll only bring you down."*

"Did you bug his office? You did, didn't you?"

"No, I did not. No need to give me that look. I didn't. Thought about it, though."

"Sam, I have a promising career ahead of me. I think it's probably best if I distance myself from you." Her eyes dropped, as though she was fixated with something on the table that I couldn't see.

Silence. Incredulous disbelief.

"Sam, I'm only joking. Do you not know how much I love you, and am committed to you?" She smiled that smile of hers, the edges of her mouth curling up.

"You should get a job on APTN as an actress. You had me completely fooled. Again. I gotta give it to you, Annie, you're good. I can see it now. *Aboriginal Peoples Television Network presents, undercover special agent, Annie Greyeyes, in, Fooled Again, with guest appearance by Sam Eagle Eyes, as her duped lover.* Stop laughing."

"He did say this, which will surprise you ... *Much as I find Mr. Stephens intolerable, he will be a copper's cop, and a damn good one at that. I just hope I never find myself in the unfortunate position of being his superior officer."*

"I hope you corrected him?"

"About what?"

"Being my *superior officer.* None of them are *superior* to us, Annie. They are merely our *supervisors,* not *superiors.*"

"There you go again, Mr. Stephens. Just can't let it go. Got to have the last word if it kills you."

"What's on the agenda now?"

"Defensive tactics. No, sorry. We can't use that word. For your benefit, Mr. Stephens, from now on we're going to call it, *OIV tactics against assholes.*"

"You make me laugh, Annie. Come on, let's go do some *OIV.*"

Chapter Ten

"It's my Band's powwow this weekend, Annie. Would you like to come? We could stay at my place on the res."

"Are you taking part?"

"Damn, right. You want to dance?"

"Sure, but I don't have my regalia with me, unless you want to drive down to my reserve to get it."

"Call your Band office and have one of the Ojibwa dancers bring it with them. They can drop it off at my Band office Saturday morning."

"I'll call my sister. If she knows I'm going to be there, she'll come. My family's dying to meet you anyway. Do I need to remind you, not to bring any weapons into the ceremony with you?"

"Of course not, I'll be among friends. I was thinking, Annie, my house is on the Port Albert Peninsular on the Cheyrone First Nation Reserve. If Dalton ever posts you to Port Albert, my place will be ideal for you. You'll be ten minutes from work."

"That's very generous of you, Sam. You wouldn't mind?"

"Not unless you brought a boyfriend with

you."

"I can't promise. Anyway, you told me you weren't controlling."

"Don't worry I wouldn't have control issues with it, but I'm not sure I could suppress any homicidal feelings toward him."

"Hard to imagine. Two weeks from now and we graduate. I can't believe how fast it's gone by. We're not going to see so much of each other once we get to our divisions. I hope our shifts are going to be at least a bit compatible. Dalton's on twelve hour shifts, two days two nights, four off. Toronto's shifts are weird. I'm not sure which I'd like better."

"Some of the shifts I've worked in the military have been pretty crazy. Especially in battle. In fact, sometimes there's no shifts at all. In the heat of it there's no time to put your head down. The only time your head goes down is when you get killed or seriously injured."

"Do you miss it?"

"Sometimes. After having dealt with so much mayhem, dead bodies, fallen brothers, and sisters sometimes, too, I'm not sure how I'm going to handle some asshole sergeant telling me I need to get more speeding tickets. I've got a feeling I might quit there and then and go back in the military."

"Well, absence makes the heart grow fonder. I'd wait for you."

"That's what they all say. Watching a young soldier fall to pieces after he receives a *Dear John* is heartbreaking. There's nothing you can do to take the pain away. They're stuck in some Godforsaken land, thousands of miles from home, fighting for their country, while some insurance broker is screwing their wife or girlfriend. No wonder there's so much suicide."

"I know, Sam. I would never do that to you."

"That's what they all say. That's why I never allowed myself to get too involved in a relationship. Can you believe it, Annie? More cops are killed with their own handguns by their own hand than are ever shot and killed by assholes. There's a lot of *PTSD* in the military, the police can't be that far behind."

"How do you cope?"

"To be honest, Annie, I don't know. Maybe I think I'm coping, fooling myself, when in reality I'm not coping at all. That scares me. Like there's a day down the road when I finally *snap*. I think in policing I'm more likely to get post-traumatic stress disorder from all the bureaucracy and bullshit, at least that's what some of the old cops tell me."

"I think you and me need to go into town this evening and take the scenic route back."

"Annie that is an absolutely wonderful idea. Hopefully, we can have an evening out together without getting into any trouble this time."

"As the Director said, *Stephens, you're like a magnet for it.* Before we get back to class, I want to clear something up with you. Don't look so worried. It's nothing bad. I just want you to know that, when I say I'd wait for you, whatever. I'd wait for you, and you can take that to the bank. If you think otherwise, then you really don't know me very well at all. It's hurtful and insulting to me that you would think otherwise."

"I'm sorry, Annie. I was out of order. You're one of a kind and I'm very lucky to have you."

"We're lucky to have each other. I don't even ask if you'd wait for me. I already know the answer."

"Fool."

"You know, Stephens, sometimes you can be such an ass."

* * *

"Do you mind if I drive tonight?"

"No, why should I?"

"It's just that guys like to drive. You know."

"Annie, I love being chauffeured. Not sure I can fit in that little sports car of yours, though."

"Sam, you'll squeeze in, I can always pull you out when we get there."

It was a smooth ride for a little car, but then I shouldn't have been that surprised. German engineering. The console looked like the cockpit of a fighter jet, all dials and coloured lights. Lots of electronic gadgetry. Too many things to go wrong. Inboard computer. Great when it's working. When it isn't, the car isn't going to be working either. I liked my old gas guzzler. Carburetor. No *inboard computer.* Simple engineering. Reliable, like an old tractor. A lot of its mechanical parts could die on you, but it would still keep on going, just not as smoothly. Simple dials, too. Speedometer, rev counter, temperature gauge, fuel gauge. Wind-up windows. Simple engineering.

In the side mirror, I saw the big Dodge Ram pick-up truck roaring up behind us. A couple of cars were approaching, so unless the guy driving wanted a head-on, an overtake was unwise. Its huge chrome grill filled the back window of the BMW.

"I hate tailgaters," said Annie. "It's an eighty limit, I'm doing ninety-five. If he gets any closer he'll be on top of us."

"How many in the truck?"

"At least four, maybe five. Young guys in their twenties."

"Start spraying your windshield washer for a good few seconds."

"That worked Sam, he's backed off."

"Good."

The chrome bumper filled the rear window again. Then the sound of the truck horn blaring. Loud and long. The driver was obviously irritated. The road ahead was clear, he could overtake if he wanted.

Then the unexpected. He nudged the rear of the BMW.

"Oh my God, he's trying to run us off the road."

"For the time being, Annie, we're on our own. Likely scenario. These are local boys, out to have some fun. Could be armed, unlikely, but I guarantee there's a shotgun in that truck for poaching. Accessible, but not lightning fast."

"What shall I do?"

"There's been an accident under the Highway Traffic Act. We must stop, render assistance if necessary and exchange information. You stop, I'll render assistance. When they exit the truck, you take off. I'll be waiting here with the driver's information when you get back five minutes later."

"I don't like that idea. Why don't I outrun them and get away, then call 9-1-1."

"If you were on your own I'd say that was a great idea. On your return, park back up the road. Flash your lights. You'll know I'm okay when you see their truck suddenly burst into flames. If you flash your lights and nothing happens, take off and call 9-1-1."

The BMW pulled onto the gravel shoulder, followed by the truck. I adjusted the rear view mirror and waited. I didn't have to wait long. Five young men got out of the truck ranging in various sizes, like a small football team. Amateurs. They didn't rush us, uncertain as to what lurked inside the BMW. They weren't expecting us to pull over. I got out. That's not quite true. I was like a balloon being squeezed through a letterbox. Small coming out, but much larger as the balloon began to expand again. Big, angry, and very disappointed. Annie drove away.

They all began to smile. I smiled, too. But

then I had a reason to smile. They'd left the shotgun in the pick-up truck. Nice truck, too. Fairly new. Big tires, shiny black metal. Across the top of the windshield the words, *If I'd wanted a Hummer, I'd have asked your sister.* Definitely rednecks.

"I'm here to exchange some information with the driver as required by the Highway Traffic Act. Which one of you would like to claim to be the driver?"

"We all are," replied the driver. The big guy. The linebacker. Too confident and too cocky.

"Well, that is good news," I said. "I think we should get down to business straight away. Oh, before we do. Do any of you smoke?"

"I do," said the smallest one. "What of it?"

"Do you have a lighter or matches on you?"

"Course I do, how d'you expect me to light my cigarette, *dumb ass.*"

They all found that funny. Diffused the situation momentarily. The big guy wasn't laughing when my right forearm slammed into the bridge of his nose, my body twisting fast. Then twisting back the other way as my left fist slammed into the small guys face, he dropped immediately. I hoped unconscious. Dead would be awkward. The other three moved in. One got a punch in against my right cheek, no real power, no damage, not like the fist that struck him full in the face. Three down, two to go. Not so keen now, but they gave it their best. Knee hard in the testicles. One left standing upright. Head butt to number five. Out for the count.

Back to number one, coming in for a second round. I was going for a solid hard punch to the breastbone, but decided against it. It had a way of sometimes stopping the heart. This wasn't a military encounter, but deadly all the same. My favourite, the brachial stun. Down and out for the count. I kicked the asses of the two retreating thugs as they hobbled away down the country road. No other vehicles. Yet.

I found what I was looking for. A red plastic Bic lighter in the small guy's right trouser pocket. A quick inventory of the truck. No other forms of life aboard, human or animal. No baby stuck down between the seats or on the floor. I opened the gas tank, stuffed a long piece of material torn from the big guy's plaid shirt down the tank and waited. Then I saw headlights approaching. Annie's BMW pulled over to the side of the road. As the headlights flashed, I lit the cloth, tossed the lighter into the truck and jogged back down the road to join Annie.

Just as I reached the BMW I heard the *whoosh ... bang* of the exploding gas tank, followed by the heat wave against the back of my neck. I squeezed myself back into the passenger seat. The pick-up truck was engulfed in flames. I was relieved to see the five men propping themselves up. That was good. Less of an investigation. All probably well known to the local police anyway. Not a priority, assuming they bothered to report the incident. Probably would, insurance purposes, they'd need an incident number before their insurance company got involved. No sweat, unless Constable Robbins was involved. He already had a hate on for me as it was. I'd be his number one suspect. Wouldn't take him long to find Annie's BMW and figure it all out.

"Spontaneous combustion. Unbelievable. Turn around, lights off, no need to illuminate the rear plate for them. Let's head back to the Academy. We'll change cars and find somewhere to eat."

"Anyone dead?"

"No. No one's dead. They requested to pay for our dinner and drinks tonight. They didn't have enough to pay for any damage to your car I'm afraid."

"You stole from them?"

"That's far too harsh a word to use, Annie. I asked them about exchanging details as per the HTA, but the language used in reply was far too profound to repeat."

"How much did you take from them, Sam?"

"It wasn't taken. Think of it as a voluntary donation. If you decide to go to war and lose, you can't expect there to be no repercussions. They decided to go into battle, fought bravely, lost, and were required to pay compensation as required by the Geneva Convention."

"As required by Sam Stephens, you mean."

"Did you get a chance to see if your car sustained any damage?"

"Not much, but the rear bumper is not as straight as it was."

“Okay, we’ll drop it off at a BMW dealership this weekend and get it fixed. I’ll pay.” I opened my window and tossed out a couple of drivers’ licenses.

“What are you doing?”

“Taking evasive action. I told the driver and the little guy that now I had their licenses, I knew where they lived. If the police came looking for me, I’d come looking for them.”

“So now I’m an accomplice to assault bodily harm, robbery, and arson, and God knows what else.”

“Did you actually witness anything?”

“No, just intelligent speculation.”

“Did you see Mr. Stephens hit anyone, officer?”

“No.”

“Officer, did you see what caused the pick-up truck to catch fire?”

“No.”

“Did Mr. Stephens tell you what had happened while you drove away and came back five minutes later?”

“No.”

“Why did you drive away?”

“Because Mr. Stephens was worried about my safety. He said he was going to talk to the driver about running into the back of my car.”

“You had a cell phone with you, why didn’t you call 9-1-1?”

“There were five of them there. One, if not all of them would have a cell phone. This is the twenty-first century.”

"Why didn't you report the accident to the police?"

"The damage to my vehicle appeared to be under one-thousand dollars. I can't imagine their truck sustained any damage, other than bursting into flames later. Why, I don't know. Maybe as a result of them deliberately ramming my car. We could have been killed. Their actions were violent and dangerous. I wanted nothing more to do with them."

"Mr. Stephens was angry when you dropped him off, wasn't he?"

"No, he doesn't get angry."

"Very good, Ms. Greyeyes. No further questions."

"It's not your fault, Sam. I'm sorry. I never even asked if you were okay."

"I'm fine. Probably best it happened really."

"How on earth do you figure that out?"

"Well, if we're, *stopping on the way home*, as you suggested. I really don't know how we're going to do it in your car."

"Do what, Sam?"

"Star gaze of course. I could show you how to find the North Star."

"Well, you're not going to find it where you're thinking of looking. And anyway, I know how to find the North Star, how to live in the wild, and navigate through it. An Inuit elder told me this about traveling through the wilderness, *Always know where you are.*"

"Want to winter camp this year?"

"I presume you mean hiking into the wild,

pitching a tent and not driving to a campsite with a heated trailer."

"I do. You're right, I really don't know you, Ms. Greyeyes, but I like you more every minute we're together."

"You know, Sam, I'd like to be able to say that my mother warned me about men like you, but how could she. I don't think *men like you* exist in the minds of average citizens. You are in a category all of your own. I'm not even sure psychiatrists have a name for your breed. You're unique. Are you listening to me?"

"Yes I am. I'm just trying to decide if I should take that as a compliment or not."

"It's just a statement of fact. Don't make too much of it."

* * *

We parked Annie's car off campus. Far enough away that if Robbins did come looking, he wouldn't find it. If he did find it, then both Annie and I would *act surprised, look concerned, and deny, deny, deny.*

After a good half hour's drive, we found a small restaurant on the outskirts. A mom and pop kind of place. Good people. Friendly. It didn't have a liquor license so its patrons were mainly older people. Local farmers and their wives, I guessed. The coffee was good. My steak was out of this world. A place that was probably the best kept secret in the area. After the truck incident I'd worked up quite an appetite, so I felt I deserved to reward myself with a big slice of homemade cheesecake. The plastic red and white gingham tablecloth wasn't your regular dollar store variety. It was as thick as drywall vapour barrier, if not thicker. I excused myself and headed for the washroom. I could feel their eyes following me. I heard someone whisper, "That's one big Indian." An old man's voice, a little hard of hearing so when he spoke, what he thought was quiet, was quite loud. Then a woman's voice, his age. "Shush, Bert, he might hear you."

I turned around and walked up to their table. "This place has the best steaks I ever tasted. Have you tried the cheesecake?" They had turned to stone, and then nodded their heads. They must have been in their eighties, if not their nineties. I called the waitress over. "Their meal is on me this evening. Please make sure I get their bill." The old lady placed her wrinkled hand on my arm, the veins sticking out. No fat left.

"You don't have to do that, young man. I hope we didn't say anything to offend you."

"Not at all. In my culture, we are supposed to take care of our elders. I have been brought up in the traditional ways of my people. Enjoy your evening." I could see Annie smiling at me, slowly shaking her head.

"That was generous of you, Sam."

"Not really. I can afford to be generous with

other people's money."

"I think your name should be Robin Hood, not Sam Stephens."

I tipped the waitress very generously.

On the way back to the Academy I followed the back roads. Then I found what I was looking for. A track leading across a large field. No houses around. The track went up a gradual incline and then dipped over the other side, out of sight from the road. It was getting dark so I kept the lights off, not wanting to draw attention. The car rolled along like a large boat on a rolling sea. Before us, distant lights, fields, trees, hedgerows, and descending darkness. There was enough of a breeze to keep the mosquitoes away. I opened the rear door and pulled out a thick woolen blanket my grandmother had made for me and laid it on the grass. The air was thick with the sweet smell of freshly cut hay. When I stood up, Annie came around from the other side of the car. She was looking down coyly, the moonlight illuminating her naked body. She stepped onto the blanket, sinking to the ground like a synchronized swimmer, slowly slipping below the surface of the water. I stopped and listened, looked all around me. Satisfied we were alone, I began to undress.

Chapter Eleven

Friday evening, on the way to Port Albert, we dropped Annie's BMW off at the dealership. When we finally arrived in Port Albert I took Annie to The Toll Bridge for a meal, washed down with a glass of red wine for Annie and a draught Guinness for me. Then it was home to my house on the Peninsular. The preparations for tomorrow's powwow were in full swing, evident as we passed the Band office.

"Nice place, it looks well cared for."

"It is, Annie. Of course, the casino helps, but it's not all about us. We pour a lot of money into the local community, like the hospital, for instance. Not a lot of people know that. We support a lot of charities, as well as helping other reserves not as well off as our own. Our casino even provides money to Dalton to help police us. Some of us, like me, think we should police ourselves like Curve Lake. We could have our own Annishnabe Police Service. Then there'd be three police services up here. The Ontario Provincial Police takes care of the casino, mainly the gaming side of things. If you work up here, they'll call you for the drunks, drugs, and assholes. There's not many of us left on this reserve. I hate that word, makes it sound like we're wild animals allowed to exist inside specified boundaries. In time our blood will no longer run pure. Hopefully, that's a long way off."

"You sound like a radical."

"Look who's talking. Like the Ojibwa, I stand up for what I believe. You're Ojibwa, you know what I'm talking about. We're neither Canadian nor American. We're North American. That's how I see it."

"I'm not disagreeing with you, Sam. Can we change the subject?"

"I apologize, aboriginal rights, or the lack thereof, gets me fired up. Before we get to my place, let me take you down and show you the land we bought. It's right on the lake. If I was ever going to get married, that's where I'd want it to take place."

I turned off down a long gravel side road, tall trees on either side of the narrow road. No street lights. Eventually we arrived at the end of the road. You'd need a four-wheeler to continue westwards. I turned right into a long winding driveway, the entrance heralded by two large fieldstone pillars that looked very phallic. It was eerie driving slowly through the park-like setting. Old statues loomed white out of the darkness as the car's headlights illuminated them. As we passed the cottage, I stopped and turned on the interior light in the car so the occupants of the house could see it was me and not trespassers paying no heed to the sign at the entrance. On the other side of the lake, the distant lights of Port Albert.

"What a beautiful place. I can see why the Band Counsel bought it."

"Ironic isn't it, Annie. We bought back land that already belongs to us, taken away from our forefathers by lies, trickery, greed, and dishonesty. And some of our own people are to blame, I'll admit. Sitting Bull was right. *I do not wish to be shut up in a corral. All agency Indians I have seen are worthless. They are neither red warriors nor white farmers. They are neither wolf nor dog.* I am a wolf, Annie."

"You don't have to tell me that, Sam. Either way, we've all got to find a way to get along."

"Agreed."

"What time is the Sunrise Ceremony tomorrow?"

"We should be there ready by five-fifteen. That'll give us time to get seated, ready for the smudging ceremony. Let's get home, we have an early start."

"Your house is like Fort Knox. Are you expecting an invasion?"

"I keep a lot of sensitive equipment here. Believe it or not, I'm a bit of a computer geek. In the military I did a lot of hacking into enemy sites. Some of those enemies are still my enemy. That's why the high-tech security."

"If I pressed in the wrong code, on the third attempt, would the house have blown up?"

"The third attempt? You'd have been lucky to have got past the second. Want to sit out on the balcony?"

"Sure. Do you have any red wine?"

"I have a nice Shiraz in the wine cellar, my lady. Be back in a minute. There's some snacky bits in the cupboard to the right of the fridge, bowls in the cupboard on the left."

"You do the interior decorating here as well?"

"I did," I said, descending the basement stairs.

"I love all the native artwork, the sculptures and woodcarvings. Very expensive."

"That's why I drive an old beater and you drive a BMW. Here you are. Cheers."

"No lake view?"

"When the white man pushed us here, we didn't get lake views."

"Sam. Why did you quit the military?"

"A lot of people have asked me that question and I've lied to every one of them. You want the truth?"

"Not if you don't want to tell me."

"When the Weatherman was killed, a huge piece of me died inside. I began taking risks. I just wanted to kill as many of the Taliban as I could. When I started taking risks with my own squadron, I knew it was time to make a change. Who knows, I might go back."

"Are you ready to go back?"

"I'm a warrior, I need action. I'll see how this police job works out. If it's not for me, then I'll go back. If they put me in traffic, I'll definitely be going back."

Alert! Vehicle entering driveway.

“What was that?”

“My security system. We have company.”

“By the smile on your face, it looks like good company.”

“It is. It’s my grandfather. I hardly ever get to see him. He’s eighty-seven and still driving.”

“An old beater like your own.”

“He’s very traditional. Likes the old ways. Wise beyond belief, you’ll see what I mean.”

I turned on the porch light. It was like watching the car giving birth to an old man, the way he struggled out of the driver’s door.

“Aren’t you going to help him?”

“No, Annie. And neither are you. He’d never come back again if we did. He’s got to be the most stubborn human being I’ve ever met.”

“Does he live on the reserve?”

“He has a house here, but is hardly ever there. He travels all across North America visiting other Bands. I guess he’s like the old medicine man, whatever remedies he’s using, they’ve kept him going this long.”

The small figure eventually emerged from the car, opened the rear door and slid out a small battered brown leather case. He looked up at the house, not moving, just staring.

“What’s he doing?”

“Thinking, probably. Assessing the atmosphere. If it’s not to his liking, he’ll turn around and leave.”

“You’re kidding me?”

“No, I’m not. Watch and observe.”

After a few minutes of standing and

watching, the frail old man, with long flowing grey hair, turned around and replaced the suitcase on the rear seat, got back into the car with slightly less difficulty than he had getting out and reversed out of the driveway, clipping the mail box with the front left corner of the fender as he turned into the road.

"I think he hates my mail box. I've lost count of how many times he's done that."

"That's weird."

"What, hitting my mail box?"

"No. Just standing there and leaving. It doesn't make sense."

"He knows you're here."

"Come on, how would he know that? That's just ridiculous."

"I have no idea. It's not some magic trick or anything like that, like the white man would imagine in some John Wayne movie. Your scent is likely still in the air and he smells it. He's like the buffalo. You put a bull buffalo in that driveway and without seeing us, he would know we were inside this house. Man and woman. That old man has retained all the traditional instincts of our ancient people. The Creator chose him to be among those few, blessed or maybe cursed, with that gift, depending on how you look at it."

"I'm sorry, that's not weird, it's amazing. I can feel his presence inside the house, when before I couldn't. This is creeping me out."

"We'll see him tomorrow, probably. He'll likely be at the Sunrise Ceremony. I don't know about you, but I need my bed. Care to join me?"

"Silly question."

* * *

"What time is it?"

"Four-twenty, Annie. Fresh coffee brewing in the kitchen." Annie was one of those very rare women who looked as beautiful first thing in the morning as she did last thing at night. It made me think about all those beautiful celebrity women, caked in makeup. You'd think you'd gone to bed with Cinderella and woken up with one of the ugly sisters.

"I'll be right out, Mr. Stephens. I don't think I could face a big breakfast this early in the morning. Coffee will be fine. I'll get something at the powwow later."

There were very few cars parked at the Band office for the ceremony. Later on in the morning, the parking lots on both sides of the road would be packed. Vehicles would be lined up bumper to bumper along the gravel shoulder on either side of the road. Powwows attracted members of the First Nations from across North America. Ours was no exception. By five o'clock the chairs encircling the fire pit began to fill. Heads turned and aboriginal members rose from their seats. I turned to see my grandfather entering the spiritual circle. He was well respected and revered. The old man approached the fire, his sacred turtle drum in one hand, in the other a large clamshell full of sage. Bending low, he dropped a small burning ember into the shell. Slowly, it began to smoke. Standing toward the east, he smudged himself by wafting the sage smoke over his head and down his body with an eagle feather, all the time chanting in an ancient tongue that I was still struggling to master myself. Then he smudged the turtle drum and sat down. This was not the time for, *How are you, Grandfather, this is my girlfriend, Annie Greyeyes.* The Sunrise Ceremony is an ancient spiritual ritual, performed over thousands of years by aboriginal people all across North America, to give thanks to the dawning of a new day. My grandfather spoke, which was expected of him.

"Long before the white man came to our shores and tricked us out of our land, slaughtered our people, men, women, and children. Before they tried to take away our own religion, forcing us to believe in theirs, tried to take our language from us, beat us into submission in residential schools. Before we were forced into *reservations,* the buffalo roamed the plains in their millions. We were at one with all things, the animals, the birds, the insects, the trees, and the flowers. The mountains, the mighty rivers, and the vast oceans. The fishes, and all the creatures that dwelt in the waters with them. Even the sky, the sun, the moon, all the planets, and the stars, in the mighty universe. The Creator taught us to respect all these things. Not to take them for granted. To only hunt for what we needed to sustain ourselves, and for every creature that gave its life in order that we should live, we should pay homage to it and thank its spirit for the great sacrifice it made. We have lost our way and must find it. The great warrior Sitting Bull said, *When I was a boy, the Sioux owned the world. The sun rose and set on their land, they sent ten thousand men to battle. Where are the warriors today? Who slew them? Where are our lands? Who owns them?* That is all I have to say."

The circle remained silent. The crackling of the fire and the irreverent sound of the internal combustion engine was all that could be heard, by us. I was sure my grandfather could hear the moaning in the wind and the great sorrow of our people that seemed to weigh down his very being.

He stood, facing the east once more, arms outstretched and began to speak in his native tongue as the sun began to peak over the distant horizon. I began to tremble. The sound of explosions, gunfire, soldiers screaming in agony, as the sun hauled itself up wearily from behind a distant mountain across a vast desert. At first I didn't notice Annie's hand squeezing mine.

"Haggis!"

Repeatedly, I heard soft words, "Come home, my son, come home. Leave that strange place behind. The wind is carrying you across the sea to me, your grandfather. You are safe now. I am here. Sit, my son. You are among friends. You are with your people."

The sensation of butterflies flitting around my face. My eyes were open, but it was a while before I could see my grandfather standing in front of me, gently caressing my face with his fingers.

Annie was kneeling beside me, still holding my hand, tears welling in her eyes. "It's okay, Sam, it's okay." I felt so embarrassed. Annie had never seen me like this before, no one had. Except for the Weatherman.

"You are a great warrior, my son. I am proud of you. Sitting Bull would have been proud of you. He is proud of you. Come, breakfast is ready. I want to hear all about this beautiful creature with you and how things are going at the Academy."

"I'm sorry. I made a fool of myself and spoiled the ceremony. I'm so sorry, Grandfather."

The old man began to laugh. "You, my son, have made a Sunrise Ceremony that no one will ever forget. How wonderful is that? Nobody got hurt. You certainly tested the strength of everyone's hearts, including mine. I was ready to go for my gun, I can tell you."

We sat together in the huge dining hall, my grandfather seated between Annie and me, holding our hands.

"You, the raven on the wind, remind me of my wife. She is in the spirit world now. But I know she is delighted that her grandson has found a young lady like you. I'm afraid, he can't be tamed, but I see in you, a person who has the spirit to try, and the will to succeed." He turned to look at me and smiled. "I will be there at the passing out ceremony. I will rid you of your demons before the ceremony begins. I cannot rid them forever. You must learn to do that. The white man has ways that can help you. I, too, have ways to heal you. I don't think shouting, *Haggis!* at the top of your voice will go down well during the Academy ceremony. Someone there is bound to have a heart attack, if not faint."

Annie looked up, a broad smile on her face. A slightly older version of Annie arrived at our table in company with a stern looking man of the same age. Ojibwa.

"Suzie, Joe, it's great to see you. How have you been?"

The two sisters embraced affectionately. "I'm sorry we're late. We planned to be here for the ceremony this morning, but didn't get up in time, coupled with the long drive. Anyway, I brought your regalia." Suzie handed her sister a bulky black dress cover. "So, this is the man you've been telling me about."

I rose to my feet and shook Suzie's hand and then extended my hand to Joe. He was a well-built man, chiseled features, tough looking, but shorter than me. Construction worker I figured, probably steel worker. Like all First Nation steel workers; proud, strong and fearless. A special breed of warriors.

"This is my husband, Joe." Suzie smiled.

Joe wanted to send a private message to me by squeezing my hand as firmly as he could. Our eyes locked and I squeezed back even more firmly. Had it just been the two of us, I would have spun around, still holding his hand and twisted it behind his back, then slammed him over the table. Just for starters. Suzie didn't know that, but Annie did. I caught the disapproving look she gave her big sister

"Be nice, Joe, Sam's family," said his wife. He released his grip. Said nothing then nodded his approval. A good man to have on your side in a tight spot.

I was surprised to see Joe hug my grandfather. I didn't know they knew each other. Briefly, they spoke in our native tongue. When my grandfather told him I was his grandson, Joe's face lit up. He nodded approvingly, and then embraced me warmly. Without saying anymore, Joe turned and left.

Annie and I returned to my house to change for the powwow. She insisted on changing in the spare room. It was like preparing for a wedding. She refused to allow me to see her until she was ready.

I stood on the back deck, the smell of pine trees in the air. It wasn't even ten o'clock and the sun was blazing. It was going to be another scorcher. I almost closed my eyes, glad that I hadn't. The intense heat was pulling me back to a place I didn't want to revisit. At least not today. I heard the screen door sliding open and turned slowly to see the most beautiful woman I have ever set eyes on, wearing a traditional deerskin dress with coloured beads intricately sewn into the leather. It was long, just above her ankles. Her moccasins had the same coloured beads, with bells attached. On her head, she wore a beaded headband, an eagle feather protruding from the back. Silently I thanked the Creator for my good fortune. I felt like the luckiest man alive.

"There are no words to describe how beautiful you look, Annie. I'm tempted to miss the powwow."

"Now you look like a real warrior. I feel so proud. The way you painted your face, you look both handsome and frightening. You have many eagle feathers. I am even more proud. We should head over before I change my mind as well."

At twelve noon, the master of ceremonies announced the *Grand Entrance.* A long procession of dancers of all ages entered the large arena and began to dance around the open space. Thanks was given to all veteran First Nations who had fought in past wars, in the two World Wars and in present day wars. Thanks, too, was given to those who had stood up for aboriginal rights. When the names of *homegrown* conflicts were mentioned, many of the non-aboriginal visitors looked uncomfortable. The singing and dancing to the sound of drums became hypnotic. Then my grandfather entered. People rose from their seats in respect. Despite his age, he was determined to dance with the rest of us. As Annie and I danced, I lost myself in another time and place, told to me by my elders in stories handed down through the centuries.

Chapter Twelve

"Evening Sam, Annie. Did you have a good weekend?"

"Wonderful thanks, Tom. How about you?"

"Quiet. Well it would be wouldn't it, what with most of the recruits and staff away for the weekend. You must be getting excited, only two weeks to go and you'll be passing out. Oh, heads up. A Constable Robbins was in here yesterday asking questions. Wanted to know what kind of car you were driving and did you have access to a BMW sports car. Seemed a nasty piece of work. Gave me a bad feeling just being around him. He wanted to know if you were dating anyone here."

"What did you tell him?"

"Well, I figured I best give him something. I told him all about that old car of yours. I know Annie drives a sporty looking BMW, but I figured he didn't need to know that. As for dating, I said, definitely not. Mr. Stephens has his nose to the books every evening. I've never even seen him with a girl. I didn't like his reply. Not professional."

"What did he say?"

"Is he gay? I said, I doubt that very much. Why don't you ask him the next time you run into him?"

"I'm going to miss you Tom, even if you were in the infantry."

"Me too," said Annie. "Before I forget. I drove my VW Golf in, here's the license number for your records. The Beamers not actually mine, it's my stepdad's. Nobody needs to know that."

"Another thing. He wanted to check the sign-out register for last week. You two are renowned for forgetting to sign out in the evening. You'll be pleased to know, as far as I'm concerned, you were both here all last week. In fact, Sam, we made a point every evening of discussing military campaigns. Annie wouldn't have been privy to the conversations on military history, because, as I've said, I've never even seen you with a female recruit. I've got a good idea as to what it's about. I heard talk in my local Friday evening that a group of thugs picked on the wrong guy and got a good hiding. Not only that, before leaving, he set their pick-up truck on fire and gutted it. They're local assholes. Everyone in the pub wished they knew who it was so they could give the guy a medal. Apparently, he was the biggest Indian they ever saw. Sorry, that's not politically correct."

"Indian's fine coming from you, Tom. Christopher Columbus, great seafarer that he was, screwed up big time thinking he'd landed in India. What makes my people mad is that you white folk think he discovered North America. How can you discover a place that is already colonized by other intelligent human beings? You can't rediscover what's already discovered."

"Well, Sam, I think we should leave that one alone. Keep your heads down you two. Mum's the word."

The week shot by. Neither Annie nor I were anxious to stay at the Academy for the last weekend. We decided to spend it in Toronto. It was going to be a weekend of cramming information into our heads. I invited Billy Big Canoe, Joe Two Rivers, and Big Jim, to come with us. They were struggling with the course and I wanted to give them all the help I could, as did Annie. It didn't matter that we were from different Bands. We were all First Nation and would stick together. The old days of inter-tribal warfare were long gone. Being their first trip to Toronto, I had to take them on a tour of the downtown. No amount of persuasion would get them to stand on the glass floor on top of the CN Tower, even with Annie jumping on it. They were speechless when I took them inside the Sky Dome. The Toronto Blue Jays being his favourite baseball team, Billy knelt down and kissed the turf, much to the amusement of Joe and Big Jim. They were both devout Detroit Tigers fans. Dale, the security guard, whom I knew well, allowed Billy to stand on the mound. He raised his arms high and let a small amount of sacred tobacco slip from his fingers. I had no idea he was going to do this. Fortunately, Dale was looking at Annie, busy snapping photographs. Then it was lunch and a beer at a Harbourfront restaurant and back to work. When we entered the condo, Billy was still smiling.

"From now on, this season is going to be good for the Blue Jays. They're going to win the World Series for sure."

"In your dreams, Billy," scoffed Big Jim.

"A case of beer says they don't," added Joe. "What do you say, Sam?"

"I'm not getting into it. Much as the Blue Jays are my team, I wouldn't place a bet on it."

Me neither, said the Weatherman. *I'm with Big Jim, Joe, and Annie, on this one.*

"Are you okay, Sam, you seem out of it?"

"I'm fine, Annie. Who's your money on, or should I say beer?"

"My money's on the Detroit Tigers."

"Way to go, Annie," shouted Joe and Big Jim together, high fiving each other.

* * *

"I trust you're all ready for the big exam?"

"Crammed full of knowledge," replied Annie. "Did you have a good weekend, Tom?"

"Well, you'll be pleased to know that Sam's name never came up once in conversation over the weekend. Constable Robbins never showed his miserable face, and as such, I had a very pleasant weekend, thank you. Good luck this week, guys. Mr. Stephens. Stay out of trouble."

"I will, Tom, I promise."

Tom pointed out toward the parking lot. "Good heavens, I don't believe it. A flying ostrich." The others found this very amusing.

"Very funny, Tom," I said, smiling.

It was a week of more cramming every evening in our pod. Me, Billy, Big Jim, Joe, and Annie. Billy Big Canoe complained his head was going to explode.

On the day of the exams, we all went outside before breakfast and conducted our own smudging ceremony among the pine trees, out of sight from prying eyes. I brought with me a round and well-polished stone, worn by years of handling. It had been given to me by my grandfather. A precious and sacred keepsake. The grass was still wet with dew, so we remained standing in our small circle. I handed the stone to Annie. We could speak our thoughts aloud if we wished, but in this intimate circle, we wanted to keep our dreams and aspirations to ourselves. By the long look Annie gave me, before passing on the stone; I knew she was thinking of us. There was so much I wanted to share with the Spirit World that I held on to that stone for a long time. My friends were very patient. They knew I carried a heavy burden.

When the exams were over, Billy, Joe, and Big Jim, looked troubled.

"Let's go get a coffee and sit outside. I don't want to be around people discussing what answers they gave. It only adds to the stress instead of relieving it. We're not going to be a part of that."

"Sam's right," agreed Annie.

All five of us sat outside on a wooden picnic table. The sun was shining, but not too hot. Just the smell of grass and pine trees. That is, until Billy brought out his cigarettes. Annie and I sat upwind from the three of them.

"I can't believe I'm saying this, but I'm going to miss this place," said Big Jim. We all looked at him incredulously.

"Have you lost your mind?" said Billy.

"I mean, all of us here together. Not the building. It's been good. We've had a lot of fun."

"And adventures," said Annie. "Haven't we, Sam?" she said, squeezing my arm.

* * *

Finally the day of the passing out parade arrived. Annie's family arrived from the reserve. This time, Joe and I greeted each other warmly. Seeing Annie's mother for the first time, I could see where Annie and Suzie got their looks. Their stepfather, Mike, gave me the third degree. Satisfied I was suitable for Annie, the atmosphere became distinctly more pleasant. I was pleased that the family was so protective of each other. I had no parents to wish me well. They were both killed in a traffic accident when

I was a boy. I felt their presence with me. It was a good feeling. The Weatherman was there, too.

During the march past, you could tell the ex-military recruits from the civilian ones. Crisp in-step marching, immaculate uniforms, and the shiniest boots. Some of the civvies marched as though they had two left feet, swinging their arms completely out-of-sync with their feet. Not professional.

Afterwards came the speeches and the various awards. I was surprised when my name was called. I hadn't expected to merit anything, not being in the Director's good books. They couldn't ignore the fact that I was top in the Academy for academic achievement, top for physical training. Despite all this, I didn't make top recruit. I was told, *Had you not been trouble, you would have done.* I shrugged it off. Worst things happen in life.

Then followed the service. A Christian service. I stood when I had to stand, sat when I had to sit, but otherwise, didn't participate. Neither did Annie, nor the guys from Turtle Lake.

At the end of the service, the Director announced there would be a service honouring members of the First Nation recruits. I was impressed. Taken aback, in fact. I was even more shocked when my grandfather took the stage wearing his traditional medicine man regalia. He was carrying an eagle feather, his sacred turtle drum, and a small bag, that I knew contained sweet grass, sage, and tobacco.

A voice behind me caused me to stiffen.

"Why do we have to sit here and listen to this pagan worship?" Annie sensed my rising anger and grabbed my arm. I turned to see who had spoken these words. One among them, began to colour, no doubt thinking I had not heard.

"Because I had to sit here and listen to your hypocrisy without complaint. You're no longer welcome here. Leave now, or I will address the matter with you personally, after our service." He didn't move, not until I began to rise from my seat.

"Go, you have insulted my people." At least when I spoke, I was whispering. Annie was furious.

Sergeant Dipper moved quickly. He knew what the problem was. "Mr. Ashton, I suggest you leave. I can guarantee your wellbeing here, but afterwards, I wouldn't count on it."

Ashton left the hall, red-faced.

The rhythmic sound of the drum, accompanied by the sound of the Medicine Man chanting in his native tongue, brought peace to the hall. I watched my grandfather, as I had done many times before, prepare our altar to the Creator. The Medicine Man unrolled a small carpet. It was colourful. I knew, though could not see from where I was sitting, that it was embroidered with symbols of turtles, eagles, deer, wolves, trees, lakes, and rocks. He placed a flat rock upon the carpet onto which he put the sweet grass. Reverently he placed the wampum belt on the carpet. He stood holding a large shell

I knew was crammed with sage. Smoke poured upward. I knew it smelled sweet and aromatic. Using the eagle feather he directed the smoke around his body and over his head, next he smudged his sacred possessions, going round and round the rock. He stood close to the edge of the stage and directed the smoke into the crowd with the eagle feather. The Medicine Man called to us in Ojibwa. Slowly, reverently, the five of us made our way down to be smudged.

We sat cross-legged in a circle around the rock as The Medicine Man lit the sweet grass. A small flame flickered, was blown out and sweet smelling smoke began to rise up and waft around us. As the Medicine Man moved among us, the smoke danced around with him. His chanting rose higher, the drumbeat grew louder. Not a sound could be heard from the audience.

I was walking across an endless prairie, tall grass all around me, swaying in a gentle early summer breeze, dressed in my traditional clothing, spear in my right hand. I was the warrior once more. It felt good. From horizon to horizon stretched the mighty buffalo in their millions. Not a white face to be seen anywhere. I was happy. Everything was as it should be. In harmony. The sea of buffalo parted and I began to walk through them. An elder appeared in front of me. He was smiling. I drew closer to hear what he was saying. *It is not your time yet, Warrior. When it is, I will come for you, and you will know. Go back now, your grandfather is waiting for you.*

My grandfather handed to each of us a small red cloth pouch, tied with string. It contained sacred Indian tobacco. He embraced each one of us. Though he looked frail, I could feel his body felt strong. I felt good, but troubled.

* * *

Annie drove with me in my old, but reliable car, back to my condominium on Harbourfront. This was going to be her home as well. For as long as she wanted it.

“I guess I’ll rent a van this weekend to move your stuff here.”

“No need. Joe has borrowed a van. They normally use it for transporting cigarettes, but we can have it for a day.”

“That’s good. Monday, I start my in-house training with Toronto. Then I’ll be assigned to my new division. Apparently, I’m going to be working the east side.”

“Monday, I’ll be at the Police Learning Centre for the same thing. After the Academy, I’m really looking forward to getting out on patrol.”

“Me, too. I’m glad they recognized you for excellence in academic as well as physical training.”

“You got me through the physical training, that’s why I got the award.”

"Annie, you put the time and hard work in. It was well deserved. Can we get the van tomorrow?"

"Already arranged. That gives us all of Sunday to relax."

It was my first trip to Annie's reserve. Pretty much what I expected. A mixture of well cared for houses at one end of the spectrum, and run down shacks at the other. I couldn't care less about the exterior of the house, what mattered were the souls that dwelt within them. Joe was there waiting with the van, already half loaded with Annie's belongings. Her mom looked sad to see her baby leaving home. Farewells were exchanged. I was reminded by many, to take good care of Annie. Not least by Annie's mom. Joe and Suzie rode in the van, Annie and I traveled together in my car, like newlyweds.

"You sure you're okay with this, Annie? Any time you want to change your mind, say you get homesick. That's okay, I understand."

"You trying to get rid of me already?"

"No, never. From now on, Annie Greyeyes, my home is your home."

Annie was the first to rise on Sunday morning. When I looked at the bedside clock, it was nine-fifteen. I could smell coffee brewing and the sound of Annie singing. Her voice was pitch-perfect and beautiful. It was like a creek, cascading over rocks. Like the sound of the water, it beckoned you and when you reached it, you became mesmerized by the spell it cast and never wanted to leave. I made my way down the hall to the kitchen and stood in the doorway. I couldn't recall the singer, but knew the song. Haunting and yet beautiful. Annie was standing with her back to me at the sink looking out the window, still singing, unaware of my presence. Lost in her own world. She looked good in the white blouse and blue jeans, her long black hair almost down to her leather belt.

"I'm only human ..."

I couldn't take my eyes off her. I couldn't even speak. I felt tears slowly rolling down my face. It would be a mistake for the white man to see this as a sign of weakness. When a warrior sheds tears, they too, are a thing of beauty. It shows a man with a true love of the earth and the Creator.

I cannot say why it is, that we sense someone or something in the room with us. We cannot hear them or see them, but something tells us they are there. My grandfather understands these things. One of the few that can sense things not only in a room, but across the vast oceans and continents, to another room in a faraway country. I do not understand these things, but I know they are true, but only to those that have that special gift, bestowed upon them by the Creator.

Annie turned around. She looked even more beautiful as she cast her eyes down in mild embarrassment. Her singing faltered, but when she saw my face she continued as before. That will always be my most precious memory of her. I mentally locked it away deep within me.

"You sing so beautifully," I said when she had finished. She came to me in the doorway and gently placed her hands against my damp cheeks.

It just came out of me, completely unexpected, as though my mouth and brain were no longer under my control. The words were not even inside my own head.

"Will you marry me, Annie?"

Her face lit up.

We kissed, hugged, and cried, in that doorway.

"I wasn't expecting to say that, Annie. I didn't even buy a ring. The Creator made me say it."

"I don't need a ring to say *yes*. Just being with you makes me so happy."

We went back to bed. The coffee could wait.

Chapter Thirteen

I knew parking and traffic would be a nightmare, so I took the subway to my new division over on the east side. The building was a mixture of the old and the new. Made me think of myself. I was in my civvies, my uniform kit in a hockey bag at my side. You'd have to be on a suicide mission to mug me, but then, Toronto is full of crazy people. It was day shift and I liked to be on time. Wouldn't do on my first day to be late. I could hear laughter coming from the parade room as I approached with the Sergeant.

Someone said, "Seeing as you're the oldest guy in the division, if not the service, we've given you the new recruit to train. We want you to pass on all that worldly wisdom. He's just a little guy, about your size."

I entered the room to fits of laughter. "What did I tell you? Constable Jimmie Callaghan, meet Constable Sam Stephens, your new recruit." The Staff Sergeant was definitely enjoying himself.

One of the constables piped in. "At last, Jimmie, you've got someone to take care of you. Sam, Jimmie's wheelchair is out in the hall. It's got lights and sirens, but don't go over twenty,

Jimmie gets dizzy at high speed."

More laughter. I was going to like this platoon.

"Sam's ex-military," said the Staff. "Seen a lot of overseas action. Welcome to the platoon, Sam. They're affectionately known as *The Misfits.* You'll fit right in. What's that awful noise? Oh, it's Jimmie's knees. Don't get up, Jimmie, the sound of your knees is making me deaf."

"You know guys, this is elder abuse, and I'm documenting every word."

One of the officers piped up, "No worries there, Jimmie, you'll never remember where your notebook is, and even if you do find it, you won't remember why you wrote it. Assuming you'd recognize your own handwriting that is."

"Okay, enough. Let's get down to business," interjected the Staff Sergeant.

Our patrol areas were assigned to us. Jimmie, who looked to be in his late sixties, if not early seventies, gave me a tour of the station. His hair wasn't grey, and he had hair, almost a full head of it. His was all white. His face, with all the lines and furrows accumulated over time, reminded me of an old vinyl record. If there was a stylus to fit those grooves, what a story it could tell. Jimmie had definitely, *been there, seen it, done it, got the T-shirt.* His face also gave away one of his vices. He liked to drink. I soon learned his second.

"Been policing almost thirty-five years. Started when I was twenty-five. All of it in

Toronto. You'll be my last trainee, Sam. Word of advice for you. Don't piss off the Brass. They've got long memories, that's why I'm still a constable on the front line. Any chance next time you're on the reservation, you could pick me up a couple of cartons of cigarettes?"

"Jimmie. You know that would be illegal. You've got to be a card carrying Indian to have those cigarettes."

"You're kidding me right?"

"Of course, I'm kidding you. Next time I'm home I'll get you some."

"Second piece of advice. The law is only there for the guidance of wise men and the obedience of fools. Got that?"

"Got it, Jimmie."

"The other thing you need to know before we do anything else is this. And you should write it down in the back of your notebook. Go on, write this down. The job's fucked."

That was my first unofficial entry in my notebook. I put it under the title, *The world according to Jimmie.*

Jimmie continued with the lecture. "Now the reason I want you to remember that, Sam, is this. Learning that from day one will help you sail through your whole career, laughing all the way to the bank and toward your pension. I never learned that until it was almost too late. Nobody told me the job was fucked. I had to find it out myself. When you find yourself typing away on a computer in the early hours of the morning on a long night shift, preparing a complicated criminal case, and the papers you need are missing in outer space, and the computer goes down on you. Not literally, they're still working on one that can do that apparently. You, unlike your other platoon members, will just laugh it off because …"

"The job's fucked."

"Precisely, Sam. Now, if tomorrow morning you haven't grasped that concept, I suggest you quit policing and apply to be a firefighter. All right. Rule number four. Three things guaranteed to get you into trouble during your policing career. Booze, broads and bullets. Rule number five. A good police officer never gets wet, cold, or hungry. So, we need coffee and breakfast. They don't pay me for what I do, Sam. I get paid for what I might have to do. Management will tell you otherwise. Don't listen to them. They are excellent in areas you wouldn't even dream of. They can conjure up paperclips and pens like no human beings I have ever met. Just don't let them on patrol with you. Not all of them. Some, the rare few are almost as good as us. Come on, breakfast calls. We can't fight the public on an empty stomach."

I liked Jimmie. He was the real deal. What you saw is what you got. No airs or graces. A man that would rather do you a good turn than a bad one, unless you pissed him off. He was as broad as he was tall, the stereotypical Irishman.

"You drive, I like to be chauffeured," he said. The Crown Vic is a big car, but it was still awkward for me to get in behind the wheel. "I can see we need to get you one of those SUV's, Mr. Stephens. Perhaps one of those Humvees you're likely used to driving."

The word *Humvee* brought the Weatherman back into my thoughts, along with the images of the Humvee rolling over and all the horrors that went with it.

"Are you okay, Sam? You've gone awfully quiet."

"I'm fine, Jimmie." I knew he was smart enough to know I wasn't, *all right,* and also smart enough to leave it alone. For today.

"Okay then, straight on, turn right at the lights and follow my directions. Try as much as possible to avoid left turns. Invariably, they lead to trouble. Here we are, Callaghan's Restaurant. Best in the city."

Some of the platoon were already seated when we entered the diner, including Sergeant Wells, who motioned me to a seat opposite him.

"News travels quickly in the police service. I heard all about what went on at the Academy." I said nothing. I wasn't surprised. It was to be expected. "The sergeant you met in the bar that night with all the bikers." It was more a statement than a question. "He's a friend of mine. We were at the Academy together, only years ago, but not as long ago as Jimmie, of course. I've been told to, *keep an eye on you* by the superintendent. Sam, whatever you thought policing was, forget it. It's all politics now. The good old days are long gone. Just ask Jimmie."

"That they are, Sergeant. And more's the

pity," replied Jimmie, a wistful look in his eyes. "Why, I remember the days when some idiot would come to the police station to make a complaint against a police officer, only to find himself thrown out on his ear by the Staff Sergeant. He didn't come back a second time, I can tell you. Now, as soon as they set foot in the door, the bloody Inspector comes running to the front counter, papers in hand to take the complaint as fast as possible. Would never have happened in my day. I blame some of those high and mighty detectives for it. They need to share some of the blame for all the wrongful convictions they've conjured up. And why? Just to keep the clear-up stats nice and high."

"And what about us, Jimmie? The front line guys in uniform."

"Don't get him going, Sam. Not this early in the morning," implored the sergeant.

"We are the unsung heroes, Sam. The soldiers in the trenches. We go out there in all weathers to protect the good citizens of this fair city. Along the way, we meet assholes. Sometimes, you just can't deal with assholes by the book, so you have to be, how can I put it. *Imaginative.* If we policed exactly by the book and followed every police directive starting from how to put gas in the cruiser, we'd hardly ever see the streets. There would be no policing. So, in order for us to do the job, the public turns a blind eye. They don't want to know about the *behind the scenes* policing methods that get results. Every so often, a leftwing, police hating do-gooder comes along and makes a fuss. The pendulum has swung so far the other way, I don't think it's ever coming back. Thank heavens, I'll soon be out of it, and God help you new guys, and I mean it."

The waitress came over to take our orders. She was at least half Jimmie's age and cute. "The usual, Uncle Jimmie?"

"Ah, yes please, Nicole, my Rose of Tralee." Jimmie looked across the table at me. "I've told her many a time, I'd gladly sell my house and all its contents if she'd run away with me."

"Jimmie, you're all talk. And who's the handsome new fella you've brought me today?"

"Alas, Nicole, Sam here is gay. Not for the likes of you."

"Jimmie, you are such a liar and anyway, one night with me and I'd soon have him converted."

"Oh, Nicole, don't let your father hear you talking like that. He'd be fit to be tied, so he would."

"Sam, welcome, and don't mind Jimmie. He reminds me of my father. Well, I guess he should, after all they are brothers. Now, will this be on separate bills?"

"It will not," replied Jimmie indignantly. For a moment I thought Jimmie was buying me breakfast. Very generous. "He's the new boy. It's tradition. First day the rookie buys his coach officer breakfast, and drinks the first evening out. Where's your dad this morning?"

"He's not back from the market yet."

"Tell him I've got a line on some cheap cigarettes. I should have 'em in soon."

"Would this have anything to do with a certain rookie?"

"I can't divulge my sources, young lady. It wouldn't be good for business."

"You didn't kiss the Blarney Stone, Uncle Jimmie, I think you swallowed it."

* * *

"Well, young Sam Stephens. What would you like to do today?"

"Catch bad guys. And I mean, real bad guys, Jimmie. I believe the streets are only there for good people. Bad guys don't need to be on them. When I find them on our streets they're going to be sorry."

"What about vagrants, Sam? Are we gonna kick their asses, too? Not to mention the poor people and those with mental issues."

"No, Jimmie, we are not. We're gonna kick the butts of gangbangers, pimps, and drug dealers, that's what we're gonna do."

"You don't talk like a recruit, Sam. You get planted here by management? Did professional standards stick you with me so you could bring me down before I retire? Head back to the station. This partnership is over."

"This partnership has only just begun. You want to quit on me? You can walk back to the station yourself. You can quit on me at the end of the day. Now don't get all pouty on me, just because you're too old to kick my ass."

"Don't kid yourself."

"Don't delude yourself; old man."

"That's it! Stop the fucking car. We'll settle this right here, right now and don't you ever call me *old man* ever again."

"Okay, then."

I pulled the cruiser over to the side of the road and wriggled my way out of the car. Jimmie, face flushed with rage, got out of the passenger side. The street was jam-packed with vehicles and pedestrians.

I knew he was going to come in hard and fast like a raging bull. I stood there on the sidewalk outside a fashionable ladies' clothing store, smiling. That made him even madder. The last thing I wanted to do was hurt him, or worst of all, hurt his pride by playing with him, which I knew I could. Like an old horse, his ploughing days were over. His problem was he just wouldn't accept it. I wasn't going to humiliate him.

He charged. His old, but powerful body slammed me into the side of the cruiser. I was impressed, if not a little surprised. I locked him up quickly before either of us got hurt.

"Jimmie. I'm sorry. I was out of order. I shouldn't have called you old man. I respect my elders, I was out of line. As for being a plant, that's bullshit. I should kick your ass for calling me that. Okay, I'm gonna let you go now."

I bobbed when I should have weaved. His fist caught me a glancing blow across my left eye. He came in with another jab. I could have killed the guy right there and then. Not good to cause serious bodily harm or death to your coach officer. At least not on your first day. I locked up his wrist this time. Painfully. And I meant it. Anymore nonsense and I was going to break it.

"Okay. I'm going to release you again. If you so much as blow my hair out of position, I'm going to put you in the hospital."

Jimmie skulked back to the cruiser and got in the passenger seat. Damn those cell phone cameras. There was no doubt we were going to be on the Internet. Were already on it. It was just a matter of time before we got the call to the superintendent's office. Not good. Not good at all.

"Okay, here's the story. Tell me what you think, partner."

"I'm listening," I said.

"We're driving along having a discussion about martial arts verses boxing. So, we decide to put it into practice, only I forgot that some of your combat skills came from fighting in the military, with some real hard-nosed guys. So, in our enthusiasm, we give it a go. Unfortunately, the venue was not best suited for the purpose, for which, *we are eternally sorry, sir.* How's that sound?"

"On its own. You'll get early retirement today and I'll likely get canned. I suggest we go get some real bad guys pronto and make ourselves look good. Let one even out the other. That way, you get to retire honourably, and I get to continue with my probation."

"My Irish temper. It's been a problem my whole career, as well as my sense of humour. About three months ago I was walking down the street, on duty, when I see this Pakistani fellow beating a carpet. So I says, all joking like, *What, having trouble starting it?"*

I roared with laughter.

"It's no laughing matter, Sam. That cost me forty hours."

"What do you mean it cost you forty hours?"

"That was my punishment. They said it was *discreditable conduct.* I had to come into work and work off forty hours without pay. I'm still working it off. When we're supposed to be off duty, I've got to come into flippin' work. Not only that, they put me on a *sensitivity* course. Our little disagreement's going to be another, *discreditable conduct.* Pretty bad you're going to end up with Police Act charges on your first day. I forgot to tell you. The platoon's had a bet going that something was going to go down on our first day together. I've already lost the bet. There goes my bloody whiskey allowance. My old lady's gonna crown me."

"You mean," I said laughing, "a woman actually agreed to marry you?"

"I know. Unbelievable isn't it. My Mary's a saint, God bless 'er."

I could hear the Weatherman laughing inside my head, tears streaming down his face. *I could have told Jimmie he was never gonna win that bet.*

"Jimmie, let's go for a walk through that apartment building."

"Are you insane? No beat cop would ever even dream of walking through there, unless he had a death wish. We don't go in there, at least not without being mob handed. It's full of gangbangers, pimps, and dope pushers."

"Perfect."

"Sam, there's stupid, and there's complete bloody suicidal stupid."

"Jimmie. This is my land. My ancestors land. I am a warrior, from a long line of warriors, and no asshole is ever going to dictate to me where I can and cannot go. You can sit in the cruiser if you like."

I pulled over to the side of the road and got out. Jimmie sat in the car shaking his head. An elderly black woman, struggling with heavy grocery bags made her way along the broken paving, toward the apartment building. I smiled at her as she approached.

"What you smiling at? Gonna harass an old woman now, already harassed all the young black kids who ain't doing nothing wrong? Why don't you harass all those gangsters inside my apartment building, an' all those drug dealers, and hookers? An old woman ain't even safe in her own home."

"How about I carry your groceries for you and we walk into the building together?"

"You on something, son? You seem like a

real nice man. If you know'd what's good for ya, you'd turn around and go back to your *police* station. Or better still, go home."

"I'm not going anywhere, ma'am. I'm going in that building. You want me to carry those bags or not?"

"No, I don't. I ain't disabled, and secondly, I don't need the likes of them in there thinking I'm a snitch." As she said this, she tossed her head in the direction of the building. I let her struggle along with her heavy bags. She was proud, stubborn. Old school, just like Jimmie was. When she was safely inside, I started the long walk toward the front door. A large, aggressive looking man with an Hispanic appearance stood outside the front door, talking into a cell phone. My eyes began to scan each and every window and balcony, every industrial garbage can, tree, half dead shrub, and brick wall. I felt like I was in a war zone, preparing to do battle with an unseen enemy. Three magazines, forty-two bullets. Forty-three, including the one already racked into the chamber of my Glock .40 and ready to go at the gentle squeeze of the trigger. I reminded myself, *You're going in there to help people, not hinder them. If they don't want to be helped, then hinder them. Remember there's a lot of good people inside that building and only a few assholes. Make sure you know the difference.*

I heard a car door open behind me, and then slam shut. I knew it was my cruiser. There were no other cars there. Then I heard Jimmie's footsteps coming up behind me.

"Well, this looks like my last day on the earth. I guess I won't need to worry about that retirement party."

I turned. Angry. "Never, ever go into battle with that attitude, soldier! We're going in there to kick ass. After shift, we're going for a well-earned beer. Got it?"

"I got it, partner."

"Let's do this!"

The guy at the entrance made the mistake of blocking my path. "You can't come in here."

"You cannot possibly be talking to me. If you are, you must have one hell of a health plan." I wasn't going to walk around him. If he stayed where he was, I was going to walk right through him. He stiffened and stayed where he was.

"You pigs ain't welcome here, now get your sorry asses outa here before you gets your butts kicked."

I hit him hard and fast with a brachial stun. My favourite move. I wasn't going to walk around him, so I walked over him like he was a human carpet and kept on going toward the entrance. He wouldn't be getting up for a while.

The inner door, to my surprise was locked. I pulled out a combination knife, with blade, pliers, and all sorts of fancy gadgets. It was a good make. Expensive. I slid the knife between the doors and pushed the worn lock in just enough to release the door. We were in.

It is incredible how much information the human brain can recall from a life threatening situation. It all happens within the confines of a moment of time, one split second is slowed down by the brain. Tunnel vision takes over. A primeval safety system. Focus on the immediate danger to the exclusion of all others. Not always a good thing. I trained and trained not to let it happen, but recognized it as soon as it began to happen, refocused, and looked for other threats. There were none. Just two agonizing pains in my chest and the sound of ringing in my ears, as the unseen gunman burst out from around the hall and shot me, twice in the chest. Had this been a military operation I would have had my weapon ready and engaged for action. As soon as that punk showed his face, he'd be dead. But it wasn't a military operation. As soon as I saw him, my weapon was drawn, but he had the edge, that part of the split second I didn't have. My Kevlar vest did its job. I worked through the pain and began firing back. There was no time for the police challenge, *Police don't move!* His next bullet might have struck me in the head.

He turned and ran, under a hail of bullets from me and Jimmie. He was already in the hallway and charging up the stairs. One of our bullets had caught him somewhere, but not in a place to slow him down. I charged after him up the concrete flight of steps, leading from the front foyer. He was bleeding, but not haemorrhaging. I had nine bullets left in the pistol's magazine. He only had two in the chamber of the revolver. He'd already fired-off four from the Smith and Wesson .38 he was carrying. At least I suspected it was a Smith and Wesson, possibly an old cop gun that somehow went missing when they changed over to the Glock. No real stopping power. If he was smart, he'd keep one for himself. The stairway door slammed open. My brain told me we were now on the tenth floor. Good to be in shape. As expected, he fired his last two rounds as I ducked out and then purposely back into the stairwell. I was running down the long hall as he fumbled with a key and entered an apartment, quickly slamming the door behind him. I doubted he had a speed loader and was probably fumbling behind the door, desperately trying to put bullets into the chamber and likely dropping some on the apartment floor in his haste. Even though I knew he was on the other side of the door, I didn't fire through it, which I would have done on a combat mission. I didn't know who else might be in the apartment, maybe a pregnant woman with a small child clutching her thigh in terror.

I hit the door with my shoulder by the lock. For some reason, it registered that the apartment number was missing from the door. Strange what you can see, even with all that adrenalin pumping through you. I was not under stress. Years of training in the military. The door exploded inwards as the wooden trim tore away from the frame in splintered fragments, nails still attached in places.

My attacker was sent reeling backwards, blood spurting from his flattened nose. He scrambled quickly to his feet, gun in hand, and raced for the balcony. No doubt hoping he could make it across to the next apartment balcony and freedom. But that wasn't to be. As I came through the balcony door, he leveled the revolver at my face. My hand clamped tightly over the cylinder so it had no chance of turning to engage a bullet, assuming he had managed to get any in there. All it needed was one in the right place to do the trick, and I wasn't taking any chances.

I snatched the gun out of his hand. His finger wouldn't have snapped had he not left it in the trigger guard. But I didn't hit him. Which sounds compassionate for a guy that just shot me twice in the chest. I threw him over the balcony instead. But not completely. I let his hands grip the railing and grabbed his wrists. After all, he was having a hell of a time holding on with his right hand.

He was screaming. That, I thought, was understandable. I wanted to make sure he didn't fall, just in case some innocent person just happened to walk underneath where his body would land. I thought it only fitting that I should begin shouting in earnest for him to, *Hang on, I've got you. You don't need to do this, you don't need to kill yourself like this!* His gratitude was very disappointing.

I lowered my face to his. "Listen. You're only going to get one chance to redeem yourself. I need information, and I need it now."

When he had told me what I wanted to know,

I let him go. It was all clear below. That was good. And the other thing that was good. I didn't have to lie by telling him I'd save him, when I knew I wouldn't. I guess he didn't know what *redeem* meant. I thought of the Gurkhas and *take no prisoners*.

Jimmie came huffing and puffing into the apartment. He was spent and couldn't have done anymore.

"The cavalry are on their way," he wheezed, bent over, clutching his knees. "I called for an ambulance. I figured you might need one. Are you okay?"

"Bruised, I suspect. Good job you called an ambulance, I think you're gonna need one. Your normal ruddy complexion is looking kinda blue. Not good, Jimmie."

"Funny guy. Where is he?"

"He decided to test Newton's Laws of gravity. I don't think he's going to be writing a thesis on it, though. Anyway, no great loss to society, though I'm sure his mom will be sad. We'll hear all about what a wonderful, churchgoing young man he was, what an asset to the community he was."

"Don't tell me anymore, Sam. I can see this going down as one of my worst days on the job in recent times. I don't even want to think about my earlier years. Jesus Christ, Sam, this is your first day on the job. What is wrong with you? Why couldn't we just go out there and give out friggin' parking tickets. What the hell is day two going to bring? Don't tell me, I can hardly wait"

I said nothing.

"Okay, we're gonna have to tape this apartment off and post someone on it. You can't do it, and neither can I. Now you're the subject officer, and I'm the witness officer, in a messy SIU investigation. Is there anything we need to, *clean up,* before the troops get here?"

"Everything is copacetic. As soon as we get this place sealed up, we've got some doors to break down and guns to seize."

"Not so fast, buddy. A sergeant's gonna arrive, separate the two of us, seize our guns and send us packing back to the station. There we'll be isolated until we get permission to go home. Once our notebooks are done, that is. It's not like the old days when you could speak to a lawyer through the association and then do your notes. Now it's notes first, then lawyer. One law for civilians and another for cops. Do not. I repeat, do not incriminate yourself. The Special Investigations Unit is going to go over this with a fine tooth comb in liaison with some of our homicide officers. I don't trust our own guys, so you can imagine how little I trust the SIU."

"There's nothing much to tell. The guy fell to his death. Too bad. So sad. I need another coffee."

"Tell your ride to drop by Tim's on your way in. If they ask, I'm gonna have to lie. *Did Officer Stephens look distraught after the incident? Distraught. He was mortified.* Wait a minute. You ain't going to the station. You're going straight to the hospital. I'll call the association and let them know. I got them on speed dial on my cell."

"Jimmie, you got a good guy in Guns and Gangs?"

"Sure. What d'ya need."

I told Jimmie the information I had. He knew how I got it, but I wasn't ever giving that away.

The sound of heavy footfalls charging down the corridor from both sides announced the arrival of our guys and ETF.

Toronto, professional as ever in a crisis, had the place buttoned-down in no time. Sergeant Wells took my gun and made sure an armed officer rode with me in the ambulance to the hospital. Despite my protests, the paramedics would not stop for a coffee, even with me offering to buy theirs. I'd have to get one intravenously at the hospital. It would all give me time to think how I was going to word my notebook. Jimmie wasn't put in a compromising position. Everything that happened at the front door could be easily explained. We had to be a little creative regarding the mouthpiece at the front entrance. Using the Use of Force Model, his aggressive action, gestures and words warranted *open hand techniques*. What happened after that, Jimmie wasn't a part of. He wasn't a military guy used to real combat. He might be *solid,* but he wasn't Malloy. Malloy, I trusted. Our secrets would go with us to our graves.

At the hospital they insisted on x-raying my chest to ensure no bones were broken or splintered. All was well. The bruising was starting to show, it wouldn't be something I could hide from Annie. I was wondering how her day was going. We agreed that, unless there was a real emergency we weren't going to call one another at work. Of course, if one of us was going to be late and heading into overtime, that was different. Jimmie was the only other officer I knew who didn't have his cell phone stuck to his ear or was texting someone. It made you wonder how the old guys got by before cell phones. Today it was like the world was going to fall apart if your spouse, girlfriend, or boyfriend, couldn't get hold of you at any time of the day or night. Relationships could be very distracting, and in a life or death situation out on the street, you needed to be focused, not worrying about picking milk up on your way home or saying goodnight to junior before bedtime.

I was lying on the hospital bed, hands behind my head relaxing, when the association president, Buzz Rockart paid me a visit. Like Jimmie, he was old school. I liked him.

"How yer doin' Sam? Do you need anything? Want me to call someone?" I shook my head.

"Okay, I got the association lawyer on standby. You know they want your notes done before you speak to a lawyer, following that dumb Supreme Court decision? You're a smart guy, I asked around about you. Don't write anything that will come back to haunt you, or your partner. Jimmie, he's as solid as they come. No worries there. I hear you had to smack a guy who was threatening to assault you. No problems there. Then some asshole shoots you in the chest. Thank heavens for bullet proof vests. No problems there. The guy who shoots you decides, who knows why, and we can't ask him now because he's dead, to throw himself off the balcony. Only you, the hero in all this, try to save him, risking your own life and with two severe and very painful chest injuries from the asshole shooting you. Unfortunately, you just can't hold on to him any longer, and sadly, he falls to his death. Amen. No problems there. Why were you there? Good old community policing. You wanted to show initiative by doing a walkthrough the building, especially after a little old lady asked for you to help rid her apartment building of gangbangers et cetera. Noble, my friend, noble. Dumb, of course. Other good news. You chose the right building to visit. Video cameras? Yes. But the cheap bastards don't actually operate them. Nothing recorded. No problems there, either. The Internet shows pictures of a gallant police officer that looks like he's trying to save a man's life, clinging onto him for dear life over a balcony ten floors up. At one point, the officer appears to whisper to the man, obviously reassuring him. Alas, gravity takes over and the inevitable occurs. Naturally, we're all very sad at the loss of this pillar of society. Get my drift?"

I smiled in acknowledgement.

"As for what you and Jimmie were doing before you even got there, I don't know what to say. A little bird tells me you have an answer for that. Try to remember this is not nineteen-sixty. You and Jimmie are going to catch some flak for it. But, I have it on very good authority that you'll skate on that one, purely because of the good work that followed afterwards. The other glorious news for the department, is this. Guns and Gangs raided a number of apartments in the same building with the Emergency Task Force and K9. Numerous illegal guns have been taken off the streets of Toronto, along with hundreds of thousands of dollars' worth of drugs, and a stash of money amounting to seventy-five thousand dollars. A number of people have been arrested, and as we speak, Canada wide warrants are being prepared for the arrest of others. I'm intrigued, but don't want to know, or even speculate, how this all came to fruition. Any questions?"

"Just one. Is there any chance you could get me a coffee? Black, no sugar."

"I'm on it. The Brass will be in to see you shortly. Don't trust them, just smile in all the right places."

By the time Buzz returned with my coffee, an entourage of senior officers arrived to see me. A few I suspected, were genuinely concerned about my wellbeing. For the others, it was the thing to be seen to do. Good PR. Not many recruits get to see the Chief on their first day on the job. Having met Chief Mick Tuohy, I understood why Jimmie had lasted as long as he had. Both with roots still in Eire, both Catholic boys, and both had grandparents from the same village.

Before leaving, Chief Tuohy placed his hand on my shoulder and whispered in my ear. "The Force is with you, Sam. You need anything, you call me personally. Glad to have men like you aboard, unlike some of these ass kissers." He winked and left the room.

Buzz looked pleasantly surprised. "The Old Man must like you. If he didn't, he wouldn't have come. I know that for a fact. He loves his uniform guys on the front line. Nobody had better touch one of his officers or say a bad word about them, without good reason. That goes for the media, too. Especially the media. Sam, it'll all work out. I have to go to a disciplinary hearing. Not my favourite venue. I'll be in touch."

* * *

When I got back to Harbourfront, I took a long hot shower. The coffee had brewed by the time I got out. I sat down at the kitchen table, and looked out over Lake Ontario. The lake was fairly calm, but with enough wind to fill the sails of the yachts tacking back and forth. Peaceful. My eyes were drawn to a gaff-rig sailing boat. I got my binoculars. It was old, as expected, but well preserved. Its teak deck scrubbed almost white. It had beautiful lines. If there was ever such a thing as a male or female boat, this beauty would be a woman. When I saw the name on her stern, I couldn't stop smiling. *Annie*. One day I was going to find that boat and buy it. Annie and I would sail away aboard her.

I looked up at the surveillance monitor. Annie was approaching the door, keys in hand. She looked tired.

"Oh, Sam, what a day I've had. Is that coffee fresh?"

"Just made it. Sit down, I'll pour you a cup and you can tell me all about it."

"We spent nearly the whole day in the station. My coach officer continually bombarded me with questions about the Highway Traffic Act. Apparently, Don, that's his name, is the guru for the department when it comes to anything to do with a motor vehicle. As if that wasn't enough, then he grilled me about the difference between suspended drivers and disqualified drivers. To round it off, we had a discussion on impaired drivers. I am not looking forward to going in tomorrow. I had to keep telling him that my eyes were not on my chest."

"Do you want me to speak to him?"

"No, of course not. He's harmless, and a wealth of knowledge. All I wanted to do was to get out on the streets and catch criminals. I don't think I'm going to be doing that for some time yet, not at this rate anyway. You're a life saver, thanks for the coffee. Apparently, so I heard, some cop in Toronto was trying to save a guy from falling off a balcony, but the guy fell and was killed. That's awful. So how was your day? You've got a black eye. How did you get that?"

"Well, my coach, his name's Jimmie, he's Irish. That's his nickname, too, but only when he gives you permission to use it. I don't have permission yet. After breakfast he and I got into it. He's an old guy, but don't call him that. I called him *old man* and he lost it. Right on the busy street. Can you believe it?"

"You didn't hurt him, did you?"

"Annie, if Jimmie heard you say that he'd wet himself laughing. No, I did not hurt him, that's the trouble. In trying not to hurt him I caught a fist in the eye. After that I was pissed and he knew it. So we got back in the cruiser and went looking for action. I was driving."

"He let you drive?"

"Sure, why not?"

"Apparently, so the rest of my platoon has been telling me, Don drives until he thinks I'm ready. And then, I'll be sorry I got behind the wheel."

"Sounds fun."

"Don't go there. So what happened then?"

"Well, the news will be on any minute. You can see for yourself. I don't want to see it, I was in it."

"Oh, Sam, is it bad? Are you okay? I'm sorry. I missed you terribly. I don't like not phoning you. Can't we just maybe call one another, once or twice a day?"

"Oh, all right, if it makes you happy."

"It does." We kissed for a long time. "I've got something exciting to tell you." She slapped me with both hands on my chest in excitement and affection. I tried not to wince, but she saw it in my eyes. "Sam, are you okay? What have you done? Show me, please."

"Tell me your news first, then I will."

"My sergeant said that, once I've got a bit more time on, how would I like to go on a domestic violence course? I told him I'd love to. Isn't that great?"

"That is good. He's not coming onto you, is he?"

"Why would you say that? No, of course not. I don't think so."

"Go watch the news, I'll sit here with my coffee."

"Oh, my God! Sam, it's you. Oh, my God. He shot you." She bolted out of the living room in tears, sobbing into my shoulder.

"I'm fine, just bruised. The vest saved me, without it, it would probably have just been a flesh wound anyway."

"Don't joke about it." She glanced through the doorway at the television. A phone camera had caught the shooter *falling* from the balcony, with me leaning over. I was pleased that I looked genuinely upset, though I wasn't. "Oh, my God, that's awful."

"No, it's not. It's just a shame he made a

mess on the concrete parking lot. Some poor sucker had to come and clean that up."

Annie unbuttoned my shirt and raised my T-shirt. "That looks painful, Sam, are you sure you're okay? You did go to the hospital, didn't you?"

"Jimmie made sure of that. Good move on his part. Gave me time to make my notes."

"I don't think I really want the answer to this, but I have to ask it. He did fall, didn't he?"

"Oh, he fell all right. He was overcome by gravity. Let's leave it at that. Remember this, he won't be able to shoot another police officer, and maybe next time, kill them. You're not immune, Annie. It could be you, but now it won't be. We have another early start in the morning, how about I get dinner ready, and you have a nice relaxing bath. I'll bring you in a glass of red wine, and if you're really good, I'll scrub your back."

"Don't let me fall asleep in the bath, I'm beat. I can't even imagine how you must be feeling. I guess the SIU are investigating?"

"Yes, they are."

While Annie was in the bathroom, I checked my cell phone. A man and a woman had just walked into the shooter's apartment. Both were smartly dressed. No doubt from the Special Investigations Unit. Neither knew I had planted a minute camera and listening device inside the apartment. I listened intently to their conversation. The man spoke first.

"I can't put my finger on it, but something

doesn't feel right about this one."

"That's because it stinks. Your first clue is staring you in the face."

"And what's that, Miss Sherlock?"

"It involves Constable Callaghan."

"There's another reason. The recruit, Stephens. He's a problem. I tried checking his military record, only to be told, *It's classified.* A couple of things I did find out, though."

"And what's that?"

"He was one of their best, if not *the* best interrogator. Apparently, his methods got results and saved a lot of lives. My source said he did some undercover work overseas, but wasn't sure where, probably Iraq and Afghanistan. He's fluent in a number of languages, including Pashto. My source described him as, *Rambo with Einstein's IQ* and cautioned me not to make him my enemy, saying, *You know when you were growing up how you were told, There's always someone bigger than you? Well, Stephens is the guy at the end of the line.*"

"So what does that tell us?"

"That the shooter didn't fall from the balcony. He was let go. I'm gonna see if I can get Stephens to take a polygraph. Can't hurt to try."

"His lawyer won't let him for one thing, and if what you say is true about him, even if he did let go of the shooter, it would be like putting one of the Mossad on a polygraph."

"What do you suggest?"

"It's going to be tough, if not impossible to

prove. The only witnesses to the balcony incident all paint Stephens as the hero, trying to save the shooter. All the pictures so far, taken by witnesses with cell phone cameras, support that. We don't even have surveillance footage, even from other apartment buildings and offices with cameras looking this way."

"Well, then. We best go see a friendly judge and get a warrant to tap their phones. We could be talking homicide here."

"I don't think you have enough to get a warrant for that."

"Well, I'll just have to take a leaf out of Callaghan's book and do some creative writing. Forensic haven't found anything useful, so we need some evidence. Are you in, or are you out?"

"On this one? I'm in."

I poured myself a glass of red wine and began dinner. Fresh chicken fried in butter with lots of fresh garlic, ginger and rosemary. Wild rice, carrots and parsnips. Annie walked into the kitchen, towel wrapped around her middle, rubbing her hair.

"Smells delicious."

"Won't be long, but take your time. I'll call you when it's ready. More wine?"

"No, thanks, I still have some, but I'd love another glass to go with my dinner." She turned and went back into the bathroom. I could hear her blow drying her hair.

I dialed Jimmie's cell phone. He answered on the fourth ring.

"We're not supposed to be communicating partner."

"I know that, Jimmie. Listen up. I'm gonna tell you something that you will not repeat. If you do, I'm going to hurt you. A lot. And don't ask me how I know these things, either. Got it?"

"Got it, partner. You definitely do not sound like any rookie I ever met or heard of in my entire life, and that's the truth. If you didn't look so young, in comparison to me that is, I'd have said our paths crossed over thirty years ago."

"After this conversation, be very careful using any telephone, especially talking to me. The SIU are planning to get a warrant to have our phones tapped."

"Those filthy cocksuckers!"

"Jimmie, calm down. I have no idea why, but they've got it in for you. I got the impression it's for all the things you've done in the past, all in the line of policing, naturally."

"Naturally."

"That you've got away with. They want to nail you on this one for past indiscretions."

"But why? I didn't really do anything. This time."

"I know that. One of them, it's a Bonnie and Clyde team, has tried to get the inside scoop on my military record. They got stonewalled because much of it is classified. But one of them has a source who gave the guy a little info, which under normal circumstances wouldn't be a problem. Under these circumstances it becomes problematic. Clyde thinks I let the guy fall to his death. Bonnie doesn't think they can ever prove that. Well, of course they can't. It's not true."

"Course it ain't, Sam. Who would even think such a terrible thing? Anyway, no judge is going to give them a phone-tap warrant."

"They will. Bonnie and Clyde are going to be *creative*."

"Good to know. Listen, Sam."

"What?"

"I always got your back, son. Always. See you in the morning. We'll have breakfast and coffee together. We'll invite Sergeant Wells, he's a good guy. He can be there to see we don't talk about it. I doubt we'll be together, but who knows. Whatever happens. Give out parking tickets tomorrow, will ya?"

"Good night, Jimmie."

"Good night, partner. You know something? You're all right. For an Indian."

"You're not so bad yourself. For an Irishman." I could hear him laughing just before he shut off his phone.

Chapter Fourteen

Morning parade was unlike the previous morning. It was so quiet. You'd have thought someone had died. Jimmie made a point of sitting next to me. As far as he was concerned, he was still my coach officer until he was told otherwise. It was Saturday morning. The Inspector was in. Early. I was told by one of the night shift guys changing in the locker room. *The Inspector never comes in early and never on a Saturday morning.* Not good. Not good at all.

They gave me a different partner for the day. A young kid. Nice enough, but all attitude and traffic tickets. Not my kind of partner. It was going to be a long day.

Before leaving, Sergeant Wells looked across at Jimmie.

"Jimmie, the Inspector wants to see you in his office before you go out on the road. Remind me to re-issue you and Stephens with another firearm before you hit the streets." Jimmie looked grim and nodded. I didn't have a good feeling about this.

Even with the Inspector's door closed, you could still hear their raised voices, particularly Jimmie's.

"As a result of your conduct Constable Callaghan, regarding the disgraceful so-called *play fight* you and Constable Stephens engaged in on the street yesterday morning, in full view of the public, as of this moment, you are no longer a coach officer. Stephens will be assigned a more capable and forward thinking coach officer. Quite frankly, you are an embarrassment to the service and the sooner you retire the better. In fact, today would be a good day to tender your resignation. I will certainly accept it gladly."

"Inspector, when I started policing, you were still in liquid form. More's the pity you didn't stay that way. You, Inspector, will always be a manager. But, you'll never be a leader."

"How dare you! You're going to find yourself heading into a lot of trouble, Callaghan."

"Are you threatening me Inspector, because you really don't want to be threatening me?"

"Get out!"

"You know the difference between a manager and a leader? In battle a leader shouts, *Follow me!* Then charges forward into battle with his men behind him. A manager whispers, *Follow me. I'm right behind you.*"

"Get out of my office, Callaghan. Get out!"

The two men were now in the hallway facing one another. Jimmie looked red with rage, the Inspector white with fear. He wouldn't be the first senior officer Jimmie had decked in his long career. We all knew that someone was going to have the unenviable task of arresting Jimmie for killing the Inspector with his bare hands any minute. I rushed forward and grabbed Jimmie, dragging him back to the parade room, Sergeant Wells on his other arm.

We had breakfast that morning for what we both suspected would be our last together at *Callaghan's Family Restaurant*. I felt sure Nicole, through her father, already had a good idea why we were so sombre, but kept quiet about it. Sergeant Wells came with us in case questions got asked by the investigators.

Jimmie smiled wryly across the table at me. "You know, Sam, I should get you a T-shirt made up that says, *I was Jimmie Callaghan's first and last recruit.* I decided before I retired that I would, for the first time in my career, become a coach officer and impart all my thirty-five years of wisdom to new recruits. You were my first and now my last recruit."

I smiled back at him. "I guess, Jimmie, there wasn't much you could remember anymore, so you gave me what you could in one shift."

Nicole overhead this and began laughing.

"That's enough from you, young lady."

"He's right though, Uncle Jimmie."

"Away with you and get the breakfast, woman. What's taking so long anyway?"

"Why don't you just retire, Jimmie? You've done more than your time."

"What? You on the side of management now, Sergeant?"

"You know me better than that, Jimmie."

"I want to get my thirty-five years in for my pension and, believe it or not, I still love the job. The pure, being a policeman on the street, side of policing. There's nothing like it. The people, the hot calls. Christ, just look at yesterday. What an adrenalin rush. I'm not talking about all the bloody bullshit from management, unnecessary paperwork, lawyers, and bloody leftwing judges waiting for a call to the Senate. I'm talking about the nitty-gritty side of policing. Out there on the streets. Never knowing what you're going to face in the shift or even if you're going home afterwards. Of course, after three decades, it all starts to roll into one. If I had the time in now, I'd give my three months' notice and hang up my hat. I still want to be pushing the prowler on my last shift, Sergeant, which I'm going to make a day shift. I'll be buying your breakfast that morning, Sam, and you are going to drive me around the next day to hand all my gear in. Rest assured. Once I'm gone. You'll never see my face back here again. And, hopefully by then, my Irish temper will have cooled, because, if it hasn't, if I see that bloody Inspector Althoff on the street or any of those other assholes like him, they better be crossing over to the other side of the street."

I believed him. Every word of it.

As we left the restaurant, Jimmie looked very tired and he seemed to have lost his posture. He looked dejected.

"I'll see ya, partner. No recruit has ever been allowed to call me Irish and gone unpunished.

Not until they've got ten years on the job. Just ask the sergeant."

"That's right. I had to wait ten years like everyone else before I got permission. Most never get it. It was like a great honour bestowed upon me when I got it."

I noticed it, but pretended not to. Jimmie's eyes looked moist. The Inspector's untrue words had hurt him. He turned away and walked to his cruiser, parked on the double yellows by the curb.

"Sam. As of this moment. You can call me, Irish. May your God bless you." He said this over his shoulder as he got behind the wheel. Sergeant Wells and I watched him drive away. I'd only known Jimmie Callaghan for a day, but as I stood there, a great sense of sadness enveloped me like a suffocating cloud.

"They don't make them like Jimmie any more. It's not that they broke the mould. They were told to break it."

"You got that right, Sergeant."

Constable Afflek, my new training officer was waiting at the station for me. Young, tall, and skinny. When I saw him, I thought of those tall runner bean poles stuck in vegetable gardens for the beans to grow up. He was already balding, either genetics or the worries of the world on his shoulders. Probably both. I figured he'd been told if he could mould me into a clone of his, promotion to sergeant was assured.

"Where have you been?" Not pleasant. Irritated.

"Having breakfast with Jimmie."

"That loser. Time he retired."

"What do I call you?"

"Constable Afflek."

"Good to know. Because, if I ever hear you badmouth Jimmie again, I'm going to bitch slap you all over this locker room. Now, let's go persecute the public and give out speeding tickets, because I know you're dying to."

He stormed out of the locker room like a spoiled child. It was to be expected. I figured he'd be straight into the sergeant's office, following the chain of command. Eventually, I wandered out into the hallway. Inspector Althoff's office door was closed. Through the glass I could see him seated at his desk. There were two chairs in front of his desk, one occupied by Sergeant Wells, the other by Constable Affleck. My day wasn't getting any better. I began asking myself, not for the first time since becoming involved in policing, why I had ever left the military. I was now seriously thinking of going back in. I wasn't sure I should share these thoughts with Annie. She was either going to be there for me or she wasn't. Distance away, mixed with alcohol can lead to infidelity. I was sick of hearing, *I love you too,* in relationships separated by oceans and warfare. It took a very special kind of person to remain faithful to their partner with separations of months on end, or sometimes, even years. To me, Annie was that special person. I knew I was.

The door opened, Sergeant Wells motioned for me to enter. The atmosphere inside the room was caustic. Afflek sat with a smug grin on his face. Inspector Althoff sat shuffling papers, not looking up. Sergeant Wells and I stood in front of the desk. Waiting. Eventually the Inspector looked up. Not a man's man. His aftershave smelled more like a woman's perfume. His fingernails were neatly clipped, his hands soft looking. He probably rubbed skin lotion into them every night before going to bed. I envisioned a soft toy tucked under the blanket of his bed, its head resting on the pillow. Like most managers, they ruled with an iron rod in the workplace, but at home they were pussy whipped. At work we basically had to put up with it. They had the upper hand. They could make our lives a living hell, stall our careers out of spite, and do their level best to get rid of us. No job. No money. It would be a pleasure to grab both Althoff and Afflek by the hair and slam their faces into the desk. I thought about it briefly. Not a good career move. Guaranteed you wouldn't be leaving with a good reference. I kept my composure and thought about what kind of cuddly toy the Inspector was likely to have in his bed. I figured a teddy bear, but changed my mind. It had to be a police officer.

Inspector Althoff began speaking. I wasn't listening to what he was saying. I kept thinking about the stuffed police doll in his bed. He'd probably used a marker pen to change its rank. I couldn't see him sleeping with a toy of lesser rank than his own. I don't know why, but then I envisaged him and his wife having sex. The comical image made me smile.

"What are you grinning at! Do you find this funny? At least Callaghan made it to thirty-five years, whereas I don't see you making it to thirty-five hours. Not the way you're going. You will apologize to Constable Afflek and conduct yourself in a professional manner from here on. Do I make myself clear?"

"I'd like to discuss this matter with my association rep before going any further with this. As for apologizing to Constable Afflek. That's never going to happen. I suggest you pair me with a more suitable coach officer, even if that means transferring me to another platoon, or another division. Sir."

"I find your tone, Constable, to be bordering on the insubordinate. I suggest you tread very carefully and choose your words and tone with equal care in future. Otherwise, you will find yourself charged with insubordination. With regard to your attitude toward Constable Afflek, I will be considering a charge of discreditable conduct. Dismissed."

"My chest is feeling a lot better today, thank you, sir. The bruising is coming out more, but the swelling has gone. I was shot yesterday, sir. Twice, in the chest. Despite that, the shooter was, *apprehended*, shall we say. As a result of good intelligence, a ton of guns are now off the street. Thank you for asking."

"I don't need another Jimmie Callaghan in

this department. He hates management. I suggest you leave my office now, before you make your situation any worse."

"With respect, sir. I can see why."

I placed my cap back on my head, saluted crisply and shouted, "Yes, sir!" I slammed my boot on the ground as I made my about turn and marched out of the office in military style.

Half an hour later Sergeant Wells joined me in the parade room. He didn't speak for a while, it was like he was holding his breath, unsure of what to say.

"Sam, are you sure you want to be a police officer? You seem to be doing your level best to sabotage your career."

"I'm beginning to have second thoughts about that, Sergeant. Tell me if I'm wrong about this. In one day I did more for the public good than Afflek has done in all his service. Mind you I haven't given out any speeding tickets yet. He must be top of the division."

"You have the makings of an outstanding police officer, Sam, if only you could have joined thirty years ago. This is day two and you're already a marked man."

"Did Afflek tell you what happened in the locker room?"

"He said, he told you the two of you were going out to do radar. You said you didn't do speeders and Jimmie was your training officer. He said that Jimmie was lost and it was probably time for him to retire. You got angry and told him you were going to bitch slap him all over the locker room."

"He was miffed because I'd had breakfast with Jimmie. When I told him, he said, *That loser. Time he retired.* Yeah, I did tell him I'd bitch slap him all over the locker room if he ever bad mouthed Jimmie again. And if he does it again, I will. Gladly."

"I figured something like that had happened. Afflek has been wanting a transfer for some time now into Traffic. He just got his transfer. My job today is to find you a compatible coach officer, preferably ex-military like yourself. Someone who is willing to make the transfer."

"Do you have someone in mind?"

"I'm working on it. I put you back with Jimmie, but only temporarily, at least until I can find someone willing to take you on. Jimmie was the perfect match. I've stuck my neck out for you, Sam. Don't let me down. I am not one of Inspector Althoff's favourites ."

"No worries, Sarge. I got your back."

"With Afflek gone, I don't know who's going to bring the Inspector his morning coffee. Perhaps you'd like to?"

"That is never going to happen. I don't do coffee runs for management. If I come across a leader, I might pick them one up."

"In that case, you won't be burning up the taxpayers' money."

I met Jimmie parked outside the station on the double yellows. When he saw me approaching the cruiser he began to laugh.

"You, Constable Stephens, remind me of

myself when I first joined. I've been battling myself through management's bullshit ever since. Sergeant Wells told me all about it. The platoon are going to love you, they've been hoping Afflek would get posted to Traffic for ages. No one can stand the guy. Management material, not leadership material like us and most of the guys on the front line. I'm proud of you for sticking up for me. That's what real partners do."

"Irish, nobody badmouths you when I'm around."

"Likewise, my son. We've got a couple of calls, not high priority, so we'll grab a coffee at my brother's place and hit the road running. How's that young lady of yours doing in Dalton?"

"She's receiving counseling."

"I figured."

* * *

It wasn't until I started my night shifts that I was introduced to my new coach officer. A stocky guy with a military haircut sat across from me in the parade room. An old looking, badly healed scar ran across the left side of his face, from his earlobe to his mouth. He had the bearing of a military man. His steel blue eyes were cold and hard looking. Not mean. He had presence. I figured him for a guy used to hand-to-hand combat on the front line. Not a pen pusher. A man with a short fuse, pleasant to deal with, but if you pissed him off—look out. He wasn't a donut eater. This guy kept in shape.

His eyes locked on mine. He smiled, the scar becoming part of the smile. It looked grotesque, adding to the disfigurement. I'd seen lots of scars. I had some of my own. The deepest and ugliest were not visible on the surface. They were the hardest to treat.

The mood in the parade room was upbeat. Electric. The streets of Toronto vibrated with life in all its various shades. The good, the extremely bad, and the exceptionally ugly.

"Sam," said Sergeant Wells. "Meet your new coach officer, Constable Rudy Jackson."

The military man got up and walked around the tables, a cluster of office tables pushed together.

"Pleased to meet you, Sam. I've heard a lot about you. None of it good. But who gives a shit anyway. I like everything I've heard about you. You and me are gonna get on just fine."

We locked hands. Not a test of strength, just two sincere men shaking hands.

"Which regiment," I asked.

"Legionnaire. Nine years."

"Special Forces, among other adventures," I replied.

"I know. I did some digging."

I smiled and sat back down. Anyone who survived the brutal training of the French Foreign Legion during the time period Rudy was there, had to be tough. I liked him. A man with a good sense of humour.

"All right, you two soldiers. Go out there and try to be policemen. Especially you, Stephens."

"No worries there, Sergeant. If I want to get into a shit load of trouble, I'll ask for Jimmie."

At my quip, the platoon dissolved into laughter.

"The platoon's already started betting on you two," said Jimmie. "I'm being generous. By the end of the shift, something's going down with you two."

Irish has lost that bet, said the Weatherman. Jimmie looked at me knowingly.

"Anytime you want to talk about it, partner."

"I'm good, thanks, Jimmie." I didn't want to call him Irish in front of the whole platoon. It didn't seem right somehow.

"You drive, Sam," said Rudy. "I guess you pretty much know Toronto anyway, living here. I'm real sorry about Irish and you. That's tough on both of you. Irish has a nose for criminals and a way of charming the truth out of them, without them realizing they just confessed their sins to him. Once we had this crazy woman under arrest, suspected of making threatening phone calls. She wasn't going to admit to anything. On the way to the station I told her Irish used to be a priest and was well used to taking confessions. Despite not being one now, the Vatican gave him special permission to still take them. Irish blessed her and she confessed everything to him. She pled guilty, which was just as well. The lawyers would have had a field day with that one."

"Creative," I replied. "I like creative."

"Let's head downtown. We can chat up a few hookers, hassle their pimps, and see how the homeless are doing."

"How do you think the homeless are doing? Pretty bad, I should think."

"You'll see. Like any big town or city, Toronto looks spectacular through the eyes of a visitor. Even to those that live here, unless they turn over the dirty rocks or stir the muddy pools, they don't see the underbelly of the city. A police officer sees a whole other world. It's like two worlds floating side by side, but in another dimension. Rarely do they cross into the other's realm, but when they do, sometimes all hell breaks loose. As you've already experienced."

"I heard some of the guys calling you Pierre. How come?"

"That's my nickname. I made the mistake of telling someone that when you become a Legionnaire, you have to change your name. I called myself Peter. So, I'm Pierre, to my colleagues, Rudy to my friends. You can call me Rudy."

From a distance the hookers looked good. If you're into hookers that is. I'm not. Most of them with long blonde hair, slim, some quite pretty, plastered in makeup, miniskirts, tight blouses or tank tops, and of course, high heels. Girls of every nationality, especially Asians with long jet black hair.

"Some of those girls, Sam, are just trying to put themselves though university. Especially, those in the escort game. Some of them are earning thousands of dollars an hour, working out of high class condos. Their security systems and doormen are in a whole different class. When I worked vice, you couldn't even get past the front doors. Trouble is, the money is that good that getting out of it becomes almost impossible, if not, impossible. Those girls getting a medical degree are never going to earn the same money as a qualified doctor as they can get in the escort game. They're all like centrefolds. Just about all of it is run by organized crime. At the sleazier end of the market, a lot of the exotic dancers are from Eastern Europe and Asia. Girls promised a better life here in Canada. When they arrive, the nightmare begins. Beatings, drugs, always the threat of violence if they don't put out. Now we have human trafficking units trying to help these girls and shutdown the pimps. I put in for that unit. My worry is I might get a bit too emotionally involved and end up whacking some of those sleaze balls. Know what I mean?"

"I think you and me should work vice together."

"There's another problem. I'm not one to get tied down, you know, get married. I like my freedom. I could never settle down with just one woman. The thought grosses me out. So, I indulge my only little vice and get an escort now and again, depending on how my overtime is looking. It's cheaper in the long run. Look. You get married, have kids, start hating each other. You end up getting divorced, she gets half the house, half your pension. Then you're paying her spousal support and child support. Christ, you might as well be on welfare. Screw that."

"Marry a policewoman. Then you're on equal footing."

"No, thank you very much. Too controlling. I don't want to be told, *what time are you coming home.* Or, *where have you been.* No. I love my selfish life just the way it is. Now, that's not common knowledge, about the escorts I mean. You and me have been in the trenches, where the real brotherhood is. There's no brotherhood in policing anymore, I'm sorry to say. One of the guys from Professional Standards told me they are getting more complaints up there from, cops complaining about other cops. Can you believe that? What ever happened to sorting it out in the locker room? Grab someone in the locker room now and before you know what's happened, you're up on charges. The department's full of guys like Afflek, just waiting to put the knife in so they can climb the corporate ladder on your back. Take my advice, wear two panels in the back of your vest when walking around the police station. Guaranteed someone's going to stab you in the back."

"Who's the tall leggy one?"

"That's Dusty. You interested?"

"I don't think so. I like to look, but I'd rather

not touch."

"Very wise around here. Almost guaranteed to go home with something you didn't have before you left. Now, if you want the higher end of escorts. Not the really high end, unless you won the lottery, midrange, but still gorgeous, just let me know and I'll set you up."

"I'll bear that in mind, Rudy. The girl I'm engaged to, were she to be an escort, she'd be way up in the high end."

"You're blind, buddy, you're brains have dropped to your balls. I'm really going to have to take you in hand and save you from yourself."

"I have a picture of her in my wallet."

"Oh please, Sam, you're killing me. I don't even think you're salvageable." I handed Rudy a recent photograph of Annie.

"Oh, my God," he said slowly. "I take it all back. This girl's a doll. Tell me she has a sister, I want to marry her. Right now."

"You see, Rudy. You just haven't met the right girl."

"Hey, Rudy. Where you been, honey? We've all missed you. Are you gonna take me away in handcuffs again? You're such a naughty boy."

"No handcuffs tonight, maybe tomorrow night. If you're a bad girl."

"I like your new partner. He's definitely getting police discount. What's your name, big guy?"

"Sam. Pleased to meet you."

"I like him, Rudy. Make sure you bring him

again, with his handcuffs next time."

"Everything all right on the street?"

"Same old. You know how it is."

I could see she was lying. Something in her eyes.

"That's not true, is it? I can tell. I don't mean any disrespect. You don't want to say, that's your right. I'm cool with that."

Rudy frowned. Dusty stared up at me. Silence, then … "You're very perceptive, Sam. I'm not sure I like that. In fact, it scares me a little. There's something about you. I can't put my finger on it. Not evil. Not bad … Merciless. That's it. Merciless."

"Dusty is clairvoyant, so she claims. Come on then, out with it. What's bugging you? You know whatever you say to me and my partner, goes no further."

"I know that, Rudy, and I respect that." She hesitated a moment before continuing. "One of the girls got beat up last week. A john picked her up in a fancy car. Looked like a rich college kid. Took her somewhere quiet, only he had three of his college friends waiting. I don't need to tell you what happened. They paid her and dropped her off across town."

"How's she doing," asked Rudy.

"Let's just say she won't be working the streets for a while. No amount of makeup's going to cover those bruises. I know what you're going to say. Don't bother asking. She don't want no police involved. Fact is, she'd be mad I even told you."

I felt I needed to hurt some people. Four people. Very badly. "You see him pick her up?"

"No, Sam, I didn't. None of us did. She was working up the end of the street. It's darker up there."

"What *can* you tell us, Dusty? Come on, these guys are gonna do it again, you know that. Probably done it before. Maybe next time they're gonna kill one of you."

"Or, someone else," I added.

"It was the aboriginal girl wasn't it? She works that end of the street. I seen her there before. What's her street name? Candy. That's it. It's Candy, isn't it?"

"Look, Rudy, you guys should leave. You're hurting business. Your friend here looks fit to be tied."

I said nothing. I thought of all the murdered and missing aboriginal women. It wasn't safe for me to be on the street. If one asshole badmouthed me, I might just rip his head off.

"Sam, let's go get a coffee, I'm dying for a Tim's."

"Sure. We'll talk about it there."

As we drove through the busy traffic my mind was working overtime. "We need to see this girl, Candy."

"She's not going to talk to us, Sam. The poor thing's probably terrified."

"I know someone she can talk to. Someone she can trust."

"And who's that?"

"My fiancée, Annie. I'll talk to her when I

get home. We can take a drive in together on our next days off. When they crossover, that is."

"All right. I'm with you on this one. Just to cover our asses, you know, cya, cover your ass, we better put a report in on this, under police information. If we don't, and anything else goes down involving those creeps, it'll come back to bite us both in the ass."

"We should put a bulletin out about it, too. Maybe some of our guys have information already."

"Good idea, Sam. But first, let's talk to the Sexual Assault Unit. We'll run it by them. I'll ask my mate in the Vice Squad if he knows Candy and where she's living. I'm gonna tell the guys in SAU that Annie is the one who should speak to her, especially as they're both Native." I nodded in agreement and swung the cruiser into the Tim's' parking lot.

"You're not going through the drive through?"

"No, Rudy, I'm not. Irish believes in mingling with the people. There's a group of old guys that he likes to sit with."

"He'd fit right in there."

"Can you believe it? One of them, Ralph, is eighty-six. Took his motorcycle license in his seventies and still rides his sixteen-hundred Harley Davidson."

"Wow, he's almost as old as Irish. Okay, let's meet and greet the people."

We found a table in the corner. I sat with my back to the window, Rudy opposite me. Just in case. Not everyone likes the police. A mother came in with her two kids, a girl and a boy about nine years old, I guessed. She came over to our table.

"I'm sorry to bother you officers when you're having your coffee, but my kids wanted to say hi. A police officer came to their school recently and spoke to their class. Now they want to be cops. Sorry, I mean police officers."

Rudy smiled. "Cops is fine. What's your names?" The two children began to slink behind their mother.

"Go on, tell the officer your names."

"I'm Mandy and he's Tommy."

I sat back and watched Rudy in action. He seemed to be enjoying every minute of it.

"Can I see your gun?"

"Well, Tommy," said Rudy. "I only take this gun out, if I intend to use it. If I took it out to show you, I'd get in a whole lot of trouble."

"I think guns are cool," replied the boy.

"No, Tommy, they're not cool. I wish I didn't have to carry one, but sometimes there are bad people out there. My job, and my partner's job, is to protect good people like you."

"Have you ever shot anyone?" This from Tommy's sister. There was a lot of hesitation before Rudy replied. He didn't want to lie to the kids, but he didn't want to tell them the truth either.

"No, I haven't," he replied unconvincingly.

"What about your partner?" said Tommy.

"He's a new guy. He hasn't had the opportunity to shoot anyone. Yet."

The lady thanked us and headed to the counter with her children in tow.

"See, Rudy, they don't bite."

"They don't, but there's others that will."

"Irish was telling me that one time he paid a visit to one of the elementary schools on his patch. At the end of his little speech there were all sorts of questions. One kid piped up in front of the whole school, *When my dad goes to work on night shift, a policeman comes to visit my mom.* Irish couldn't think of anything better to say than, *That's nice.*"

"Cops are such whores, Sam." He took a sip of his coffee. "You miss the military?"

"Sometimes. With all that's going on lately, I wish I was back there. From what I've seen so far, I think there's more REMFs in the police service than in the military."

Rudy laughed. "Haven't heard that one in a long time. Rear Echelon Motherfuckers. Pen pushers, desk jockeys."

"You miss it?"

"Like you. Sometimes. I don't miss the desert, that's for sure. Almost got my head blown off by a sniper. My own fault."

I didn't like to ask questions. The desert held unhappy memories for me.

"I was in the Saudi desert with my detachment of *Regiment d'Infanterie* on an operation in the Gulf. I finished whatever soldiers do during the day, and as I didn't have any guard duty, or other such nonsense, I wanted to have some … alone time before I got some kip. It was really dark in the desert."

"I know," I replied.

"Of course, you do. Anyway. Being around mostly cities my entire life, I never experienced anything like it, and with the no light rule it was an inkwell. So with that cover, I made my way out to the trench holes we dug into the perimeter for base defense. I knew we weren't supposed to be out there, but if there's one thing that trumps the discipline of the French Foreign Legion, it's a young man's nature. And for that I needed some alone time. I would take my lumps if I got caught. You might say I was about mid-stroke, when I heard somebody coming out of the base. *Who goes there?* he called. It was the lieutenant. A good natured enough fellow. Most officers were to be honest. They had their underwear washed by Legionnaires for crying out loud. I would be good natured too if someone washed my underwear. I got myself together before he was on top of me and quickly identified myself. I gave some lame excuse about, *News from the home front* and *needing some alone time.* We walked back together with some words about, *Not going out that far,* et cetera, but that was about it. The lieutenant was solid enough and nothing came of it. The next day, we were running a 10k wearing S3P suits, that got black charcoal all over your skin and there was next to no water to wash it off with. Anyway, the Turkish sniper was footing beside me and he started asking me questions about the other night in the foxhole. He told me he had me in his sights, and was about to squeeze off a round when he got curious about the repeating up and down motion going on. He went through his lieutenant for authorization to take the shot and thankfully explained the reason for his hesitation. I felt weird and explained everything to him. We both laughed. I imagined a letter going back to my mom explaining what a brave soldier I was with my war medal and all that, being taken out by my own teammate. Of course, she would never learn the truth and hopefully they would put my combat pants on proper before they carried me out."

Even before Rudy had finished his heroic story of unarmed combat on himself, I choked on my coffee sending a spray of liquid across the table and began to howl with laughter, tears running down my cheeks.

"What? That never happened to you?"

"No, Rudy, it didn't. That's one of the funniest stories I've heard in a long time. Who knew that playing with yourself could turn out to be so dangerous. Just think, you came and went all at the same time."

"Funny guy, Sam."

"With stories like that you should write a book on your bizarre military experiences. It would be a best seller."

"Most of them I'd rather forget, thank you. Okay, partner, let's go check on the homeless."

We drove to another area of our division,

parked the cruiser and began walking the back alleys behind a row of shops. Under the glow of what was either a low wattage bulb or one caked in dirt, three disheveled looking men and one woman were bedding down for the night under a canopied loading dock bathed in yellow light. They had placed thick cardboard packing cases, folded flat on the concrete floor as insulation. Their bedding, of assorted quilts, blankets, and sleeping bags, on top. In case of rain, a thick sheet of polythene lay nearby.

"We brought six hot chocolates and some muffins," announced Rudy as we approached the small group, huddled in a small circle. A strong odour of clothing worn and unwashed for a year, drifted into my nostrils. I'd smelled it many times before. It was like the smell of marijuana. Once you smelled it, you never forgot the smell. Unlike the smell of marijuana, this was an unpleasant smell.

"Hey, Rudy, how ya doin'?" The old guy began hacking uncontrollably, until he got his breath back. His deeply lined face was weather beaten and dirty. His long grey hair matted under a red woolen Christmas toque. Christmas was still months away. He took another drag on a cigarette butt, likely discarded in the gutter.

"Who's ya partner, Rudy?" The woman's voice was hoarse from years of smoking and hard living.

"Betty, this is Sam. He's the new guy. I'm showing him the ropes, though most of them he's already climbed. And how's the Major this evening?"

"Can't complain," replied the old guy in the Christmas toque. "Free accommodation, fresh air, cigarettes, and booze. What more could a Christian man ask for?"

"And good company," said Betty.

One of the other men, much younger than the rest, pale and gaunt looking, smiled when he saw Rudy. "Haven't seen you down at the soup kitchen lately, Rudy. You been away?"

"Yes Sean, I was away on a course for a week on mental health. Before I forget, I got you all some decent cigarettes."

"That's an oxymoron if ever I heard one," I said.

"And some fresh matches," continued Rudy. "Any problems lately? Anyone hassling you guys?"

"It's been pretty good lately," said the Major. "I think the word's out there that the police are keeping an eye out for us. We don't get hassled nearly so much now, since you been looking after us, Rudy. Not all the cops are so friendly though, you know that."

"But as soon as we mention your name, Rudy, they leave us alone."

"That's good, Sean. I'm pleased to hear it."

"We been clearing up our mess every morning like you said, Rudy. It's only fair."

"That's good, Major. Anyone else hassles you guys, you can mention Sam's name, too. He'll keep an eye out for you. Okay, we're gonna do a little foot patrol around here. You guys stay safe and keep warm. Before I forget. Keep your eyes open for four young guys driving a fancy car. That's all I got so far. They like doing bad things to women."

"We'll take good care of Betty," said the Major. "If we see or hear anything, I know where to find you."

It was good to be out on foot, though our ears were always tuned to our radios. We didn't stray too far from the cruiser, just in case we got a hot call and had to leg it back to our wheels.

"Rudy, you sure have a soft spot for those street people."

"Sam. Every one of them has a story that'll break your heart. Can you imagine losing everything? Your job, your home, your family. No money. No hope. Suffering from mental illness. You don't even have the will to kill yourself. You just exist in this nightmare world of poverty that runs alongside a world of plenty. But you can't ever quite make the transition from one world to the next."

"That thought scares me. Good for you, though."

"No, good for you, too. That was nice of you to chip in."

"Well, partner, where you're concerned, still waters run deep, that's for sure."

We continued our slow walk through the alleyways, talking as we walked, putting the world to rights as cops do. How we'd like to be part of a small group of secret undercover police officers, sanctioned by the government to eliminate our worst criminal elements. Permanently. It was a surprisingly quiet night. I was okay with that. We got back to the cruiser and began to patrol the streets like a shark swimming through the water looking for prey.

Chapter Fifteen

Violent domestic on ten-twenty Aberdeen Street, unit four. Woman screaming for help. Ambulance en route. Rudy snatched up the radio and marked us on the call.

"Lights and sirens, Sam. Let's get a move on. When he hears the sirens it might stop him, and when she hears them, it'll give her comfort. Don't spare the horses, buddy. Just don't pick-up any human hood ornaments on the way. The paperwork will kill us."

I slammed my foot on the gas, the long hood on the Ford rose up and we were flying, rear tires biting into the tarmac, sirens blaring, emergency lights bouncing off the shop windows. It was like bumper cars, only we weren't permitted to bump into anything. Not on this call. I took the green light at the intersection, steered hard right, the car began a four-wheel skid as I steered left into the skid and we were off again down the street, weaving in and out of traffic. Rudy was screaming obscenities at drivers who took their time pulling over. They couldn't hear him anyway, but one look on his face and they knew he was seriously pissed-off.

The light ahead was red. A quick stop, check

the intersection and floor the gas again. It made me think of Irish. *We never used to stop for anything once those lights and sirens were on. It was, Get the hell out of the way! All the way. Those were the days.* The last thing I wanted to do was to seriously injure or kill an innocent citizen, especially a child, or my partner. I wasn't too fond of hurting myself, either. I kept the cruiser under control all the time, limited my risks, stopped at every red light, as required, but let it rip when I felt it was safe to do so.

"Good driving, Sam! Way to go, buddy. You nailed it. Okay, make a right up ahead by that red neon sign. The apartment building should be about halfway down the street on the left."

I pulled the cruiser into the curb, just short of the entrance to the brick apartment building. As we exited the car we could hear the sound of sirens approaching in the distance as other units converged on our location. The sound of a male voice shouting obscenities could be heard above us, together with a woman pleading for her life. The entrance door was locked. I whipped out my multi-tool, inserted the blade between the door lock and jam and applied pressure. It was just enough to clear the lock and we were in, running up the stairs. We burst through the stairwell door and charged down the hallway to unit four. I hit the door with my shoulder still at a run and took the whole thing down.

The commotion was in the bedroom. As the door went down, a large male stood in the bedroom doorway wearing a grubby white *wife-*

beater T-shirt, appropriate for the occasion. He was big and muscular and very sure of himself. Shaved head and stubble. Heavily tattooed. Probably never lost a fight in his life.

"Oh, look, the pigs have arrived. You assholes can't come in here without a warrant."

I could just see past him into the room, a woman was lying on the bed whimpering, covered in blood. I kept going, not in the mood for conversation and hit him hard and fast with a right punch to the face, avoiding his mouth. Teeth carry a whole range of infections that the host may contend with, but if they puncture your knuckle it can lead to a whole world of medical complications. I was impressed, very impressed. He remained standing, wobbling like a drunken sailor, disoriented. But still on his feet. Now, he was a bloody mess. His T-shirt had a huge red blotch for a logo, where one wasn't before. A hard left fist to the solar plexus did the trick, and down he went. Rudy was already moving past me and into the room. I could hear the sound of feet running along the hallway toward us. Military instinct caused me to draw my weapon. Finger off trigger. It could be the enemy and I'd be ready to open fire if need be. Or, it could be our backup. Four members of my platoon rushed into the room, sliding to a halt, eyes wide as saucers as they saw my gun, now being re-holstered.

I grabbed *wife beater* by the ankles and dragged him into the living room, rolled him over, handcuffed him and for good measure secured his ankles with a three-foot piece of nylon cord I carried in my pocket. Now he couldn't kick out at any of us. I was sure he was going to try. Hogtieing was not permitted anymore. It could lead to positional asphyxia, particularly when the arrested party was placed face down in the rear of the cruiser. Placed might be too fine a word for how they actually got in there. Their entry and exit into and from the *police taxi* was all subject to their politeness toward the police.

The paramedics arrived, an older guy, looked like he was desperate for retirement and a young woman full of piss and vinegar.

"She's in the bedroom with my partner."

"What about him?" The female paramedic looked horrified when she saw my bloodied prisoner lying on the floor cursing and swearing through bubbles of blood.

"He's fine. We'll drop by Emerg with him on our way to the station. Go take care of the girl. She's the one in rough shape."

The grey-haired paramedic who had seen it all before a thousand times, shouted out from the bedroom.

"She's in real bad shape. We're gonna need a police escort and get some units to keep the intersections clear. It's gonna be touch and go."

I radioed dispatch and told them what we needed. One of the units was going to stay at the crime scene; the other was going to escort the ambulance to hospital. Fast. SOCO was en route. I wanted to dig a deep hole and bury this guy alive.

"What's the scenes of crimes officer's ETA," I asked.

"Ten minutes," came back the reply from SOCO.

When they put the young woman on the gurney she was unconscious. Rudy had been amazing. Gentle, kind, and spoke with a soothing voice, doing his best to reassure her. He truly cared about people who couldn't take care of themselves. Beneath his tough black exterior was an immensely compassionate man. He reminded me of the Weatherman.

A little later we arrived at Emerg with the assailant. The woman was already being treated. When the nurses and doctors found out our guy was the one who had inflicted the horrendous injuries on her, their hostile attitude toward us changed. It was obvious they thought we'd beaten up some guy who didn't deserve it. One nurse even muttered, *police brutality* under her breath.

Half an hour later the Emerg doctor, middle-aged, pretty, and very professional called us out of the waiting room. She looked tired and worn out.

"In India, where I'm from, this sort of thing happens all the time. It's disgusting." I was shocked to see a tear roll down her dark cheek. "I'm sorry, gentlemen. She didn't make it. We tried our best, but her internal injuries were just too severe. And now I have to treat *him*." She said the word with venom.

I placed my hand on her shoulder. "Thank you for trying, Doc. We know you all did your best. You always do."

For a moment, I thought she was going to bury her head into my shoulder and start crying. She composed herself, nodded, and walked away. I liked her. I liked her a lot. Rudy seemed to have been struck dumb. He stared blankly ahead. One too many deaths for him to cope with. I could see it was having an impact on him. One day it was all going to be too much for him. His heart was too big, it was going to bring him down eventually.

"Better call the Sarge and let him know, Sam," he said wearily. "He'll call the Duty Inspector and homicide will get called out. Better make a start on our notes for this one. There's two things I'm sorry about. One she died."

"The other?"

"You didn't kill him." There was a long silence. "I hate this job."

"No, you don't, Rudy. You're an awesome cop and a great partner. You need to come with me to the res and go to the sweat lodge. My grandfather will help heal your troubled soul."

"Man, you're too deep, brother. Can we get drunk after?"

"Probably best to do that before, then we can sweat it out afterwards."

"All right, you're on. Next days off, can you fit me in?"

"Sure. My grandfather will be there."

"Is Annie going to be there?"

I smiled. "I was going to say no. But, I think when you see her you'll feel a whole lot better. Just remember. You can look, but don't touch."

"I never touch a fellow brother's woman, especially his wife. That's just plain ignorant. You gotta be a real asshole to do that. Besides, I have no desire to be staked out by you in the hot sun and tortured for days on end, then roasted on a giant spit over a huge wood fire and eaten."

"You have a vivid imagination, Rudy. How did you know I was going to do that to you?"

"Now you're scaring me, Sam. I need another coffee, this is going to be a *long* shift, my friend. A long shift."

I radioed the information through to our sergeant. Then we sat and waited. There was a lot of just sitting around and waiting in policing.

As if Sergeant Wells could read our minds he called back. "You guys are gonna be stuck there a while. What d'you want in your coffees? You hungry? I can pick you something up."

Not just a sergeant. A great sergeant, taking care of his men. Not a manager. A leader. Rare. Almost extinct in policing. I hadn't been long on the job, but I already knew I'd go through fire for this man. Irish was right. We were damn lucky to have him on our platoon. The more I worked with him, the more I liked and respected him. I gave him our food and beverage orders and sat back in the chair staring at my prisoner. Dark thoughts on my mind.

"You're a dead man when I get outa here. I'll

come looking for you."

"I hope so," I replied with a smile. "Trouble is, I don't think you'll be coming out for a long time. But don't worry. When the time comes, you won't have to worry about looking for me. I'll already be waiting for you. I hope you can breathe underground."

"Yep, you worry me, Sam. I hope I never piss you off."

I looked at Rudy sitting in the other chair next to me. "Don't worry, I'll give you a long straw."

"You're sick, do you know that? But I like your thinking."

I returned to my dark thoughts that were now even darker, and suddenly remembered something I had promised I would do and hadn't yet followed up on. I took out my secure phone and sent Malloy a text message.

You still out near Lake Eerie?

Yep

Need you to pay a visit to someone with a burned out pick-up truck

Ok. Gotcha

Needs to be advised that it's not a good idea to proceed with the venture. Unhealthy

Is there any damage?

No damage ... Just needs to be ... advised

Roger that

If I said I was going to do something, I liked to keep my word. Idle threats were like trying to scare someone by throwing balls of cotton wool at them. Pointless. Annie sent me a text. She still loves me. My dark thoughts evaporated.

We'd just finished our coffee and burgers when two well-dressed Italian-looking men entered our room. They looked like Mafia, both in Armani suits, beautifully tailored. I stood up. Sitting down is never a good starting point for a confrontation.

"Hey, Rudy, how's it going?"

"Peachy, Bruno. Just peachy. Gabrio."

The other man, Gabrio nodded. "This the perp?"

"That's him," said Rudy.

"Is this the infamous Constable Stephens?"

"Yes, Gabrio, it is."

I shook hands with the two men.

"Sam, let me introduce you to Toronto's finest homicide officers. Detectives Bruno Moretti and Gabrio Santoro. Better known as, S and M." The two men smiled.

Moretti handed me a cardboard tray with two large coffees, a brown paper bag with sugar and creamers and another bag with two muffins. A simple gesture for *the uniforms* as the guys in plain clothes liked to call the downtrodden misfits in uniform. Three leaders in one shift. A miracle.

"So you don't fight over the muffins, I got you the same. Blueberry," said Moretti. "What happened to this guy, you drop him over a balcony, Stephens? You know this is becoming a pattern with you. Not that I gotta problem with that. Hell, it's been rumoured, unfairly I might add, that S and M have dropped a few ourselves. Accidentally of course, ain't that right, Detective Santoro?"

"Apparently, Detective Moretti. People say the most unkind things. Unbelievable. Two saints like us."

Rudy chuckled. "He ran into Sam's fist."

"Ouch, what a mess," replied Santoro.

"Well deserved, though," added Moretti. It was like watching a well-rehearsed double act listening to these two detectives.

"Fuck you!"

The detectives looked at each other in amazement and said in unison, "It speaks."

They beckoned us out of the room.

"Who's the arresting officer," asked Moretti.

"Sam is," said Rudy.

"Okay, Sam. Let's hear it from the top."

I told the detectives everything that happened from my perspective and then Rudy did the same.

Moretti turned to his partner. "All perfectly justified I'd say, Detective Santoro, wouldn't you say?"

"I concur with your learned conclusion, Detective Moretti. Quite justified. In fact, I'd go so far as to say, throwing said individual off the balcony would be quite justified."

"I agree, my learned friend. That said. Sam, arrest this piece of shit for homicide, read him his rights to counsel, exactly by the book, plus the secondary caution. As soon as he gets medically cleared, bring it back to the station, book it, and if it wants to speak to a lawyer or duty counsel, make sure it does."

"You want me to arrest him?"

"Why not, Sam? You're a policeman still, aren't you? He didn't resign without me noticing did he, Detective Santoro?"

"I don't think so, Detective Moretti."

"Rudy, for continuity purposes, you're gonna have to go to CFS with the body. Get your sergeant to send another guy up to replace you. We're pretty high up here, I don't want Sam to *accidentally* drop our man. You didn't hear this from me, Sam, but apparently the SIU got nothing on you."

"Thanks, Detective Moretti. Not that they would have."

"Bruno. Call me Bruno. You already earned that right. I been talking to my old pal, Irish."

"Thanks, Bruno."

"Any time. Okay, see you boys back at the factory later. Remember. Good notes. We're gonna take a look at the crime scene. Nice job buttoning that down by the way. Enjoy the coffee and muffins."

"CFS? What's that, Rudy?"

"Centre for Forensic Science. They'll do the autopsy there. You ever been to an autopsy?"

"No. I've seen enough dismembered bodies to last me a lifetime."

The Weatherman got inside my head again. *Yeah, the Centre for Forensic Science. That's where they took me. We drove all along Highway 401 from Trenton to Toronto. People*

I'd never even seen before lined the bridges over the highway. Moms and dads with their kids, old people, young people. There were cops in uniform, and veterans, firefighters, paramedics, emergency vehicles with all their flashing lights going. And as we approached each bridge they all saluted. Yeah. I remember that. It was so beautiful.

"Sam. You okay, bro?"

"Yeah."

"Wanna talk about it?"

"No."

It became an awkward moment for both of us. But I knew he knew, and he knew I knew he knew.

"Okay, Sam my man. Don't you forget our sweaty lodge date."

I smiled. "It's called a sweat lodge, Rudy. Not a sweaty lodge, though believe me, you'll sweat more than you ever did in the desert. I presume you got a strong heart?"

"Strong as yours, brother. Maybe even stronger."

"Rudy, I'm not even going to contradict that statement. Know why? Because I think it's probably true. If not stronger, it sure is bigger."

"You, Sam Stephens, are a man I never wanna tangle with. Even if you was blind and had no arms. I think this guy oughta escape out the window. What do you think?"

"I couldn't agree more. But I think it's a little too soon, considering the other one."

"Nurse! Help! They're gonna throw me out

the window."

The ward nurse entered the room. "Mr. Simpson. Keep the noise down or I'll help them throw you out the window."

"Bitch."

"Shall I open the window for you, officers?"

"It's okay, nurse, we can manage," said Rudy.

I looked at them both. "I have a better idea. Where's the incinerator, nurse?"

"That's restricted access. But tonight, I can make an exception. I saw you chasing him down the hallway, and somehow he disappeared. Never to be seen again. Of course, that silence will have to be paid for."

"How much?" She looked at Rudy's name tag.

"Large coffee, two cream."

"Expensive, Alyson," he said, looking at her name tag. At least, I think he was looking at her name tag. "Are you single?"

"Might be."

"How could the most beautiful black woman in the whole universe be single?"

"Are you single?"

"Might be."

"I don't date married men."

"Me, neither."

She began to laugh. "A comedian. I like that. And single."

It was like the human version of two birds of paradise in a mating dance. The chemistry between them was electrifying.

"You free this weekend, Miss Alyson?"

"I am, Rudy."

"Wanna go to a sweat lodge with me?"

"Sure. What is it?"

"Tell her, Sam."

So I did.

"Sounds great. I'm always up for a challenge."

"Alyson," I said. "We were going to get slightly intoxicated first though, especially after this shift. But, we could cancel that if you like."

"No way, you guys. Count me in. We're a team. Just don't forget that coffee."

* * *

When Rudy's relief came, with Alyson's coffee and two chocolate chip cookies that Rudy thought would entice her even more, he took off to the CFS in the ambulance with twenty-three year old Susan Marshall. I wondered if she would remember the trip like the Weatherman. I doubted it somehow. When we first arrived at the hospital, Rudy was so low, depressed even. Now, after meeting Alyson and cementing their first unofficial date with two chocolate chip cookies, he was on cloud nine and rising. If this wasn't the right woman, there never was going to be one. If there had been a preacher in that room right there and then, the two of them would have got married on the spot.

Once Simpson had been medically cleared, we took him back to the station and lodged him, awaiting the arrival of homicide. We bagged and tagged his clothes and gave him a white *bunny suit* to wear. A paper coverall. Then I went into homicide to talk to S and M.

Before going off shift, Detective Moretti called me back to his office.

"I read through your general occurrence report, Sam. Very impressive. Detailed. I like detail. Creative writing regarding your encounter with Simpson."

"What's he saying?"

"Not much. He spoke to duty counsel, and didn't want to answer any questions. At first, that is. Eventually, he came up with a story. He arrived home late to the sound of his girlfriend screaming, as he rushes into the room, a guy wearing dark clothes and a hoody rushes out past him and takes off down the back fire escape. There's no surveillance camera coverage there."

"It would catch him coming through the front entrance, though."

"It would, only Simpson thinks he saw him climbing up the ladder, but couldn't be sure. I guess our mystery man likes to use the fire escape. Probably believes in safety and wants to make sure it's always in good repair."

"Convenient."

"Very, Sam. Anyway, she's in a mess, he's trying to help her, is about to call 9-1-1 when he hears sirens coming to his rescue. He tries to explain to the big, he actually said *huge* police officer, first on scene what has happened. He doesn't even get a chance to explain because the officer punches him in the face and stomach. He goes down and remembers little after that. Of course, he now wants to sue the police department for millions, and can't wait to hear the news that you've been fired."

"What about Susan's dying declaration?"

"Sam, you and Rudy have already done your notes. There's no mention in there about a dying declaration. You know why? Because there isn't one. There was a time, given these circumstances, when S and M would have heard that *voice from the dead.* Contrary to popular opinion, defense lawyers aren't stupid. As the years have gone by, they've evolved and have got a lot smarter. Stop and think about it. What's the average education level of a cop? High school diploma? Well, some of these lawyers have graduated from Harvard. A tiny percentage of them are near genius level, then there's the super smart, and finally we have the bottom feeders. The scum-sucking asshole crawling creeps that are no better than the people they represent. Fortunately, they're as rare as the geniuses. Some of these people are out to get you and to make a name for themselves. To discredit you, the police, and having you locked up is a great advertisement for future business. A handful of those you come across, know what's needed to do the job and keep society safe. These guys will go out of their way to protect you on the stand from hurting yourself, but there's only so much they can do. These are the guys you can share a beer with later and won't stab you in the back. Until you know your ass from your elbow, when it comes to policing, don't trust any of them. Be careful, Sam. You're running before you can walk. There's no doubt in my mind you were a hell of a soldier, but you had to learn your craft. You'll get there, Sam. One of my jobs is to make sure you don't trip and fall flat on your face. I like your style. You'll do well, but, in these days being smart isn't enough. You gotta be super smart, too."

"Good advice, Bruno. Thank you."

"Come with me, my son. All is not lost. Gabrio is going to enter the interview room shortly with some heart-wrenching photographs of Susan Marshall to show Simpson his handy work. He's gonna drop them on the table, turn around and leave, without saying a word. Let the magic begin."

I walked over to where the TV screen showed Simpson sitting back in a chair inside the interview room. He looked cocky, like he didn't have a care in the world. Detective Santoro entered the room and set a stack of photographs on the table in front of Simpson. Like an experienced card dealer, he fanned out the photos across the table, turned and left. No words were exchanged between the men.

At first Simpson didn't even look at the photos, but, unless he closed his eyes or turned the chair around, they were staring back at him. A petite, not unattractive young woman with long dirty blonde hair, caked in blood stared lifelessly back at him.

I watched intently. Fifteen minutes went by and still he remained sitting back in the chair looking up at the ceiling. Half an hour went by. Still nothing. No emotion.

"Be patient, Sam," said Detective Moretti. "These things take time. You can't rush these things. It's all about who can play the waiting game longer. You probably know from your military experience, that when you've reached the end of an interview and you can't break your subject and you're about to give up, your subject has reached the same point about the same time. That's when you dig deep and you keep going for at least another ten minutes. When I discovered that nugget of wisdom, my confession rate went through the roof. Look, he's starting to fidget in the chair. He's not so sure of himself now. Not such a cocky sonofabitch anymore. Watch and wonder, my son. It's poetry in motion, my friend, poetry in motion."

Simpson's head began to drop and his eyes rested on the array of grotesque photographs. They were like a magnet. He couldn't stop looking at them. His chest began to heave. Detective Santoro joined us for the *waiting game.*

Now he was crying, his chest rising and falling with every wave of grief and remorse.

Then he picked up one of the photographs and clasped it against his chest.

"I'm sorry, Suzie. I didn't mean to, I was so drunk I didn't even know what I was doing. Please forgive me, baby. Oh God, I'm so sorry."

He collapsed onto the table, his arms and chest covering most of the photos, wailing out loud, no longer able to contain himself. It was almost pitiful. I still wanted to kill him. I didn't notice Santoro leave, then I saw him entering the room.

He was kind and gentle, his hand rubbing Simpson's back, telling him how sorry he was that it had all come to this. Simpson was sucked-in. I knew Detective Santoro, under another regime, would have drawn his gun and shot Simpson through the head. It didn't take long before Simpson made a full confession to the detective. Before Santoro left the interview room, the two men hugged and Simpson thanked him.

"You know," said the detective. "At a time like this, writing a letter of apology to Susan, telling her how sorry you really are can sometimes be therapeutic. I thought you'd like to do that, so I brought you some paper and a pen."

Each page was numbered so the detective knew exactly how many pieces of paper he had given Simpson. If you didn't do that, sometimes they would scrunch up one of the pages because they didn't like what they'd written and stuff it in their pocket. If you weren't watching closely, that possible piece of damning evidence was gone for good.

"What shall I say? I don't know what to write."

"Write what you truly feel," said Santoro in a soothing voice. "I'll leave you on your own so you can have some time alone to do it."

Detective Santoro gathered all the photographs together, with no more emotion than a real estate agent picking up papers from a desk, and left the interview room. Shortly afterwards, he returned to the homicide office, straight faced. When he saw his partner he burst into laughter. The two experienced detectives high-fived each other. Moretti opened his desk drawer and pulled out a bottle of Canadian Club whiskey and three glasses. Moretti glanced up at the monitor.

"Good work, Detective Santoro, your man's busy writing his confessional."

"Thank you, Detective Moretti."

"You realize, Sam," said Moretti. "If the great Detective Santoro had not got that confession, you and Rudy would have had to get two new note books and copy your old ones into the new ones, only this time, with the *dying declaration.*" He winked at Santoro. "Only joking. These days they can do ink tests and determine how old the ink is on the paper in your note book. Perjury carries a long prison sentence, and being a cop, you'd get the full whack and no breaks for previously being a pillar of society."

"And remember," added his partner. "If you tell the defense lawyer you made your notes standing on the street, outside your cruiser, he or she will have already checked to see what the weather report was like for that time and day. If it was raining, there better be some smudge marks in your notebook to reflect that."

"Quite so, Detective Santoro, which brings me to another point my esteemed colleague."

"And what is that, pray tell me, Detective Moretti?"

"If the defense lawyer asks how long it took you to make your notes and you say, *Thirty minutes, your Honour.* Don't be surprised if the lawyer gives you pen and paper and with the leave of the court, times how long it takes you to write out your notes. A lot of cops have been caught out with that one. If you're still struggling an hour later, your credibility will be out the window, not to mention that all your times in your notebook will be out by half an hour. As I said, perjury carries a long prison sentence."

"Admirably put, Detective Moretti."

"Thank you, Detective Santoro."

I liked these guys, they treated me like an equal, which of course I knew I wasn't. These guys were way out of my league.

Moretti looked up at me. "Sam, you're on our team. If you were more experienced I'd let you continue here with the paperwork and I'd go get the coffees. Our machine's broken. Would you mind?"

It's funny. With some guys I'd tell them right up front, just so we all knew where we stood. *Yes, I do mind. Get your own, I'm not your lackey.* But with these guys, I didn't feel that way.

Chapter Sixteen

It was the first weekend in ages that Annie and I were off together. Rudy and Alyson arrived Saturday afternoon at my home on the Peninsular. Annie and Alyson took to each other immediately and became inseparable. It was like watching two very close sisters, who hadn't seen each other in ages, getting together again. Rudy and Alyson helped Annie and I set up the sweat lodge at the rear of my house. As we were adding the finishing touches, my grandfather arrived to preside over the sacred ceremony. Afterwards, we all headed over to the casino for dinner and to lose some money. Alyson defied the odds and won five-hundred dollars. I gave Alyson the spare bedroom, Rudy slept on the couch.

Sunday, Annie and I headed back into Toronto. I had unfinished business to attend to. Rudy and Alyson went sightseeing.

Annie and I climbed the stairs of a dingy apartment building. The elevator was out of order. As we walked along the hallway, I could feel the soles of my shoes sticking to the threadbare carpet. I didn't even want to think about what was ground into it. There was a smell of cabbage rolls and curry wafting down the hallway, mingling with stale cigarette smoke and urine. It wasn't pleasant. We stood outside Orysia's apartment, listening. We could hear someone shuffling about inside. I listened for the sound of a second, or maybe a third person. There was only the sound of one person. Not a heavy person, female likely. Annie and I looked at one another and then she knocked on the door, gently. A woman's knock, not a man's. Not demanding entry. Requesting permission to enter.

The shuffling footsteps approached the door. The person was looking through the peephole directly at Annie on the other side of the door.

"What do you want?" The voice almost a whisper. Frightened.

"My name's Annie. I heard what happened to you Orysia. I've brought you some groceries, I figured you could use some."

"How do you know my name? I don't know you. Go away."

"I've come a long way to see you, Orysia."

"Then you've wasted your time. Now please, leave me alone."

"I was told to come here by a great elder from the Cheyrone First Nation. We know you are hurting and my people want to help you, because you are one of us. Under the Creator, we are sisters. Please open the door and at least take my gifts and I will go."

Silence. A rasping, painful cough. The sound of the deadbolt drawing back into the door, then the door opening, but only a little, its progress halted by a chain. False security. One good shoulder barge and the chain would either snap or be torn from the door jam. I remained out of sight, having retreated back down the hallway.

I knew Annie would be smiling at the figure in the doorway. A disarming smile. Then the sound of the chain being removed and the door swinging open.

"You better come in." The sound of Annie inhaling a breath of shock and stepping inside.

"Thank you." The door closing behind her and the deadbolt sliding back into the door frame.

I put the earphone in my left ear and listened. Looking at my phone screen, I could see the small figure of a young First Nation woman, her face swollen, both eyes blackened and almost sealed shut. Her lips were swollen. There was so much bruising on her face, it was hard to see the natural colour of her skin. She was just a little thing. I breathed in and out slowly, trying to calm my rage.

An hour had gone by. These things cannot be rushed. Annie was working her magic. The two women sat together on an old couch. I could make out Annie's arm around Orysia. Street name, Candy.

They were now in a tiny bedroom, Annie packing things into my old hockey bag for Orysia. One hour and forty-five minutes later, the apartment door opened. As planned, I began to walk slowly back down the hallway. Both women were expecting me. I purposely let my long black hair fall around my shoulders so she would know, too, that under the Creator, I was her brother.

I nodded. Gently I picked this fragile, damaged creature up in my arms and held her to me. She did not resist. Her head fell against my chest. She began sobbing gently, her tears of relief soaking into my shirt as I carried her down the stairs. I turned to look at Annie. She was crying. Annie held the rear passenger door of my pick-up truck open, then ran around the other side and together we gently manoeuvred Orysia into the back seat. Annie got in beside Orysia, cradling her in her arms.

Alyson and Rudy were both waiting for us as planned at the hospital emergency entrance. Alyson was all business, as she and another nurse helped place our patient on the gurney and whisked her quickly inside the hospital. There wasn't going to be any waiting to be seen. Not because we were getting preferential treatment. Orysia was in urgent need of medical care.

It was hours before we got any news. She was in stable condition, but was going to need months of surgery to reconstruct her battered face. She was seriously malnourished and dehydrated. I looked up to see Dr. Aiesha Ahsan heading toward us. She looked even more tired than when Rudy and I had seen her on our night shift.

"You saved that young woman's life you know. It's going to take a long time for her physical injuries to heal. Even longer for her psychological injuries. And then what?"

"That's already arranged Doctor," said Annie. "We're going to take care of her."

Her face lit up. "Bless you. I mean it. Bless you all." She placed a hand on Annie's shoulder and began to walk away. Stopped, turned around, and said, "At least we've saved one little sparrow this time." She smiled and carried on down the long hallway.

* * *

Thanks to Annie, we now had something to go on. The car was likely a newer model red Ford Mustang with tinted windows and tan leather seats. Orysia remembered the *new car* smell. We had a reasonable description of the driver who picked Orysia up. The other three were a bit vague. They were all white males, in their mid to late twenties, and smelled of expensive aftershave. The driver's clothes were casual, and expensive. Orysia had good taste in clothes. *It was like he'd just stepped out of a Sears catalogue,* was how she put it. She remembered the smell of marijuana and booze. Like a mixture of whiskey and beer and drugs. The driver had blonde curly hair. It looked like he'd stepped out of the shower and hadn't bothered to comb it. His eyes were a piercing blue. Though at first, he was really friendly and nice, laughing and smiling, his eyes remained cruel looking.

He drove Orysia to the outskirts, until they reached a winding road that led into a heavily wooded ravine. It was dark. From her description of how they got there, it sounded like it had taken place somewhere in the Rouge Valley. The driver took out a blanket from the trunk and a flashlight. Together they walked into a small clearing and the horror began.

Of the three other males, she remembered one was big and fat. She could feel his grotesque body on top of hers as she struggled to breath against his weight. She tried to scream and remembered nothing more until the driver dropped her off, stuffing a wad of cash into her purse with the words, *I have your driver's license. I know where you live. If you tell anyone, you won't be coming back from your next drive.* She remembered one last nugget of information. One of them called the fat guy by name. *Get off her, Rob, you're gonna smother her. There won't be anything left for us.*

Rudy and I stopped off at the station before heading to Harbourfront. Annie and Alyson remained at Orysia's bedside.

"How did it go?" said Detective Morton, as we entered the Sexual Assault Unit.

"Good and bad," I replied.

"Start with the bad and then let's finish off on a good note," said the detective. "I need some good news, I've had a shitty day. Want coffee, there's still some in the pot? There's creamers in the fridge."

"Well," I said, pouring myself a coffee. "She's in rough shape. Thanks to Annie, we've got her in the hospital as we speak. She'll live, just." I brought him up to date on everything we had.

"Will she let one of our SOCO's take some pictures?"

"I think so. The hospital took a load on our behalf anyway. That Dr. Ahsan is a godsend for women."

"She's the best," he replied. "All right. You done good, and in your own time. This won't go unnoticed. Now we've got something to go on."

"In my culture, Detective, we don't look for rewards when we do noble things. We just do them. It's reward enough to have saved her life."

He smiled.

"Call me, Johnny. You're a good man, Sam Stephens, and so are you, Rudy. Rudy, you should put in for a skills attachment to the SAU. You'd be good at it. You got my recommendation."

"I was thinking about putting in for the Domestic Violence Unit."

"You'd be good at that, too. I'll put in a good word for you. Pity you don't have much time on with us, Sam. We could do with you in here, too. Anyway, sorry to be a pain. Can you put something down on paper for me before you go home? This is too hot to sit on and too dangerous for the public. I want you guys working closely with me on this one. I'm gonna speak to your sergeant, and see if he'll let you do some follow-ups for me. That's if you don't mind? Stupid question, forget I said that. He's not going to assign you to this office, we just don't have the manpower. I doubt the Inspector would sanction the overtime for you to come in on your day off."

"You need me, Johnny, I'll come in anyway. This isn't about money. For me, it's personal."

"Count me in, too, partner. I mean it," said Rudy.

"All right. I'll let the powers that be know that. They won't go for it though. Liability and all that crap."

Rudy spoke for the two of us. "Call us anyway."

The detective smiled again. "Let the investigative work begin. I'll start with a Ministry of Transportation check and see how many Canadians own a similar vehicle. Then, I'll put out a CPIC information request to all police services across Canada. These assholes might already be tucked away somewhere inside one of our systems. It's just a question of finding them. One of them at least has got a speeding ticket or a liquor ticket. You any good with computers, Sam?"

"Lead me to the machine and it'll sing to you like you've never heard before."

"You're kidding me, right?"

"I can hack into just about anything, but that's military classified. I might be big and can lift heavy things, but I got a brain, too."

Detective Morton sat me down at one of their specialized computers, gave me the clearance to enter along with a few brief instructions and when the screen lit up said, "Do your magic, big guy. Make this baby sing."

"I'll start the supplementary report, while Maestro here does his thing," said Rudy.

An hour and a half later, paper was spewing out of the photocopier with information that needed to be checked and re-checked. It wasn't long before we had information overload.

"This guy's a flippin' genius, Rudy. "I've never seen anything like it. Does anyone inside the department know the level of your computer skills?"

"They don't need to. I don't want to be posted to computer crimes staring at child pornography all day. If that happens, I'll quit."

"Fair point. Okay. I want you guys in tomorrow morning. I know it's your day off. It'll take me days to process this lot on my own. Hang on, I'm gonna phone my boss at home and get the okay for you two to come in tomorrow morning on your day off. She's an awesome boss."

Johnny phoned his Detective Inspector. They obviously had a great rapport by the initial humorous banter back and forth.

"Okay. We're good to go. See you in the morning, say, eight o'clock. When my partner comes in I'll bring him up to speed. The coffee will be on when you get here. And by the way, you'll be sticking an overtime card in, or you won't be coming. My boss's words, not mine."

When we got back to the hospital Orysia was sitting up, groggy from all the pain medication. I smiled down at her.

"Orysia, I expect Annie told you, when you get discharged from the hospital you're coming to stay with us until you're well again. You'll be safe with us. The other good news is, and Annie doesn't know this herself yet, I spoke to my Band Counsel and they've agreed to let you stay in one of the townhouses on the res. They have a condition that goes with it. You have to attend college. The Band will help you financially. I have an old pick-up truck you can use to get around. We're all going to fix that broken wing of yours so you can do more than fly again. You can soar, like an eagle."

Watching the tears of joy rolling down her bruised and swollen cheeks was a beautiful sight.

"May I kiss your forehead before I go?"

Her eyes lit up. I bent slowly and gently kissed her. "You are safe now, little sister. You need not worry about anything at all. The Creator has delivered you into our safe keeping."

In the corridor out of hearing, I told Annie about our plans for the next day. She and Alyson would visit Orysia and keep her company.

* * *

"Coffee's fresh, boys. Grab a desk and let's get to work. You guys already know my partner, Detective Phil Swane."

"Johnny's brought me up to speed. Good work, guys. Thank Annie for us, Sam, she's been a great asset. Thanks to her, SOCO was able to go over to the hospital last night and grab some pictures. Ident's already got the rape kit. They're testing the bank notes in their lab for fingerprints using ninhydrin. Later this morning the Public Order Unit and K9 are conducting a search of the ravine, based on what Orysia told Annie. It would be nice to find the crime scene. Dalton have sent over some extra manpower from their Public Order Unit to help us, as well as their helicopter. It's already up and flying over the Rouge Valley as we speak. There's nothing in our database on these guys. Not a thing. Even feeding information into our major crime data base hasn't revealed anything. My hunch is, these guys have been flying below our radar. The reason we don't know about them, is because they're just getting started."

"Well," I said. "If this is how they're starting, I hate to think how they'll be finishing. We need to catch these assholes before they escalate. They're going to get bored with beating the hell out of hookers and are going to move into new territory."

Detective Morton returned to his desk with another mug of coffee. It had a big smiley yellow face on it with the words, *Worlds Best Dad Ever* in a variety of bright colours. We all had lives outside the job. I figured Morton for a great dad with a patient wife. She would have to be, given the long hours these guys worked and the frequent callouts. A relationship not for the faint hearted. He sat down and looked over at me.

"I'm with you on that one, Sam. Very perceptive. These assholes have no regard for human life, they see women as nothing more than play things for them. It's going to become like a drug for them. Now they've tasted it, they need more of it to satisfy themselves. Every police parade room across the Greater Toronto Area is going to have the current information we have. We need eyes and ears on the ground from the uniform branch. Okay, let's get digging."

Rudy and I began pouring over the computer printouts, looking for newer model red Ford Mustangs. An hour later we had half a dozen possibilities.

"What you got, Rudy?" said Detective Swane.

"Four possibles. One in Peterborough. One in Brampton. One in Midland the other in Kitchener."

"I've got one in Oakville, the other in Kingston," I said.

"Okay," said Swane. "We'll start there before opening the net wider."

"These guys could have driven in from another province, had their fun and gone home.

This could take forever."

"Rudy, we have to start somewhere. Johnny's already sent out a CPIC message across Canada asking for assistance. There's only so much we can do with what we've got. That's the Canadian Police Information Centre, Sam, you probably already know that anyway." Detective Swane began rubbing his chin in thought. "Okay, Sam, Rudy, grab one of our cars and take a drive up to Midland. That'll take you the rest of the day. Let's get that one knocked on the head. Johnny and I will take a drive to Oakville, then Brampton, and lastly, Kitchener. Tomorrow, we'll take a drive out to Peterborough, and then on to Kingston. Any problems, call me on my cell. I couldn't get you guys in tomorrow, so enjoy your days off and come back and see us next day shift. Good work."

Day shift soon came around again. After parade Rudy and I wandered into the SAU. Detectives Swane and Morton were drinking coffee at their desks.

"What do you think about Midland, then?" said Detective Morton.

"When Sam and I got there, the registered owner had just got back from an overseas trip with his wife. They'd been in Europe and were there during the time frame of the crime. Their passports confirmed that. Very helpful, but very pissed off. They were waiting for the Midland Police to show up and take a report on their house being broken into while they were away."

"In your message you said the thief, or thieves, smashed the window pane in the back door, got into the kitchen, took the car keys hanging on the hook by the door, opened the garage and drove off in their new red Ford Mustang. That may well be the car we're looking for," said Detective Swane.

"Hasn't shown up yet," said his partner.

"It will," said Rudy. "Burnt out in some pit, I bet. Trouble is, if that's the case it could take forever to discover that, and of course, forensically, there'll be nothing left. How was your trip?"

"No red flags as far as Brantford and Kitchener are concerned. The Brantford car is in the scrap yard. During the timeframe we're interested in, it got T-boned at an intersection, confirmed by the registered owner who survived the accident with cuts and bruises, but his pride and joy was written off. The hospital reluctantly confirmed it. *We can't tell you anything without a warrant.* Fortunately, one of the nurses heard us telling the staff nurse what happened to Orysia. As we were leaving, the nurse followed us out and told us what we needed to know. It brought back memories of the old days. The Kitchener car is in the garage. The son borrowed his dad's car, blew the transmission and during the timeframe we're interested in, the car's been in the local garage. We confirmed it with a visit to the garage. We got a call from the Peterborough Police this morning, saved us a trip out there. That car belongs to a nurse at the local hospital. Nobody drives it but her. The officer confirmed this information with the nurse's mother, who happened to be visiting. We saved ourselves a drive to Kingston as well. I phoned Kingston this morning. Staff Sergeant Siggs answered the phone. Low and behold, the red Ford Mustang belongs to his grandfather. The Staff has been driving it for the old man because he just lost his license on medical grounds. He said if we needed to see it, he'd drive it down right away for us and we could take a look at it if we wanted. I told him not to bother. If we keep getting dead ends, we'll head up and take a look. "

"And, Oakville?"

"That's the interesting one, Sam," continued Detective Swane. "See what you two make of this. We arrive at this house, Johnny and me."

"You'd hardly call it a house, Phil, it was more like a bloody great castle. I bet it was worth somewhere between ten and twenty million dollars. Right on Lake Ontario. Magnificent, like something out of Hollywood."

"You're right, Johnny. It was out of this world. Unbelievable. Oozing with wealth. Anyway, we arrive at the huge wrought iron gates. Closed of course. Johnny pressed the intercom button, surveillance cameras all over the place. A male voice said in a snotty English accent, *Can I help you?* You tell them the rest, Johnny."

"I tell, Shriveled Balls the butler, who we are and request permission to enter, and he replies,

Do you have an appointment? I tell him we're the police and we don't do appointments. He says, *We do not allow unsolicited persons to enter. I suggest you make an appointment, but I doubt it will be worth your while.* I ask him why that is. He replies again in that irritating voice, like he's chewing on a bread roll full of marbles, *Mr. Jansen-Simms does not involve himself with the police unless they have a warrant on their person, requiring him to do so. Good day.* I kept pressing the buzzer, but he wouldn't answer. Next thing one of those military-size Hummers comes flying round the corner, all shiny black and menacing. Four muscle-bound thugs get out, black fatigues and sunglasses, ball caps, batons, and pepper spray at the ready and handcuffs. Probably at least one of them was carrying. Anyway, the front seat passenger, I guess he was the guy in charge, says, *You're on private property. You've been asked to leave and you haven't left. Now, you're trespassing. I don't care that you're the police. We're past that now. I'm going to ask you to leave once more. If you don't, as much force as is reasonably necessary to remove you, will be used. Putting it simply for you two dumbasses. If you resist, you're going to get hurt. Now, last time. I request that you leave the property, immediately.* Phil had to have the last word. *Are you guys on steroids?*"

"Yeah, sorry about that, Johnny."

"Those assholes grab us out of the car, frog march us to the end of the driveway, hitch our car to the Hummer and drag it back out onto the road. Wouldn't be surprised if they damaged the tranny."

"We need to go back there. Now. This time take me with you. I'd like to see those assholes try and drag me out of the car and not be hospitalized afterwards."

Detective Morton looked a little embarrassed. "Sam, sometimes you have to pick your battles. We were lawfully there, but the homeowner or his representative has the right to tell us to leave. If we don't leave, it would be argued in court that we were now trespassers, and as such, despite being the police and not in possession of a warrant to enter, we could be made to leave. And as the security thug said, *using as much force as is reasonably necessary.* In this day and age and with all the leftwing police haters out there, we'd lose. Had you been there, you'd have ended up getting arrested."

"Put surveillance on them," I suggested.

"We can't," replied Detective Swane. "Surveillance is swamped on other projects."

I helped myself to a coffee. "So, we don't know anything about the car we're looking for that's registered to that address, to Reginald Jansen bloody Simms."

"I've done some background on him," said Detective Morton. "He's a billionaire property tycoon. Property all over the world. Owns casinos around the globe, especially the Middle East. You name it, he's linked to it. He's married to Jackie Wallace, supermodel. Two kids from his first wife, Marilyn and Nicholas, both in their late twenties. That's about it. Couldn't find any more. No idea if the kids live with him."

"Surveillance is near impossible," said Detective Swane. "The security team made sure we were well away from the property before they stopped tailing us. We managed to persuade a local boat owner to take us on a little trip along the bay. When I mentioned the name Jansen-Simms, he spat on the ground. *That asshole. I wouldn't sell some property to him. What's he do? He buys the lot on the other side of me, builds a house there and fills it with degenerates. Made our lives a living hell. It got so bad we couldn't even go out into our back yard. Wild parties day and night. Local police and township, bloody useless. My wife got so sick in the end with the stress, we had to move. She died six months ago. I blame that bastard. Thinks money can buy him anything he wants. That son of his, the arrogant sod is no better.*

They must have seen us coming. Two Zodiacs were deployed with security. I don't mean some old guys making sure Santa doesn't run off with the Christmas presents from the department store. These were built like the ones in the Hummer. They almost swamped us. Finally, I'd had enough. I fired a warning shot in front of the bow of one of them, only I missed and it hit the inflatable. It roared back to harbour, but didn't make it. The other one had to rescue them. Someone in that boat pulled out a rifle and pointed it at us, another guy pushed it down and away. Then they went after their stricken buddies with one chamber inflated and the other, dragging in the water. I'm surprised the shit hasn't hit the fan yet. To cover my ass I put in a Use of Force report for drawing and firing my weapon. I'm expecting to be suspended any moment now. Why are you looking so happy, Sam? This is serious shit, man. I could lose my job."

"No you won't, Phil. You should be proud of yourself. I don't blame you for leaving the gate without a fight. A couple of reasons. One, you're too little to be awkward. Two, you're out of shape. The same goes for you too, Johnny. Three. You were outnumbered. You redeemed yourself, Phil, sinking that Zodiac. If you were in the military on my squadron, we'd be singing your praises. Hell, we'd have a medal made for you. You my friend are *The Man.* Way to go, Zodiac Man. Come on, you guys, we're going for breakfast. Zodiac Man, you're breakfast is on me."

"Okay, you're on. Keep the Zodiac incident under your hat, would you guys?"

"We're solid, Phil," I said. "Did you get any more info from the guy who gave you the boat ride?"

"Glad you mentioned that. He's coming in this afternoon to make a statement about the security detail swimming lessons and give us everything he can on Jansen-Simms. His name's Charles Banbury. Retired stockbroker. He wants to be our eyes and ears. I told him officially we can't do that and not to put himself in danger. If that security detail ever got hold of him, he'd be feeding the lobsters off Newfoundland."

As we walked past the front counter the Staff Sergeant stopped us. "One of our homeless people called in yesterday, asking for you, Rudy. What he said makes no sense to me, but he said you'd know. He said, *Tell Rudy the Major called. Treeman's gone missing and we're all worried about him. We haven't seen him in days.*"

"That's not like Treeman," said Rudy, looking concerned.

"His exact words, too," said the Staff. "Oh, before I forget. One of your girlfriends was in, too. A hooker named *Dusty.* Rudy, you're starting to worry me. I think you're taking this community policing a little too far, if you don't mind me saying. Anyway, the lovely *Dusty* wanted to know how, *Candy* was doing. I told her you'd be in touch."

"Thanks, Staff."

"You're welcome, Constable."

"Shit. I hope nothing's happened to Treeman. Love that guy. That man knows everything you could possibly know about trees and more, especially native Canadian ones. He knows all their Latin names, where they grow, how to grow them, tree diseases, pests, and cures. The man's a walking tree encyclopedia. He's the guy that was wearing the Maple Leaf toque the other evening when we were talking to the Major. He never said a word. Very shy. Hates being around people, until he gets to know you and trusts you. He wouldn't hurt a fly."

"Unless it was eating one of his trees."

"You're right, Sam. Unless it was eating one of his trees. Okay, breakfast at Callaghan's and then let's go find the Major."

Chapter Seventeen

We eventually found the Major, sitting on a bench playing his harmonica, cap upturned on the sidewalk.

"He always comes to this plaza," said Rudy. "It's busy, the people know him and he makes good change."

"He sure can play that harmonica, too."

"Morning, boys. You got my message, I see. Guess you were off duty when I called in to see you."

"Yep. First day back," replied Rudy. The old guy looked at me.

"Name a tune, Indian. Don't mind if I call you Indian, do you, son?"

"Major, no one calls me Indian. But you can. I guess you being called the Major, you must have been in the military."

"Damn right, son. British Army, Parachute Regiment. Retired in good standing as a sergeant. Got promoted to major vicariously when I hit the booze and the streets. The rest is history, something I'd rather not talk about. You?"

"Canadian military. Special Forces. Usual stuff."

"I can see just looking at you, son, there's

nothing *usual* about you. Whatever it is about you, it seeps out through your pores. Now, name a tune."

"Can you play Moon River?"

"Can I play Moon River, he asks."

The Major was lost in his own music. The melody was both beautiful and haunting. He hit every note just right. Before long we had quite a crowd around us. I threw a couple of Toonies into his hat. By the time he'd finished playing, his hat was overflowing with money.

"You better come again, Indian. You bring good luck."

"Only to good people, Major. There are those who wish they'd never met me."

Rudy became serious. "Okay, Major. How long has Treeman been missing?"

"Three, maybe four days, now. I can't keep track of time. It's not like him, you know that. Said he was going to Allan Gardens. You know how much he loves the gardens, especially the conservatory. The staff all know and love him there. Who doesn't love the Treeman? Except when he gets drinking."

"Had he been drinking when he left?"

"No, Rudy. You know he don't drink when he's going to the gardens, especially when he's going to be drawing. It was late evening when he went. I offered to go with him, but you know the Treeman. He likes to be alone when he's visiting the parks."

"Why so late?"

"It was a full moon, Rudy. Said he wanted to

capture the atmosphere of the gardens in moonlight. Took his sketchpad with him, his pencils, and that pocketbook on trees you bought him. I figured maybe you guys picked him up, or he got sick and is in the hospitable."

"I checked before we left the station," said Rudy looking concerned. "Me and Sam are gonna take a drive over to Allan Gardens and see what we can find. We'll catch up with you later."

On the drive to the gardens, Rudy remained silent. He seemed upset, but didn't want to talk about it.

"We'll find him, Rudy, don't you worry." He didn't answer.

As we entered the park on foot, I stopped.

"What are you doing, Sam?"

"Absorbing the atmosphere of the gardens. My grandfather taught me these things. *Don't rush across the unfamiliar plain. You might not see the abyss.*"

"All right. I'll be up at the conservatory. It's still early, but there might be a staff member on site."

The park was beautiful, full of magnificent trees, their leaves beginning to change as fall drew nearer. The hydrangea shrubs, though still in bloom, were beginning to lose their brilliant whiteness, but not their rich perfume. I made a mental note to bring Annie here. I still hadn't bought her an engagement ring, our lives had been so crazy.

I had a bad feeling about Treeman. Rudy

returned with a member of staff.

"Well, any thoughts, Sam, you being the spiritual guru?"

"None, Rudy, only we should search the park."

"I'll help you," said the staff member. She smiled. "We all know Treeman. He's probably asleep under a bush, at least that's where I found him last time."

We split up, dividing the gardens into three areas. After an hour we had found nothing. I stood in the middle of the park and slowly turned in a circle, my eyes tracing every leaf, flower, branch, shrub, and tree. Then I saw it. It was easily overlooked. I missed it myself. I looked across the gardens at the huge hydrangea border. Near the middle, some of the delicate stems were broken. As I approached, it was obvious to me that someone had gone through the shrubs and come out again the same way. Twigs had been carefully bent back. Like someone had chased their dog in there, come out again, realized they had caused some damage and wanted to conceal their unintended vandalism.

The woman and Rudy were talking up by the conservatory. No doubt he was telling her to keep her eyes open and to let the rest of the staff know. I walked slowly across the lawn to the shrubs. The perfumed smell of *Quick Fire* hydrangea filled my nostrils. I had some growing in my front garden on the Peninsular and recognized the scent. It was beautiful, but the scent was soon lost when I looked down between the stems and saw on the earth, a small book. *The Pocketbook of Canadian Trees.* Footprints leading farther in. More than one person. Going in and coming out. An attempt to conceal the impressions by sweeping the soil with probably a branch. I looked around. A fresh tear in a nearby branch of an overhanging evergreen. Snapped by hand and torn away, leaving the telltale rip in the bark.

"Rudy! Over here."

As Rudy ran toward me, I was confused by the expression on his face. A mixture of shock, anger, and hurt.

"What is it? What have you found?"

I told him. To my surprise he pushed past me. I grabbed his arm tightly as he tried to brush me away.

"Rudy. What are you doing? This could be a crime scene. You're gonna mess it up blundering in there like that. Let's go around the other side where they haven't been."

For a brief second, there was comprehension in his eyes. He stopped struggling and came back onto the grass. I let go of him and he ran around to the other side like a madman.

"Rudy! What the hell's got into you?" He was already gone and through the bushes. I shook my head in disbelief at the lady helping us and told her to stay put and guard the main point of entry into the hydrangeas. She nodded, a worried look on her face.

The loud cry of someone deeply and

emotionally hurt, followed by loud sobbing filled the gardens. When I found Rudy he was huddled over the unrecognizable body of Treeman, crying uncontrollably like a child. I just stood there dumbfounded.

"Jimmie, that you?"

"Go ahead, Sam. What's up?"

"Rudy and I are in Allan Gardens. We just found the Treeman. He's dead, beaten to death. It's a mess." Silence. "Jimmie, you still there?"

"Yeah. How's Rudy?"

"That's why I'm calling you. I can't get him away from the body. I tried to pull him away from the crime scene, he went berserk. The guy's lost it."

"Have you called it in yet?"

"No. Not yet. I wanted to talk to you first."

"Don't call it in until I get there. I'll call the sergeant. Bernie Wells and I will be over shortly. Meanwhile. Leave Rudy alone. That homeless man beaten to death on the ground is his father."

For a brief moment, I was in shock. I called Alyson and told her.

"I'll be right over, Sam. He told me about Treeman being his dad. He was going to tell you, but he said he wasn't yet ready to do so. That's why Rudy volunteers at the soup kitchen. That way, he gets to have lunch with his dad once in a while."

"What shall I do? The crime scene's compromised, but who gives a shit at the moment."

"Comfort him. He trusts you and respects you. Leave him with his dad to grieve."

I placed a hand on Rudy's back and told him to take all the time he needed. He raised his right hand and I held it. He grabbed my hand like I was a lifeline and I was the only thing stopping him from falling off the edge of a crevasse into a dark abyss, from which there was no return.

I could hear sirens approaching as Jimmie and Sergeant Wells made their way over to us. When they entered the gardens, they were both carrying a carton of *Police Line Do Not Cross*, yellow plastic tape with bold black lettering.

"He's in there, sobbing his heart out."

"Thanks, Sam. You done good," replied Jimmie.

"I got his girlfriend coming over. You remember me telling you about her?"

"Yeah, Alyson. I know her from the hospital. Lovely girl. That's good she's coming."

"What can you tell us, Sam?"

"Well, Sarge, they dragged him in here, I believe. The pocketbook on trees that Rudy gave him is in there. There may be two, three, or even four, of them. But there's at least two of them. They tried to cover their tracks and pushed the broken twigs back."

"Good eyes, Sam. Good eyes," said Jimmie.

"When I told Rudy what I'd found he tried to go in through there, but I stopped him. He ran around the other side and found his dad. He's been in there since I called you."

"Sarge, I'm going in to see him. I'll be careful where I tread. You guys might as well start taping the place off. Does that lady know anything or did she see anything?"

"No, Jimmie. She works here and was helping to look for Treeman. They all know him. She hasn't seen anything."

"Good. Everyone knows Treeman. Ident are on the way. I called S and M. They've dropped everything and are heading over. It wasn't their call, but they're taking it anyway. They know Treeman very well. It's personal, like taking out one of our own."

"Jimmie?"

"What, Sam?"

"I think whoever did this are the same people that beat and raped Orysia."

"Orysia?"

"Street name, Candy. I told you about her."

"I remember now. The hooker. Sam, if anyone else told me the two cases were connected like that, I'd probably laugh at them. Coming from you, I'll sit up and take notice. Better tell that to S and M when they get here. That's good to know. Before I go in there. How bad is it?"

"Bad, Jimmie. Very bad."

While Jimmie walked in to the shrubbery to comfort Rudy, Sergeant Wells spoke to me.

"Sam. Don't take this the wrong way, but don't you think you're getting too close to the people you're dealing with. I heard about the hooker. That's pretty bad, but bringing her back to your home to convalesce, what are you thinking? You'll be the joke of the division."

"Sergeant. That *hooker,* is one of my people. Her name's Orysia. I'd like you to call her by her name. The first person I find out who is laughing behind my back, I'm going to hurt. That includes you."

Silence.

Sergeant Wells inhaled a deep breath. "I'm sorry Sam. You're right. I didn't realize she was First Nation. That's understandable. If I hear anyone badmouthing you, I'll advise them accordingly by explaining it could be injurious to their health. Heads up, Ident's here, looks like S and M are pulling in behind them. Sorry you didn't know Treeman was Rudy's dad. Not too many people know. The older guys like Jimmie and me, who he trusts, know. He would have told you himself, when he felt the time was right."

Detectives Moretti and Santoro walked slowly across the gardens toward us. They both looked like they wanted to kill someone. Other officers began arriving to help with the scene containment. A K9 truck pulled up, the officer exiting the vehicle without his dog, awaiting further instructions.

Two Ident officers began unloading equipment.

"What kind of scene containment is this, Sergeant Wells? This is a balls up. Get those men out of my crime scene."

Moretti looked like he was going to explode,

but somehow kept his composure.

"The dead homeless man in there is Constable Jackson's father. He found him. So, in the nicest possible way, leave him the fuck alone, until he's ready."

The Ident officer went pale, gained his composure, his face turning red with anger.

"Well, you can explain that to the judge. I'm sure you'll all get some good box time on this one."

"There won't be any box time, as you put it," I said. Moretti and Santoro looked at me in amazement. The two Ident officers looked dumbfounded.

Sergeant Wells spoke for all of them. "I know you're upset, Sam, but keep those thoughts to yourself. Be professional."

From the corner of my eye I saw Moretti and Santoro smiling at me. My kind of men. I liked them. I liked them a lot.

Alyson arrived and rushed across the lawn to where we had all gathered.

"Thanks for coming, Alyson. We can't let you go in there, but we can't coax him out. Can you try?"

"Of course, Sam. How near can I go?"

"Come with me. You don't need to see what's behind those bushes."

"Rudy, it's me, Alyson. I'm so sorry, sweetheart, but I need you to come with me now. You have to be brave and say goodbye to your dad. You have to let your friends do their job now. I can't come in there because I don't want to spoil the crime scene. I want the police to catch whoever did this. Sam's going to come and get you and I want you to come out with him. We'll give you a few more minutes. Okay?"

I watched the crows flying overhead. Listened to the sound of birds singing. The sun shining in a blue sky with white clouds. It was a beautiful day. People were now entering the park, but only into the conservatory. Little children were laughing. A baby cried. Traffic flowed, horns blared. Life was going on all around us. Just as I had been told … *There are two worlds in the world of policing. The world of everyday life. It's like an old carpet spread out across the city. Some areas remain thick and rich and colourful. Other areas are worn and threadbare, just like the people living there. But underneath is another world altogether, of despicable human beings, of misery and untold acts of savagery and cruelty. It is where you will find Dante's Inferno.* Behind the sweet-smelling hydrangeas, Satan had been sadistically busy.

I was back in Afghanistan, trying to guide an uninjured soldier away from his dead comrade. *Be gentle Sam,* said the Weatherman. *He may not be injured, but his heart is broken. He is ready now, take his arm.*

Jimmie took immediate charge. "Rudy, you're going home with Alyson. Give Sam your gun belt and radio. I'll drop by later and pick up your uniform."

Sergeant Bernie Wells nodded his approval.

"Don't worry about anything, Rudy. We've got it taken care of. I'll make sure your dad's treated with dignity. As soon as Bruno and Gabrio release your dad's personal effects, especially the book on trees, you'll get them. Now go home and try and relax. Take as long as you need. Here's my personal cell number and my home number. Call me any time of the day or night. I mean that. You need anything, anything at all, call me."

It's like he's shell-shocked, said the Weatherman. *That boy's in a world of hurt.*

"Sam, you still with us? Earth to Sam."

"Just thinking, Jimmie."

I gave Rudy a hug. He still hadn't spoken to any of us. Not even to Alyson. No emotion now at all. He stood rooted to the ground, staring blankly ahead. Not good. Not good at all. Gently, I undid the keepers on his gun belt and then removed the belt with all his use of force options still attached. Detectives Moretti and Santoro patted Rudy on the shoulder.

"We'll get whoever did this to your dad, Rudy. We all loved Treeman. We'll keep you updated. Don't worry, we'll get them."

"Damn straight, Gabrio," said his partner. "Like Bernie said. You need anything, call us. We're here for you, buddy. Golden rule. You don't touch one of us or one of our own. Take care of him, Alyson." She smiled back at him, tears in her eyes.

One of the Ident officers called out. "Bernie, can we get a quick photo of Rudy's boots before he goes? I want to eliminate his footprints from the scene. I'll need Jimmie's and the new guy's, too."

Photos of the tread pattern on our police boots were taken with measurements. Then the Ident officer dusted the soles of our boots and had us stand on a piece of white paper. "We don't have a photocopier, so this will do. Thanks gentlemen for your help. Rudy, I'm so sorry. My partner and I had no idea he was your dad."

When Rudy had left the scene with Alyson, we all got down to business. There was an air of outrage among us all. For the first time since being a police officer, I felt that feeling of camaraderie. The *Brotherhood.* It took an outrage such as this to bring it out.

Sergeant Wells called Jimmie aside. I could hear them whispering. "I'm worried about Rudy. When you can clear this scene, head over there as quickly as you can. I think he's had a breakdown."

"Alyson thinks the same. She's going to get him into civvies. She's already called Dr. Ahsan. She wants her to bring him in. Alyson's gonna call me when she's en-route. I'll meet her up at the hospital."

"Good. I want this kept private. We don't need the Brass getting wind of this. They'll ground him and his career will stall."

"Well, obviously they need to know his dad's been brutally murdered. I can see the Chief giving him a load of compassionate leave so he doesn't have to use his sick time up. He's good like that. I hope they don't put him in the psych ward. That will be awkward."

"Don't even say that, Jimmie. Call me as soon as you have any news. Don't be too long here, we've got enough guys to cover it. Good call, by the way."

"Thank Sam. He's on the ball that one."

Ident erected a canopy over the body. Small orange plastic cones covered the scene. They must have taken a thousand photographs. Sergeant Wells handed me the Major Incident Log, to record the time everyone entered and the time they left, next to their name. I was now the official keeper of the log until I got relieved and handed it over. It gave me time to write my notes and to think.

It didn't take long for the media to arrive. They arrived just before our Mobile Command Centre pulled into the gardens.

"Detective Santoro."

"Yes, Detective Moretti."

"I hear one of our officers has psychic powers. He thinks this case relates to the hooker case."

"That's amazing, Detective Moretti. I only wish we had those powers of deduction."

"You guys should be on stage. You know that don't you?" I said.

"Joking aside, Sam. Jimmie told us what you said. Why do you think they're connected?"

"Bruno. My grandfather taught me everything I needed to know about hunting and fishing. About the animals and the birds, about all the creatures and how everything is interconnected. It has nothing to do with psychic powers. It's all about observation. My grandfather would take me into the wilderness for days on end, traveling on foot, and would show me things that the white man and many of my people have long forgotten. But he still knows these things. He can tell you, by looking at a freshly killed deer, which wolf pack brought down the animal. Not psychic powers. That's insulting. I can tell you, through my grandfather that the injuries sustained on the body of Orysia, please don't call her the *hooker,* are not unlike the injuries sustained by Treeman. And when you remove his clothing in the morgue, compare the two sets of photographs and you will see I am right. This is a *thrill kill* by four men. That has not been confirmed yet by Ident. Ask them how many sets of footprints there are at the scene belonging to the attackers."

"They think two, maybe three," said Detective Santoro.

"I can see four. Very subtle differences, but four. Very hard to see."

"Show us." Detective Moretti didn't sound convinced.

Ident let me back into the crime scene with the two homicide detectives. Neither they nor Ident could see what I could see.

"Those two impressions are hardly noticeable, Officer. They look pretty much the same as these here," said one of the Ident officers.

"But, they're not," I replied.

"I'm not convinced. We'll take pictures and measurements, but to be honest, where those almost invisible impressions are concerned, we don't have anything really to work with. They're too faint and there's no detail."

I turned away and headed back to my post. "Four men, one heavier than the other three. Much heavier."

I went back to thinking. The two Ident officers were talking to the two homicide detectives. I watched as Moretti and Santoro shrugged their shoulders, and then walked back to their car. The Ident officers looked in my direction. I saw the slight shake of their heads and the look that said, *He's out to lunch.*

Rob, the fat man, I said to myself, *is the most out of shape of the four of them. Sedentary job. Sits at a desk all day. Computers, banking, office worker, insurance, business, stockbroker. I'll call him Frub. Fat, revolting ugly bastard. Maybe an out of shape police officer. There's enough of those dough-boys. He's the one with the soft squishy hands. He's the one with the broken knuckles. Not used to the heavy bag, like our Nicholas. Not used to punching. Punches like a twelve-year old girl. He's the one that's gone to the hospital for x-rays. Which hospital? Linked to a red Ford Mustang. Oakville area, or Midland? Or who the hell knows where. If Oakville, that car's long gone to the scrap yard. Daddy will have made sure of that to protect his darling Nicholas. Where's the stolen Midland car?*

My cell phone rang. "Sam, that you?"

"Who's this?"

"It's Johnny Morton, SAU. We found the missing Midland Mustang. Burnt out, nothing left of evidentiary value. It was found on the outskirts in a disused quarry."

"Rudy was right," I said.

"Yes, he was. Phil and I went up ourselves to take a look. Nothing, just a burnt-out rusting lump of scrap metal. We're still working on how to get to see the Oakville one."

"I shouldn't bother, Johnny. You won't get in there. I reckon Daddy's already got rid of it for junior. My theory on that one is, it's either scrapped or, when Daddy sent two of his security team to scrap it, they changed their minds. They couldn't bear to scrap a new car, so they paid off the scrap dealer, gave their boss a receipt and the cash value of a scrapped Ford Mustang and one of them kept the car and gave his buddy some *hush* money. He either kept the car for himself, a friend or relative, or he sold it. I think it's still out there."

"Interesting, Sherlock Holmes. Where are you now?"

"I'm in Allan Gardens guarding a homicide scene. A homeless man by the name of Treeman got beaten to death behind the hydrangeas."

"Oh, shit. That's Rudy's dad. Does he know?"

"He knows. He was the first one to find

him."

"Oh man, that's terrible. How's he doing?"

"Not good at all. He's gone home, he's with his girlfriend. Jimmie's calling in on him. Probably already there."

"Who's working the case for homicide?"

"S and M."

"Thank God for that. Great investigators."

"I got another theory. I told S and M about it, but I got the impression they think I'm nuts."

I told Detective Morton about the crime scene and how I believed this case was linked to Orysia's.

"Let me tell you something about S and M, Sam. The one thing you need to know about those two, apart from all the legendary stories. If someone tells them something, it doesn't matter how stupid it sounds, they always pay attention to it. You may think they've blown you off, but they haven't. I guarantee they'll be heading into this office to speak to me and Phil. Speak of the devil, they're both here. Gotta go. Talk to you later."

It was a long shift. Longer for Ident, and far longer for homicide. Moretti and Santoro would be on this until they cracked it, with little to no sleep, so I didn't feel so bad having to do a couple of hours overtime.

It was Annie's day off. I didn't want to spoil it until I got home. Dinner was ready when I walked through the door, a glass of red wine already poured, sitting on the table. She knew me too well.

"Sam, what is it? What's happened?"

"Sit down, let me pour you a glass of wine. It's a long and unhappy story."

By the time I'd finished telling her, she was in floods of tears. I gathered her up in my arms and hugged her.

"You should have called me, Sam. You should have at least called me. I need to phone Alyson. Oh, my God, poor Rudy."

"No. I saved you a whole day of hurt that you didn't need. If I thought it would have helped to call and tell you, I would have done so. Don't be angry. Call Alyson. If she needs us, we'll go. I'll eat while you call her."

Annie was angry. She went into the bedroom to make the call. The wine tasted good. I could hear her talking to Alyson. *I can't believe he didn't call me. I don't know what he was thinking. How are you and Rudy doing?* She must have realized I was listening and shut the bedroom door.

I drove Annie to the hospital. Alyson, thanks to some finagling by Dr. Ahsan, had managed to keep Rudy on the general ward. The staff nurse stopped me at the door to the ward.

"I'm sorry," she said in a thick Scottish accent. "Doctor's orders. No police officers allowed to see Rudy until he's feeling stronger. I'm sorry, Mr. Stephens. Rudy's fragile at the moment. We're trying to get him not to focus on anything to do with policing. I know you mean well, but your presence will only make things worse. You, young lady, on the other hand, not being directly involved with the event, are welcome to see him. Just try to focus on anything not police related."

I sat in the hallway, thinking. Planning.

Chapter Eighteen

"Annie. I'm going to be in and out over the next few days. You're working, and I'm off. I'm going to be following up on some leads in my own time."

"What kind of leads, Sam?"

"It's better I don't tell you. Safer that way. Better for your career you don't know anything."

"I don't think I want to know. Please be safe. Don't do anything stupid, I've just found the man of my dreams and I don't want to lose you."

Silence. A flicker of rage in her dark eyes. "Find them, Sam. Kill them."

On a hunch, I rode my Triumph 2300 Rocket III motorcycle to the Oakville General Hospital emergency ward. It was a nice day for a ride, a chance to blow the cobwebs out of my mind and open up the powerful 2294 cc engine. I explained to the three nurses on duty behind the counter who I was and showed them my badge. A couple of paramedics were hovering around chatting to the nurses. Like any emergency room, it was busy, but being the morning, the night time rush hadn't yet started.

"I'm looking for any males who may have

been in since last Thursday with an injured hand or hands. Maybe badly bruised or broken, sustained probably by punching something with a lot of force. Like a human being."

"That doesn't mean anything to us. We've just come back on shift. None of us would have been on."

I looked at her name tag. "Mary, could someone check your records. It's important." She sipped her coffee. Mary was an older woman, likely been a nurse all her life. Probably was going to save the world when she first joined, but just like cops, eventually your outlook on life becomes jaded and you just don't care anymore. You just want the madness to be over, to be retired and get away from the nightmare.

The younger nurse, Janice, not yet cynical and jaded, smiled. "I'll take a look. Just hang on there." She returned a few minutes later. "We had three in. One was an industrial accident. The guy crushed his hand under a press. The second guy, not connected, had a DIY accident at home. He was building a gazebo when a six by six fell on his hand. The third guy was in a fight. Maybe he's your guy."

"Got a name and address?"

"She can't give you that," snapped Nurse Mary. "If you want that sort of information, you'll need a warrant."

"The guy I'm looking for was involved in the beating of these two people." I threw a selection of colour photographs on the counter. "She lived. He's dead. I don't have time for a warrant." The nurses gasped.

"We have to follow protocol," snapped Nurse Mary.

"I'll let the injured woman know that, and the family of the dead guy. I'm sure they'll be gratified to know we have their best interests at heart."

Nurse Janice was reading through some notes. "I don't think the third guy's your man. He was already in police custody. Apparently he punched another prisoner. Sorry."

"Thanks, Janice. It was a long shot."

"Wait a minute," said one of the paramedics. A tall, young guy. "I was on nights last week. My partner and I had just brought in an overdose. There was a guy waiting at Triage. Rob Prusinowski, I went to high school with him. His hand, which one was it now? His right, yeah his right, was swollen like a melon. I didn't have time to talk to him. It was a crazy Friday night, busy as hell. Triage was jam-packed. I bet he got fed up waiting and went home."

"What's he look like?"

"Big fat guy. Last I heard, he was still living at home with his mom and dad in Oakville. Apparently, he's got a good job. Stockbroker in Toronto. Makes megabucks. It couldn't be him, that's laughable."

"Why's that?"

"He couldn't knock the skin off a rice pudding, let alone fight his way out of a brown paper bag. The guy's a wuss. If Rob's hand swelled up like that, it was probably due to excessive masturbation."

Apart from Mary, all the nurses began laughing. I smiled, my mind spinning.

"You're probably right. Thanks for your help. I guess it's back to square one and start again."

I straddled my motorcycle and began doing some research on my smartphone, scrolling through the 4-1-1 phone directory for Prusinowski living in Oakville. There were a lot of them. His number was probably unlisted. Then I began searching Google, Facebook, Linked-In, and PQ. There he was, this year's Stockbroker Award winner. Now I knew where he worked. I had an extensive list of his friends. Among them, Nicholas Jansen-Simms. Who were the other two? Now I needed his address. I wasn't going to go through police records. Running any kind of police check created a trail. Not good. I dropped by the Ministry of Transportation office. It was busy, so I waited for a wicket. I was lucky, the most charming young lady behind the counter was all too keen to help customers. Especially cops with big smiles and a happy disposition, for this occasion anyway.

"My in-car computer's gone down. It's pretty urgent. Do you have an address for Rob Prusinowski? He's probably in his mid to late twenties, lives in Oakville."

"I'll have a look. I probably shouldn't do

this, but seeing as you're a cop, sorry, *police officer,* I'll make an exception." She went to work on her computer keyboard. "Here we are." She slid a yellow sticky note across the counter, lent forward and whispered. "Don't tell anyone." I winked at her and smiled.

Rob Prusinowski and his parents lived in a nice neighbourhood, but nothing like where Nicholas Jansen-Simms lived. There wouldn't be any change from a couple of million bucks for the house, that's for sure. Beautiful detached homes, large driveways and sweeping lawns with mature trees and shrub borders contained between large granite rocks. Very nice. Alarmed, of course. Didn't appear to have a dog. No yellow stains on the front grass. I'd have to check the back. Triple garage. No doubt expensive cars behind those doors. I parked my motorcycle well away from the estate. If the police were called and ran my plate, it wouldn't come back to me anyway. As I jogged past the house in my tracksuit and nondescript T-shirt, I glanced down the side of the house. It backed onto crown land. Lots of trees and cover. I needed to know where their alarm box was located. Once I entered the house, I'd have thirty-seconds to find and disable the thing before the alarm went off. Hopefully, it wasn't a hi-tech model connected to their cell phone or Internet. If I got it wrong, I'd be hightailing it through the woods.

It was a long ride to Bancroft, to my cabin deep in the forest. I parked my bike in the barn and drove out my old Ford van. Nothing fancy. A dark blue colour, not the sort of van that would warrant a second glance, except for maybe the tinted windows. Plates registered to another invisible owner. A different driver's license for a different vehicle. I phoned Annie, she'd just got back from work.

"Where are you? Are you okay?"

"I'm good, Annie. I may not be home for a few days. I'm setting up surveillance on a target. I'll call you again when I get a chance. Nothing to worry about."

"I miss you, Sam."

"Miss you too. How was your day?"

"Crappy."

"That good, eh?"

"Alyson's coming round for dinner then we're going to see Rudy. She saw him this morning and said he seemed to be doing better. He was asking after you. I think when you get back he'll want to see you."

"Just tell him the soldier's on a mission. He'll understand. Love you. I gotta go. Long drive ahead."

"Love you too. Be safe."

It was the early hours of the morning before I got back to Oakville and parked my van near the Prusinowski's house, but not directly in front. Under the windshield wiper blade on the driver's side I put a note, one easily seen. It read, *Broken down, will be moved hopefully by the weekend.*

At 7:15 a.m. one of the garage doors opened.

A sleek looking silver Cadillac reversed out, backed around in the large driveway and headed out. The overweight guy behind the wheel was no doubt, Rob Prusinowski. I took some photographs and made a note of the license plate. He had to be on his way to work and I doubted he came home for lunch. Ten minutes later, another garage door went up and out drove another Cadillac, black and shiny with an older man behind the wheel. Prusinowski senior I guessed, on his way to his dental practice. From my research, that left Mrs. Prusinowski still inside the house. A woman flitted past the front room window in a red housecoat. That had to be her. At 9 a.m. I phoned the house.

"Good morning, this is FYT Security, specializing for over fifty-years in household security systems, especially surveillance cameras."

A woman's voice. "No thank you. We already have a perfectly good system."

"But, do you have cameras?"

"I don't think that's any of your business, quite frankly."

"I'm sorry, you're quite right. At the moment we are having a huge sale on cameras with free installation."

"I've already told you, our system works perfectly well and we don't need cameras." She hung up the phone.

Cameras, or no cameras? Nothing visible on the outside of the house. The inside might be a different matter. By the sound of it, they probably didn't have cameras. As long as I was in and out without setting off any alarms, I should be all right. I couldn't disguise the size of my body, but I could do something to alter my appearance. I waited.

At 10:15 a.m. the third garage door went up and out drove a mid-size white Mercedes, driven by I presumed Frub's mother. I took some more pictures. As soon as the car disappeared down the street, I walked up to the front door in my brown UPS uniform, package in hand.

The front door lock was old and worn. It wouldn't take long to pick it. I figured, if they were all leaving through the garage, the alarm control box was not going to be by the front door. It was a long way from the front door to the garages and they only had thirty seconds to set it and leave. It had to be right by the door leading into the first garage. On the wall. It might still be by the front door, which was where most people had them located. I set the second hand on my watch to count down twenty-five seconds. I jiggled the lock, opened and shut the front door behind me. I noticed there was no alarm box on the wall on either side of the front door, as I ran down the long hallway toward where I expected the door into the garage to be.

My heart was pounding. There was the panel on the wall to the right of the door. Screwdriver in hand, I pried the box open from the top, then using a small screwdriver, I unscrewed the clamp holding the phone and power lines in place, disabling the alarm system. Then my watch alarm went off. My heart missed a beat. I breathed in, and breathed out slowly and was back in business. I put the cover back on, just in case someone came back in the house. Ran back to the front door, locked it, straightened my brown wig and raced upstairs. It didn't take me long to find Frub's room. His laptop was still on his desk. Nice room, too. Large, overlooking the back garden. No yellow patches in the grass. I didn't see any security cameras, unless they were well hidden, or of the pinhole type. First job was to hide my listening devices and minute cameras. Then I went to work on the laptop.

Contrary to the movies, hacking into a computer by trying to work out the password was not as easy as they made it out to be. A simple password like *Chris* could be cracked in seconds. Add a few numbers after that and now you were into a little more time, but not much. Make the password *Christopher07* and you were going to be there way beyond your lifespan and your children's children.

I plugged my USB flash drive into the laptop. Powered up the laptop and pressed F12 *Boost Menu.* Then pressed *Boot from USB.* The screen lit up with the image of a feather, as I expected. I opened the file folder, highlighted all the files and copied them to the flash drive. There were a lot of files. It was going to take a while. Getting into the e-mail was going to require some work. I'd have to install another flash drive and send in my *Trojan horse.* When Frub opened his e-mail it would be mine, too. It was going to be a waiting game. I made sure to install a flash drive with plenty of memory for all the files that were downloading. Half an hour later it was still downloading. Then I heard the sound of one of the garage doors opening. I glanced out the hall window using a small mirror I'd put on the windowsill to see what was going on outside, without showing my face at the window. The white Mercedes had returned with Mrs. Prusinowski. I checked my watch. It was now 11:05 a.m. If she entered the bedroom I doubted she would be concerned about a flashing plastic item stuck in the side of her son's laptop. She might, however be concerned about the screen being lit up. She'd either turn the computer off, or more likely phone her son at work and ask him about it. Like the flash drive, she might not be concerned. I lowered the lid so it was not so obvious, looked around to make sure there was no trace of my presence, gathered my UPS package and slid under the queen-size bed. I had to exhale my lungs to get my chest under the wooden side panel. Then I heard the door open leading into the house from the garage. There was no sound coming from the alarm panel as the woman pressed the disarm code. That could be a problem.

At 11:55 a.m. the front door bell rang. I was still under the bed.

"Mrs. Robson, come in."

"Good morning, Mrs. Prusinowski. Would

you like me to make a start upstairs?"

"Would you. Vacuum the bedrooms, there's a dear, and of course make the beds."

The sound of someone coming up the staircase. It led upwards from the huge hallway and divided into two staircases. Mrs. Robson turned on the vacuum cleaner outside Frub's bedroom. Shortly afterwards the bedroom door opened. Mrs. Robson followed the *Dyson* into the room.

As a child, whenever I played hide-and-seek, my friends invariably discovered my hiding place. Not because they could see me or even hear me. They could *sense* me in the room. I would stay frozen, thinking of them trying to find me and they were tuned in to my thoughts. When I stopped worrying about being discovered and thought about other things, like sitting beside a campfire roasting marshmallows, they stopped being able to find me, other than by sheer luck.

I knew if I began thinking Mrs. Robson was going to find me hiding under the bed, she would feel *the presence* of something, or someone, somewhere in the room. She would automatically be drawn to the bed, raise the overhanging duvet, look underneath and discover me. Before she entered the room I was on a hiking trail, walking on a sunny fall morning, the sun glistening through the leaves. The leaves had changed from green to yellows, and golds, browns, reds, and crimsons. There were no mosquitoes or deerfly buzzing around my head. The only sound was the breeze blowing through the trees, whispering to me. In the distance I could hear the faint sound of running water. As I drew closer, the sound became louder. It was now a roar, a torrent of cascading water. The trees gave way to granite rocks, smooth, ancient, and magnificent. Lichen covered huge areas of the granite. Here and there a small, but ancient oak tree or evergreen grew out from within a fissure in the rock. The grass was dry and brown. Patches of Michaelmas daisies grew in and around the rocks, their purple flowers centred with yellow. As I crested the top of the granite plateau, there below me was the waterfall, powerful, dangerous, and beautiful.

I always love coming to this place, Sam. I'm real glad you brought me here again. It's just nice the two of us. Let's take a seat by the falls and have a bite to eat and a cup of coffee from that thermos I know you got with you. Just like old times, partner. I smiled and nodded to the Weatherman. We sat down next to one another. The Weatherman unwrapped the sandwiches as I poured us both a hot delicious smelling cup of coffee.

The bedroom door closed. The sound of Mrs. Robson and her vacuum headed off down the hallway. I had the vague sensation of the bed having been made, the sensation of the mattress being raised slightly as she tucked in the blankets. The sound of pillows being ruffled and replaced. Her pink fluffy slippers. The sound of her humming a tune. What was it now?

At 2 p.m. Mrs. Robson left through the front door. The sound of a blender. Mrs. Prusinowski was making something in the kitchen. Noise. That was good. I exhaled again, slid quietly out from underneath the bed and retrieved my flash drive, inserting another with the *Trojan horse*. My bladder was fit to burst. I pulled out a medium size plastic sandwich bag with a zip-type seal and urinated into the bag. As the bag filled, I began to wish I had used the larger bag. I tried not to think about dropping the bag, or fumbling with the seal. The carpet was a plush creamy colour. It wouldn't be improved by a large yellow stain. The colour of my urine showed I was getting dehydrated. I had a bottle of water with me, but didn't want to risk drinking too much. I would have a hell of a job trying to piss into a sandwich bag lying underneath the bed. I was hungry. I grabbed a handful of mixed nuts, good for protein and high in calories, took a mouthful of water, retrieved my second flash drive and slid back under the bed. I held that water in my mouth as long as I could, letting droplets slowly drip down my throat. If one drop went down the wrong way, a coughing spell would send the bed heaving off my chest and the game would be up. Simple bodily functions could spell disaster for a clandestine operation. Unless Mrs. Prusinowski left the house, I was temporarily trapped underneath her son's bed. The thought of him laying his fat body on top of me, despite being separated by a thick box spring and mattress wasn't comforting. I wondered how much the bed would sag onto my chest. An unpleasant image formed in my mind about medieval punishments. Of men lowering slabs onto the chest of some unfortunate secured on the ground on his back. As more weight was applied, eventually the wretched creature would be unable to inflate his chest again and would suffocate. I was hoping I wasn't going to suffer the same fate. I had no intention of dying such an ignominious death. That was not a warrior's death.

At 5 p.m. I figured I was doomed to stay where I was if I wanted this operation to be a success. I thought about my military training and realized this was really a breeze. I hoped I wasn't getting soft.

At 6 p.m. I sent Annie a text. *Don't ask ... am stuck under target's bed trying to get out of house without being discovered. Looks like a long and miserable night. Won't be able to make contact until morning when they all leave the house. Your eyes only! I miss you.*

Sam. Be careful. I'll be worried about you all night. Stay safe. Please! I hope when she takes her clothes off, she's pretty. MU2.

Funny. It's a guy. If you only knew. Have to go.

6:30 p.m. The faint sound of the garage door opening. Son or dad?

"Hi, dear, dinner's ready. Robert won't be home tonight. He's staying over at Nick's"

"What a day. Am I glad to be home. How was your day?"

"Quiet. I zipped out after you left and did some shopping, then Mrs. Robson arrived. Oh, the alarm doesn't seem to be resetting."

"Call them tomorrow morning, would you. Have them come over and get it fixed, we pay enough for it."

"I'm going out in the morning for coffee with Samantha. I'll see if I can get them here for the afternoon. Which reminds me. I got a call this morning from an alarm company. They're having a sale on cameras. I told them we were quite satisfied with our system."

"Not anymore. We ought to think about updating. Cameras might be an idea. Did you know you can keep an eye on your own house from Florida on one of those fancy cell phones? Might be an idea when we're away on holiday."

"Roger. The last thing we need to worry about when we're on holiday is the house, or anything else for that matter. We're well insured, for God's sake."

"You're right. I gotta tell you though, I don't like what's going on with Robert lately, not since he's been hanging around with that Nicholas Jansen-Simms and his buddies. And as for getting his hand accidently slammed in a car door, I think that's bullshit. We're going to have to have a word with him. He's hardly home these days. Might as well move out and get his own place."

"I know."

"He needs a girlfriend. What's the matter, Eileen? Did I say something wrong?"

"I don't know. I walked into his bedroom the other evening, I wasn't thinking and forgot to knock. You know how mad he gets if you don't knock and await *permission* to enter."

"Go on."

"Just as he slammed the cover of his laptop, I caught a glimpse of a very disturbing image."

"And?"

"It was of a young woman, naked, bound, and gagged. It looked more like an horrific rape scene. There were a group of men around her. It's amazing what the eye can see and the brain register in a split second."

"What did he say?"

"He lost his temper with me for not knocking first."

"The bloody Internet. Curse of mankind."

"That's sexist, Roger. It's *humankind*."

"Whatever. Have you joined the twenty-first century Suffragette movement?"

"Not entirely. You won't see me chained to the railings outside the parliament building, if that's what you mean."

"I certainly hope not, my dear. Okay, what's for dinner? I'm starving."

10 p.m. At long last, the two of them finally went to bed. I closed my eyes and went to sleep. I felt thirsty, but daren't take another sip of water. I had the uncanny ability to imagine I was staying in a high-class hotel, in a ten-thousand dollar a night suite. After all, once the

lights go out, you could be sleeping anywhere. In the morning I would lodge a complaint with management about the unbelievably hard bed I had to sleep on.

Chapter Nineteen

The sound of buzzing. 6 a.m. Eileen getting up to get breakfast for Roger, no doubt. The smell of coffee. If there was any left in the pot I'd heat some in the microwave before I left. Morning pleasantries. Goodbyes.

7:27 a.m. The sound of the garage door opening. Roger on his way to work.

10 a.m. Another garage door opening. Eileen leaving the house. I waited a few minutes to be sure. Frequently targets returned to the house minutes later having discovered halfway down the road they'd forgotten something. But not today.

I slid out from under the bed, raced to the en suite bathroom, plastic bag in hand, and sat it on top of the quartz countertop. It looked like a transparent balloon, full of dark yellow liquid about to burst open. I pissed like a thoroughbred stallion. The relief was memorable. I closed my eyes briefly and let out a long sigh. The bedroom had to be searched quickly for trophies and any other incriminating evidence. Evil people sometimes liked to keep something to remind them of their victims. Looking at it, even months or years later, it would fill them with the need for sexual gratification. A shock of hair, a piece of jewellery or clothing. It was there somewhere, but I couldn't find it. Time was not on my side. Anything I needed was likely on that laptop. I hoped it was now on my flash drive as well. I scanned the room carefully to ensure there was no trace of me ever having been in there. At least, not to the naked eye. Even my empty urine bag was not left behind in the bathroom trash can. Take evidence, don't leave it. That is, if you're not going to plant any.

The coffee was lukewarm. I grabbed a mug, downed it, rinsed and dried the mug, and replaced it exactly where I found it. When I finished resetting the alarm and left by the garage, I was glad to remove the thin plastic gloves. My hands were sweating. It was good having an empty lot across the street. No prying eyes. My van was still parked down the street where I had left it. As I walked toward the van I mentally put myself back on the hiking trail. I didn't want to give off a guilty aura. People can detect that a mile away. The way you walk, turn your head frequently, acting unnaturally. I opened my van door as though I had just returned from the trail, got in, started it up, and drove casually away. I was glad to rip the wig off my head, it was hot and itchy.

I needed a huge mug of hot coffee and a large breakfast to match it, but not in Oakville. I decided to drop by Callaghan's and eat a hearty breakfast. Nicole and I would flirt with each other, all in fun. She always made the customers feel special. You just couldn't help but like her.

By the time I turned onto the street, found a parking spot and began walking to the restaurant, I was famished. It was closed. It was never closed, but the lights were off inside. No movement. *There must be a mistake*. I tried the door. Locked. I had a bad feeling. Callaghan's as far as I recalled, was closed only on Christmas Day and St. Patrick's Day. Today was not one of those days. Not even close. I'd find out the gossip tomorrow morning on day shift. I grabbed a burger and a coffee at a fast food restaurant instead and went home to change. Annie would be at work. I called her and left a message. *Dinner's on me tonight. Too exhausted to cook.*

* * *

The security guard was sitting in a modern looking guardhouse to the left of the barrier leading down to the private underground parking lot that I needed access to. The stock exchange where Frub worked. I needed access to his car, assuming it was down there.

"Morning. I'm from Toronto Hold Up. I was wondering if you could help me." I flashed my badge.

"What can I do for you?"

"How long you been in security?"

"Two years."

"I figured a fit looking guy like you would be

applying to the police. Toronto needs guys like you."

"Yeah, I was thinking I'd apply. I'd heard they weren't looking for white guys. They wanted *visible minorities.*"

"Don't believe all you hear. What's your name? I'll put a word in for you. You help me, I'll help you."

"It's Peter. Peter Watkins."

"Okay, Peter. On the QT. I need to take a look at a selection of cars in your parking lot. Need to know basis."

"No problem, Officer. You think you can help me? Get in the police, I mean."

"I can put a good word in for you, sure. Best get your application in soon though, they've started hiring again, now all the baby boomers are retiring. Are you keeping fit?"

"Yes, sir. Fifty pushups, every morning."

"If nothing else Peter, that's good for your love life." He chuckled, his face once pale looking developed into an embarrassed blush. He was young and naive.

"Speak any languages?"

"French."

"Mandarin would be better." I laughed. "But good for you. Fluently?"

"I hope so. I'm from old Quebec. Help yourself down there. You have to sign in first."

"Peter, we're dealing with organized crime. Hold Up doesn't sign in anywhere. You'll get to know that once you're in the department." He had that *stupid look* expression on his face.

"Don't worry. Once you're in, I'll take you under my wing."

I walked past the barrier and made my way down the ramp. This was nothing like any parking lot I'd ever seen in my life. No *old bangers,* no run of the mill cars. Some of the fancy ones were worth more than my condo. Bentleys, Rolls-Royces, Mercedes, high-end Cadillacs, Porches, BMWs, Ferraris. I guess it must be Murphy's Law. You can't find the thing you're looking for immediately. It can't be the first one you see. No, you have to look for it. Up and down the rows of cars. It was like dropping your car off at the airport multistory. Forgetting which level you'd parked it on and trying to find your car again.

There it was, the silver sports Cadillac. Right plate number. Robert Prusinowski's car. Alarmed of course. The low design of the parking lot ceiling made it impossible to locate the security camera any higher. Reaching up, I stuck a wide piece of duct tape over the eye, then sprang into action. I stuck the GPS tracker underneath Prusinowski's car. Slipped the *slim-jim* down the rear right passenger window into the door, carefully pulling back the plastic strip and keeping my head well back. I'd heard of a tow truck driver opening a modern car the same way and set the car door airbag off. Unfortunately, his head was looking over the tool at the same time. The *slim-jim* shot up like a bullet, entered his skull and killed him. Not the way a warrior wants to die. I'd dodged death by being crushed by a fat guy and I wanted to dodge this one, too. I did. As soon as I opened the door, the alarm went off. As expected. Quickly, I put the listening device under the front passenger seat, closed the door, ran over to the security camera, ripped off the tape and returned to the guardhouse. The copy of the police magazine I'd given young Watkins to read, was open in front of him. Hopefully he hadn't noticed the temporary malfunction of one of the cameras. Being a good citizen I told him an alarm had gone off somewhere in the parking lot, but I didn't know where it was coming from.

He thanked me. We shook hands and off he went to investigate. I left him the magazine and made a note of his name. The fake moustache and wig were driving me mad. I couldn't wait to get home and remove the blue contacts.

When I got back to my condo I had a long, hot shower. I'd keep the van in Toronto for a while. I had no desire to drive all the way back to Bancroft to pick up my motorcycle. I was tired and emotionally exhausted. There wasn't time to take a nap. I had a flash drive to download and go through. Surveillance equipment to monitor. I wasn't going to get it all done tonight. I wanted to, but I kept nodding off.

I woke up when Annie entered the condo.

"Sam, you look all in." We hugged for a long time. "You sure you're up to going out? We don't have to, if you're that tired. I can cook."

"Nope. You've done a long shift, you're tired, too. Come on, as soon as you're ready let's go. We won't stay out late. You're on nights tomorrow, so you can lie in. I'm on days. Got to be up early."

"How's *your* investigation going?"

"Between you and I? Good. Listen, Annie. You cannot tell anybody about any of this. I don't need a search warrant executed on our home."

"Our home. I like the sound of that. Sam, you and I are soul mates. You don't need to worry about me."

"I hope you understand that I can't tell you everything. There are some things I keep secret from you. Not bad things. Places where I keep some of my equipment. I'm only telling you this, because if anything ever happened to me and you found out about it, you might not feel the same way about me."

"Sam, I don't have to know. I don't need to know, and I don't want to know. However, if you ever have an affair in one of these *secret* locations and I find out. I'm going to cut your balls off. What's so funny?"

"Nothing, just that I know I don't ever have to sleep with one eye open around you, because it'll never happen. Ever."

* * *

I never liked to be late for work. I loved the banter inside the locker room. As we all changed, the conversation was always about hockey and football. The way the guys talked, it was like they were personal friends with these overpaid sports prima donnas. Bashing management was another favourite topic. It was a mixture of the night crew getting ready to leave and day shift taking over. A coming together of ethnic diversity, all in one small space. Two of the night guys were stuck at a crime scene and would be late getting off. One of us would be relieving them soon.

The joking continued into the parade room. Guys behaving like young bulls, barged against each other as we made our way to the parade room. A friendly tussle in the hallway. It reminded me of high school. You'd have to be a cop to understand.

No sergeants, yet. Unusual. We looked around at each other wondering who was in the shit today. No Jimmie Callaghan this morning. I had a bad feeling. The laughter died away quickly. We all had a bad feeling.

"I was by Callaghan's restaurant yesterday," I said. "It was closed. It's never closed." We sat quietly and waited.

Sergeant Bernie Wells walked in with the Staff Sergeant, Detectives Johnny Morton and Bruno Moretti were with them. No one spoke. Not for a while. An awkward silence. I figured we were all thinking the same thing. *If Jimmie had died, why were Detectives Morton and*

Moretti at parade? How come the night shift didn't tell us anything? Detective Morton spoke first.

"You all know Jimmie's niece, Nicole. She was found yesterday morning, not far from her apartment. Unconscious. She'd been savagely beaten and raped. She's still in the hospital on life support. Condition. Critical."

A feeling of deep hurt and rage filled the parade room. Outbursts of anger and threats to unleash unspeakable pain upon the perpetrators of this outrage circulated the room. I fell silent. While I was stuck under one of the suspect's beds, he had been out there with his friends and attacked someone I cared a lot about. I was sure of it. Someone everyone in this room cared a lot about.

"We believe this attack was committed by the people that did the same thing to one of our local *ladies of the night.* She's still in hospital, but making a good recovery. We are not ruling out the possibility that these people are responsible for the murder of Treeman. If you don't already know, you might as well know now. Treeman was Rudy Jackson's father." The younger officers looked at each other, trying to process this information.

Detective Moretti spoke. "So far, no great leads, but a lot of possible suspects. Get out there, guys, and shake the trees. I don't care how small the bit of information is. We want it, and we want it straight away. Don't bother going to Callaghan's for breakfast this morning.

It's closed. Can you believe it? Jimmie's brother said to say sorry. The Callaghans love the police. They are our friends. So, forget about your fucking traffic tickets for a while. Concentrate on getting these motherfuckers."

Moretti wasn't angry, he was furious. Had anyone else said that other than Moretti, the Staff Sergeant might have had something to say about it. The front line uniform guys got the impression, that from management's point of view, *Tickets trumped criminal arrests.*

Sergeant Wells called me into his office. "I was going to have you work with Jimmie today. You're nearly ready to go out on your own, anyway. We've got plenty on today. You can float around on your own if you like."

"I'd like to take some time off, Sergeant. It's very important, otherwise I wouldn't ask. I'd like to take it right now."

"With all that's happened, Sam? I find that odd, to say the least. I figured, if anyone, you'd be out there searching for these guys."

I stared at him blankly.

"Okay. How much time do you need?"

"I should be back next block. If I'm not, I'll have to have some annual leave advanced."

"Management won't like that."

"I told you, Sergeant. If it wasn't important, I wouldn't ask."

"Sam. Don't do anything stupid. I'm not a mind reader, but I can see you're up to something."

I nodded in appreciation, turned, and left his

office. I was in and out of that locker room in record time and on my way back to my condo.

It was still early morning. Annie walked out of the bedroom into my office.

"Sam, what are you doing home?"

I told her all about Nicole. Annie had met her a few times when we had gone in for breakfast on our days off. They liked each other and had become friends. She sat down, put her head in her hands and cried.

"Annie. No time for tears. We've got work to do. Call in sick, I can't do this on my own. I've set up cameras and listening devices, GPS trackers. I need you to help monitor the equipment. I'm on them, but we have to act quickly, before they hurt someone else."

"Okay. Just show me what to do. I'll get changed quickly."

"Would you mind making breakfast and coffee for us? It's going to be a busy few days and nights with little to no sleep. I'm not taking any phone calls or answering the door until this is done. You have to do the same. And remember. You don't have to do this. If it all goes wrong. Tell them I forced you into it."

"No. I'm doing this because I want to. I give you my word. Whatever happens, I'll never breathe a word of it. Ever."

"Well, let's get going, partner."

We ate breakfast in the office. An endless supply of coffee was on at all time. Frub was already at work. Annie was going through the computer downloads looking for evidence. I replayed his bedroom monitor. He had stayed at home last night. Before he entered his bedroom, I could hear the sound of shouting. He and his father had got into an argument. His mother was trying to calm them down. The bedroom door opened.

Don't worry, I'll be out by the end of the week, then I won't have to put up with you two bitching at me! The sound of the bedroom door slamming. A cell phone ringing.

Hi, Nick ... Yeah I'm fine. Had a big bust up with my parents. No big deal. About time I got my own place anyway. I'm going to look for a condo down on Harbourfront ... Really, that cute, eh? American Indian. I like the sound of that. You got pictures? Send 'em over, buddy ... What's the problem? ... Well, we'll have to nab her when he's not around. He sounds like one big guy ...Indian, too, eh?... Gotta go, someone's coming up the stairs.

Annie looked at me in horror.

"They're talking about me, aren't they? Cute Indian girl, big Indian boyfriend. Harbourfront. That asshole took pictures of me when I was out jogging, I bet."

"Focus, Annie. You don't leave this condo until this is over. You don't answer the door. At some point, I have to go out into the field. I won't be able to concentrate if I'm worrying about you. I'll make mistakes. I can't afford to make mistakes."

* * *

Frub goes to the door and locks it. Opens a bedside drawer and pulls out a magazine. As he grabs a handful of tissues, Annie says, "I don't need to watch or hear this." I turn off the monitor and shut off the sound. Nothing else interesting happens that night. Last night. When his alarm clock goes off, I check the equipment installed in his car and wait. Breakfast is quiet, like it is after a heated argument the night before.

The sound of a car door opening. A person getting in. The door closing. Frub is in his Cadillac. The sound of the garage door going up, the engine starting. Powerful. We're on the move. I check another monitor. The GPS installed under his car is working. A road map of the whole area and a tiny image of a car moving along the road. Frub's car. Hopefully, it is Frub behind the wheel.

Cell phone ringing. I hope it's hands free.

"Nick, you're up early ... Okay, I can do that. Mike and Jason going to be there? ... I've never been to your family's cottage, where is it? ... I should have known it would be in the Muskokas. E-mail me directions ... Okay, this Friday night's good. I'll bring some booze ... That's good we've got the cottage all to ourselves for the month. That gives us time to meet up with our Indian girlfriend and bring her up to the cottage for a couple of weeks. I don't

know if she'll like it, but I know we all will ... Yeah, that was a lot of fun the other night. Wish I'd taken pictures ... Nothing unusual my end, buddy. Those shares you were going to buy? Don't. I heard the company's going down the shitter ... No, I would never do anything illegal like that, what kind of a guy do you think I am?... See you tomorrow afternoon at the cottage."

* * *

"Sam, I'm scared."

"Don't be. I have to go out for a while. Keep monitoring and checking those computer records. Anything, yet?"

"Just that he's one sick bastard. He likes weird, degrading, porn. I think some of those girls actually get killed. Tell me, they don't."

"That's a snuff porno movie. Yeah, sometimes the girl dies. Are you sure you're cut out to be a cop, Annie?"

"After seeing this? I don't know anymore. I can't believe there are monsters like these guys out there."

"More than you realize."

"Do you really have to go?"

"Yes. I can't organize a drone strike. I have to go out and defeat the enemy. You're safe here. If you're that worried, I have a handgun available. It's a Ruga LR .22 semi-automatic. I think the Mossad use them. Don't forget to tap and rack if the casing doesn't eject properly. Anyway, you know what to do from your training. It's got a built-in silencer. Remember, it's small calibre and doesn't have great stopping power so don't be afraid to keep pulling the trigger."

"Get it, please."

The doorbell rang. I put my finger to my lips and checked the monitor. Detectives Moretti and Santoro were outside my door. They kept ringing the bell. I muted my cell phone. They left a message for me to call them. They didn't give up easily. Moretti put his ear to my door and listened. He must have stood like that for a whole minute. Now, they were going to check the parking lot for my car. I was sure they would. These guys were thorough. If anything happened to me or Annie, I'd want these boys on the case for sure. My end game would be different to theirs, of course. But, maybe not. A lot of rumours about these guys, especially from the old days. Maybe they'd found God now. But I didn't think so.

I waited half an hour before leaving the apartment, taking the back stairs down to the parking lot. I had a few things to organize. I didn't want to make any purchases too close to home, or anywhere near where my targets lived, or had access to. I'd take a drive out to my people and buy locally. That was the right thing to do. Look after the little mom and pop operations. Likely no cameras, and those that had them, didn't even have them connected to a monitor. All for show. Not too keen on talking to the police, either. All good.

It was late in the afternoon by the time I got back to the condo. Annie threw her arms around me as though I'd just got back from war.

"I dropped my van off and picked up my truck. I want to be ready to follow Frub to the cottage. With the GPS I don't even have to have him in sight. Did you find anything?"

"Yes, a photo. Three men in a dark alley. A woman's body on the ground. I think it's Nicole. None of the men match Frub's description."

"He must be the one taking the picture, only I don't think they realized he'd taken it."

"Why?"

"His personal insurance. Now he's got something on them they can't refute. I'll download the picture and take it with me tomorrow. That guy's Nick, I don't know who the other two are. Probably Mike and Jason."

"What are you going to do when you find them?"

"We've been over this, Annie. Don't ask. That way you don't have to lie if you ever get asked if you knew what I was doing. Because, in all honesty, you don't. You can guess, but you don't know. Think of the aphorism, *Three can keep a secret if two are dead.*"

"What, you're gonna kill me now?"

"Annie, that'll never happen. You're too cute for that."

"Nick and Frub think the same thing, only they will," she hesitated. "Kill me."

"Not going to happen. Trust me. Okay, when I'm on the move, you'll have to update me on what Frub's saying inside his car. The car will still pick up some sound even when he parks it. Unless you hear something like, *You're a dead man now, Sam Stephens,* followed by the sound of gunshots, don't call the police. There will be times we can't communicate because of giving away my location. If you haven't heard from me by ten o'clock Monday morning, call Detective Moretti. Here's his number. At least you know what he looks like now. I repeat, don't leave the condo, not until you see me standing outside the door, or Detective Moretti is standing outside that door on Monday morning after you've called him."

"Okay. I don't think I could be married to you if you were back in the military overseas. I'd be worried sick every minute."

"Pity. I was going to apply to the GRS."

"That sounds okay. Isn't that something to do with tax evasion in the US?"

"You're thinking of the IRS. GRS is the CIA's close protection unit. It stands for Global Response Staff. I'd fit right in there. But if you think it's got something to do with tax evasion, that'll keep your mind at ease. The guys in that outfit are nearly all ex-Special Forces."

"Doesn't sound like tax evasion, so, no. Definitely not. Well. If that's what you really want to do. I'd cope with it."

"Good money."

"I don't care about the money, Sam. I care about you. About us. Got it?"

"Got it. Okay, I'll give you a run down on how everything works. Grab a pen and paper to make notes. You'll need them."

"I was going to be on nights tonight, so why don't I take the night shift so you can get some sleep. You're going to have a long day tomorrow and probably through the night, too. You need your rest. If anything comes up, I'll wake you."

"Annie, the next few days and nights are going to be long for both of us. But you're right. I'll take a nap. My gear's all ready to go."

Chapter Twenty

Friday 6 a.m. I took over from Annie. Nothing exciting had happened during the night. Frub went home. No arguments. Peaceful dinner. All friends again. After breakfast, the target took off for work as usual. Annie made coffee and breakfast. She'd been able to sleep through the night on the foldout bed in the office.

Nothing on the drive to work. Frub was listening to a radio talk show. The news came on at eight. The brutal attack on Nicole was mentioned. No response from Frub, just heavy breathing. He was excited.

I heard the security guard's voice.

"Morning, Mr. Prusinowski."

"Morning, Peter. Lovely day."

The sound of the barrier rising. I pictured the car driving down the ramp, negotiating concrete pillars and parking between a Rolls and a Bentley. Frub was going to have to work a little harder if he wanted one of those. The sound of the car door opening, Frub squeezing out, grunting. The door closing, then that electronic sound as he activated the remote security lock system. Not likely anything more to listen to until he got back in his car.

2 p.m. Annie called me. "Frub's leaving the office early today."

"It's Poets' Day, Annie."

"Poets' Day?"

"Piss off early, tomorrow's Saturday."

"Very funny."

"Okay, we're on the move. He said he was bringing booze, so likely he's stopping off at the LCBO. Maybe the Beer Store. These guys aren't rednecks. It'll be the LCBO. Wines, spirits, and beer, if they want it."

"Good luck. I love you."

"Love you too."

Annie was on shift in *The War Room.* I fired up the old Ford and set the computer GPS system to follow Frub. I'd been waiting in a *Pay and Display* parking lot a couple of blocks away. The Ford was an old F150, uninteresting grey colour. Another nondescript vehicle. I didn't want it shiny and new, or too old and rusty. That drew attention. People would remember a shiny new pick-up truck. Their eyes would be drawn to it. People noticed old bangers, too. Nobody was interested in *an old truck.* Only the outside looked old. Everything else was in mint condition.

It was about one hundred and sixty-five kilometers from Toronto to the Muskokas, straight up Highway 400. I didn't want to be too far from my target. There was a chance the cottage was on an island. I figured that was a good possibility. If it was on the mainland, the target's car would be in or near the driveway. If it was on an island, I'd find the car parked in a gravel lot on the shoreline. Finding which cottage on which island would be near impossible in the timeframe I had. No doubt his friend Nick would pick him up in a fancy speed boat. I didn't bring the canoe. Even I couldn't paddle that fast. I brought along a sturdy inflatable boat. It fit nicely in the truck bed. A powerful outboard attached. Timing was everything.

It was the LCBO, just on the outskirts of Toronto. Frub wasn't going home; he was going straight up through Barrie, then onto Bracebridge. After that, I didn't know, but it wouldn't be that far from there. Allowing for traffic, I figured we'd get there around four-thirty, five o'clock.

Annie called me. "Looks like you were right. The cottage is on an island. He's just called Nick and told him he'd be at the dock in twenty minutes."

"Thanks, Annie."

"The phone's been ringing non-stop. Moretti and his partner were back at our door again. Persistent, aren't they?"

"That they are. Once he's on that boat, I've only got a small window of opportunity to launch my own and follow them. I'll call you again when I've found the cottage. I've got to make sure there are no innocents there, otherwise I'll have to go to plan B."

"I didn't know there was a plan B."

"There's always a plan B."

I took a series of narrow winding bends up and down hill. I couldn't see the Caddy, but it wasn't very far in front of me, according to the GPS. Over the crest of the next hill the lake came into view. I stopped the truck and backed it into a space that had been cleared to aid oncoming vehicles to pass each other. There were trees on either side of the track with thick brush. I moved as fast as I could through the trees, being careful not to make a lot of noise. I reminded myself of how fast a black bear can move through such vegetation, with little or no sound. I would have to do the same.

I got down on my belly and slid to the edge. The dock was to the left of the gravel parking lot. There were quite a few vehicles parked there already, mainly high-end SUV's and pick-up trucks. Their occupants somewhere out on the lake. A fancy fibreglass cabin cruiser was pulling up against the dock. Nicholas Jansen-Simms at the wheel. Two men jumped onto the dock.

Frub was getting out of the car and waved to his friends. "Mike, Jason, good to see you guys! Hey, Nick, nice boat buddy."

The two men secured the gin palace and helped Frub with the boxes of booze as he carried his bag to the boat.

As I crested the hill in my truck, *Bikinis Only* was pulling away from the dock. I parked, grabbed the inflatable, plonked it in the water, dropped my kitbag in, and started the engine. As it roared to life, the bow on *Bikinis Only* rose high in the water and sped away, with me following at a distance in her wake. As we snaked among the islands I was relieved to have brought my handheld GPS. Without local knowledge of the area, it would be a challenge to get back to the dock. In the dark, it would be virtually impossible.

Twenty minutes later, *Bikinis Only* settled back in the water and changed course toward an island. The cottage was not some 1970's rustic structure, but a million dollar home, not including the price of the island. The boat approached a sheltered floating dock and moored up. There were no other houses on the island. It was time to pretend I was fishing. I had the wig back on with a hat pulled well down on my head. At every opportunity I glanced over at the island, scanning it for other signs of life. So far, no *innocents.* Then I saw one. A huge, shaggy German shepherd, his coat golden brown. He was the Sam Stephens of the dog world. The dog barked ferociously as the four men made their way up to the house. It was tethered to a long chain affixed to the front of a large wooden kennel. Nobody went near the dog. It was ignored like it didn't exist. It wasn't there to be petted. A problem. A big problem. Not an insurmountable problem. A barking dog, particularly one like this handsome specimen, spoiled the element of surprise. I wanted to give these guys a monumental surprise. It seemed only fitting. The thought that Nicholas Jansen-Simms had been taking pictures of Annie was one thing. What they were all going to do with her when they kidnapped her was another. Unforgiveable. Given the time, I would have liked to inflict the sort of pain upon them that my ancestors were experts at inflicting upon their enemies. Over days, weeks even. But, I didn't have the time. I had enough grounds to arrest them all, of course. That wouldn't take much time, just opportunity.

I made a call and waited for my message to be conveyed. Eventually the person I wished to speak to came on the line and agreed to my request. By the time I had circled the island and seen what I needed to see, the sun was going down. I returned to the dock, secured the inflatable and waited in my truck. A long time.

In my rearview mirror I saw headlights bouncing over the hill and descending toward the parking lot. A large car, headlights spaced wide apart. It was still bouncing when it reached the flat gravel. Shock absorbers needed replacing. An old Pontiac Parisienne. My grandfather's car. He parked his car next to my truck and got out. When he saw me, he merely nodded. A man of few words, then he looked up at the sky as if pondering the universe. Not a casual glance, but a long stare as if memorizing the position of every star in the sky. No compass. It was all in his head. No cloud cover tonight, a beautiful star-filled sky and only a sliver of a moon.

"Always know where you are," was all he said as we walked to the inflatable.

As we headed out onto the lake under cover of darkness, I checked my GPS settings.

"Not much good when the batteries go flat. Don't be like the others and forget the old ways."

"No, Grandfather. I still remember the old ways and I still use them when I need to."

"Good."

As we approached the island I stopped the engine. The wind was getting up. Our little floating island bobbed up and down as each wave caught the side. No running lights, just a flashlight in case a passing boat was about to run us down. It appeared that we were the only boat on the lake. I took out my night vision goggles and studied the island, the house, and the occupants. Still only four people on the island and one large dog. The dog was lying in the entrance of the kennel, its huge head on its paws. Resting, but not asleep. The four targets were sitting around a campfire, laughing, drinking, and eating.

2 a.m. They all finally staggered into the house. I began to row slowly closer to the island.

3 a.m. The inflatable bounced gently off a smooth rock in the lee of the island. I snagged a tree root and secured it. Grandfather hopped onto the rock and disappeared into the darkness. As he did so I took out my *acquired* M110 semi-automatic sniper rifle, with suppressor and thermal imaging. If you popped your head up at one thousand metres, you'd never know what hit

you. I scanned the windows for movement. No doubt there were firearms in that house. As soon as I saw the barrel pointed anywhere near my grandfather, I was letting go a kill shot. All hell would break loose then. I'd have to go to Plan B. Storm the building and take out the other three. Like the Gurkhas, I wasn't taking any prisoners. Except, maybe the dog.

It was a long fifteen minutes. As I waited, I applied black face paint, not because I was a warrior. The soldier was still inside me. I began to wonder if my grandfather had had a heart attack out there. That would be awkward. Distressing, but awkward. Then I heard him whispering quietly in our native tongue, leading the *wolf* on a piece of string looped through its collar back to the inflatable. My grandfather merely smiled, petted the huge dog on its head and ordered it into the boat. He sat with the dog between his knees as though they had been part of one another all their lives. The dog sniffed at me, wagged its tail and allowed me to ruffle my fingers through the thick fur around his ears. It was my turn now. I nodded at the old man. He nodded back as I pulled the barbecue cylinder out of the inflatable, the hose still attached. It was full.

I didn't trust my skills of navigating through the darkness. With my night vision goggles strapped to my head, I set off toward the house. Every ten paces I stopped and listened. Just the sound of the water lapping against the granite rocks around the island. A shooting star flashed across the sky. A good omen. I thanked the Creator. I didn't have to search all around the house for what I was looking for. I had a good idea where I would find it from my reconnoitering last night out on the lake.

A foot off the ground in the wall. The dryer vent. Three thin plastic flaps. Carefully, I removed each one and set them aside. In my pocket I had my fail-safe insurance policy and slowly lowered it down into the vent pipe on a long piece of string, uncoiled the rubber hose and stuck that as far down the vent as I could get it. Opening the gas cylinder valve too wide would be noisy as the gas whooshed out under pressure. I cracked it open bit by bit until I was satisfied the gas was pouring into the house efficiently, and as silently as possible. Mission almost accomplished.

As I approached the inflatable, I heard the dog growl menacingly, then my grandfather's calm voice, then silence, apart from the blood pounding hard through my body, loud in my ears. We cast off and drifted away from the island. Away from the place where Annie Greyeyes would have suffered unspeakable horrors, with nobody to hear her cries of terror. The distant lights twinkled. They were pretty. Reds, oranges, yellows, whites. Even a blue light. My grandfather remained silent, stroking the dog.

I didn't have time to wait until either the gas reached the furnace and exploded, or one of the targets switched on a light. That could take a long time. By then, maybe they would smell the gas and evacuate the house. That would be a failure. A disaster. I'd have to go to plan C. Pick them off one by one with the rifle. By then there would be people around. Not good. I waited until we were a kilometre away.

"Lay low, Grandfather. It's time."

I removed the electrical switch from my pocket, took off the plastic cover exposing the switch and crouched low in the boat, my back toward the island. *Click.*

The night sky lit up with a ball of orange and yellow light, followed by a massive explosion. I felt the blast wave as it hurtled across the lake, for a split second the temperature rose and fell again. When I looked back at the island, the whole house was engulfed in flames. I took out my binoculars and looked for any signs of human activity. I could see none. As I returned the binoculars to my jacket pocket, my grandfather sat across from me, smiling.

"Time to go."

He was right. I revved the engine and raced back to the dock. It wouldn't be long before emergency service vehicles were on scene. We didn't need to be witnesses, or worse, suspects.

"Grandfather, we can't take the dog. It might have one of those GPS chips embedded in it somewhere. You don't need a visit from the police. It would really put a damper on things and lead to some difficult questions." He nodded.

I landed the inflatable by the truck. As I

hurriedly put it and the outboard back in the truck, my grandfather found what he was looking for. An insecure vehicle. Not one of the suspects' I felt sure. That didn't matter. A Buick Rendezvous. The dog would be very comfortable in the back.

It leapt up on to the backseat at my grandfather's command, and lay down. The old man petted the dog tenderly and gave him a couple of dog biscuits. He nodded in my direction, got in his car and drove away. I could hear sirens approaching, coming fast. I surveyed the immediate area for accidently discarded incriminating evidence, pulled off the tracking device from under Frub's car, smashed the rear right passenger door window, grabbed the electronics from under the front passenger seat amidst the sound of an ear piercing alarm and left the parking lot quickly, but carefully. It wouldn't do to have an accident with a tree or large rock on the way out. I called Annie when I was miles away from Bracebridge.

"Sam?" She sounded groggy.

"Annie, I'm on my way out. I have to drop something off, and pick something up. Mission accomplished." Silence. "Annie, are you okay?" I could hear tears of relief as she let out all the pent-up emotion of the last few days.

"I thought I heard a muffled explosion. Then later, the sound of an outboard motor. Voices, a car starting and driving. Then the car window being smashed and the door opening and closing." She was sobbing, catching her breath as she spoke.

"I'll be home about lunch time. There's nothing to monitor so you may as well get some rest. You've been amazing. I love you."

"I love you, too. Come home as soon as you can. Please?"

"I will. By the time you wake up I'll be at the door."

I dropped the truck off at my cabin on the outskirts of Bancroft and replaced it with my motorcycle. Before leaving I made sure the barn was alarmed and well secured, then took a long shower before riding back to Toronto. On the way, I threw my old clothing and boots into various garbage cans along the way. Only an idiot keeps his footwear.

By the time I walked back through the door to my condo, I was wired, glad I still had a few days off. Annie was so pleased to see me she was bouncing up and down like a little girl.

"You must be exhausted, Sam."

"No, too much adrenaline in the bloodstream."

"Good." She took my hand and led me into the bedroom.

That evening we cooked dinner together. A good steak and a glass of excellent red wine that looked like velvet in a glass, was hard to beat. I didn't want to hear any news on the radio or the television. Instead, we sat cuddled together in the living room watching Elf. Christmas was not quite on the horizon yet, but this was Annie's favourite Christmas movie and we both needed something lighthearted and funny to take our minds off the past events.

“You might be on the *naughty list* this year, Sam.”

“No!”

Chapter Twenty One

Night shift parade was upbeat. Nicole had come out of her coma. Orysia was able to leave the hospital in the morning. Annie and I would be there to collect her. Annie was now on her days off, so hopefully, I wouldn't get held over with an arrest at the end of shift. Rudy had been discharged from hospital during my *absence* and had moved in with Alyson. He'd applied for a teaching job at the Academy and been accepted. He and Alyson were moving down to Lake Erie. She'd get a job at the local hospital, no problem. It would mean that Rudy could still be a police officer and wear his uniform with pride. He'd be seconded to the Academy, but could always come back to Toronto and teach the new recruits here. Somehow, I didn't see him ever coming back on the road. I was going to miss him as a good friend and colleague. Annie and I agreed, we would take a road trip down to see them at least twice a year and they would come and see us.

Nights was a series of bar fights, domestics, gang violence, impaired drivers, robberies, shootings, stabbings and drug arrests. You name it. It was a busy set of nights. I was relieved when my days off came around. Annie would be back at work, but we'd be off together for the last couple of days.

We took Orysia to see her new townhouse on the Cheyrone reserve, on land belonging to my people. My old truck was parked in the lot. I handed her the keys.

"When you're ready, this will be your new home. My house is just around the corner. If Annie gets transferred, she'll be staying over sometimes. Come on, we'll take you up to the Band office to meet the Chief. You'll like her. And we've got a job waiting for you at the casino. That'll bring in some extra cash for you. On the way home, we'll show you the college you'll be enrolled in."

Orysia stood in the parking lot, tears rolling down her cheeks. Nobody in her whole life had ever shown her real love and kindness, without having ulterior motives. She hugged me with every ounce of strength she could muster from her tiny fragile body. Annie was smiling with pure happiness. It was a good day. A rewarding day. A great to be alive kind of day. This little bird was nearly ready to fly, her broken wing almost healed.

Somehow, I knew my first day shift was going to be interesting. I could feel it. Sergeant Wells made an announcement.

"You will all be pleased to know that Nicole continues to make excellent progress. She is, of course, still in hospital. Her father and our Jimmie have been overwhelmed by the acts of kindness and generosity pouring out from this police department, especially this division. As of this morning, Callaghan's is now open for business. It's breakfast as usual. Ordinarily, we don't like to see cruisers parked all along the street and have asked you all to be, discreet. This morning, park where the hell you like. If the Brass question it, direct them to me." The parade room erupted into cheers and loud applause. "Sam, before you head out. S and M are in early. They'd like to speak to you." I nodded. No emotion. No increase in heart rate.

Good job, said the Weatherman. *I'm proud of you. Keep it together, Sam. Don't let them rattle you.*

"Thanks, Leroy." The whole parade just stared at me. Sergeant Wells gave me a strange look.

"Are you all right, Sam?"

"I'm fine, Sergeant. It's a good day."

As I made my way down to homicide I heard someone say, "Who's Leroy?"

"No idea. I think Sam's losing his mind."

I stepped through the door marked *Homicide.* S and M were huddled by the coffee percolator.

"The wanderer returns," said Detective Santoro. "Where have you been, Sam? Bruno and I have been phoning you, leaving messages, and banging on your door constantly."

"I've been, *away*."

"Away where?" said Detective Moretti.

I looked at them both, a stern look on my face. "I've been to a place we *Indians* call, *Away*."

"Detective Santoro. Have you heard of this mystical place called, *Away*?"

"News to me, Detective Moretti. Is it like one of those *Far, far away places,* like in a children's fairy tale? I'll call in at the travel agents on my way home and see if I can pick up a brochure."

"What a splendid idea, Detective Santoro. Are you sure you don't mind?"

"Absolutely not, Detective Moretti. No trouble at all."

They heard my exasperated sigh.

Moretti smiled. "Coffee, Sam?"

"Sure. Black. No sugar."

"Detective Santoro and I have been following up on some interesting developments in your absence. All based on your hunches. That's why we were trying to contact you. We wanted you to give us a hand."

"You were right," said Santoro. "The brand new Ford Mustang was never crushed. One of the security guards kept it himself, just like you said. We found him, and the car. The car's with Ident. This time they've exceeded themselves, probably because they want a free breakfast at Callaghan's. They found hair fibres and blood matching …"

"Orysia's," interjected Moretti.

They knew I didn't like them referring to her as a hooker.

"Yeah, Orysia's. So, we executed a warrant at the Jansen-Simms mansion. This time we took our SWAT team with us. We heard what happened to Detectives Morton and Swane during their visit. His security team didn't want to play with ours. At first, the old man was a complete asshole. But once we confronted him with the gathered evidence, he looked hurt, disappointed. *Do what you have to. I won't stand in your way,* is what he said. Not long after that, he telephoned our Chief, personally and advised him he was withdrawing his civil suit against the department over the boating incident. We seized his son's laptop. Our guys found some interesting and disturbing stuff on it. E-mails back and forth to a guy by the name of Robert Prusinowski and two other guys, Mike Edgerton, and Jason English, as well as some images." He slid across a bunch of photographs. "Do you know these two people?"

I stared at the photos, trying to keep my composure. Most of them were of Annie out jogging on Harbourfront. Annie out shopping. Annie and me walking hand in hand by the lake. The two detectives continued to stare at me, waiting for me to say something.

"That's my fiancée. Annie Greyeyes. We live together."

Santoro spoke. "They had a plan to abduct Annie, take her to Jansen-Simms' cottage up in the Muskokas. I'll leave the rest to your imagination. They even had a dumpsite prepared for her body, somewhere up near Huntsville, down a logging trail, apparently. We need to find it."

Moretti continued. "We also executed

warrants at the homes of English, Edgerton, and Prusinowski, and seized their computers. Prusinowski kept a special file on their activities. I don't think the other three knew about it. He was either going to blackmail them with it, probably his friend Nicholas, he's the one with the money, or keep it as an insurance policy against them in case one of them ever thought about going to the police. Take a look at this picture."

The detective pulled a colour photograph out of a brown manila envelope and handed it to me. I'd already seen it. Nicole on the ground, unconscious, beaten, and bloody, Jansen-Simms, Edgerton, and English, looking down at her, smiling.

"We had the picture blown up," said Santoro. "If you look closely, there's a window just behind Edgerton's shoulder. Now, look at the enhanced photo." He tossed another photograph on the desk. "Prusinowski taking the picture through a hole in his ball cap. Both clever and stupid at the same time."

"Good detective work, you guys. I'm impressed." I would have liked to have said, *If I'd had more time I might have caught that.* Either way, I should have noticed that straightaway. Note to self.

Moretti spoke again. "We found their vehicles by a lake in the Muskokas. It's where the Jansen-Simms cottage is located. Out on some island. They've all been towed away and Ident are busy going through them." Both detectives continued to stare at me. "Prusinowski's Caddy had the right rear passenger window smashed in. We don't know yet if anything was taken. Funny thing, though. Nicholas Jansen-Simms owns a guard dog, huge German shepherd with no sense of humour. According to Jansen-Simms senior, that dog hates people, even its owner. It's normally tethered at the cottage when Nicholas goes there. Nobody can go near it. Why it was in a nearby SUV, with no connection to any of our four suspects, is open to speculation. The OPP had a hell of job getting the thing out of the car. A couple of their K9 guys finally got a noose around its neck and took it to the pound. The old man told them to have it put down. He didn't want it."

"Other good news. You were right again, Officer Stephens," said Santoro. "English and Edgerton were not so meticulous at cleaning out their cars. We found earth and plant debris stuck in the driver's floor mats. It's currently at the CFS."

"Centre for Forensic Science, in case you didn't know," said Moretti. "Our Ident boys have told us that, from the preliminary tests, it's from Allan Gardens, exactly where Treeman was killed. We were hoping to seize their footwear, but that's not looking too hopeful. The footwear we did seize from their homes, doesn't match the impressions at that crime scene."

"We got a call from a security guard where

Prusinowski works," said Santoro. "Prusinowski hadn't been in for work, I guess he was worried. He mentioned a detective from Hold Up had paid him a visit, but didn't know his name. Said he was huge, North American Indian, blue eyes, brown hair and a moustache. Funny thing, when you were down in the underground parking lot, the alarm in Prusinowski's fancy Cadillac went off."

Detectives Gabrio Santoro and Bruno Moretti stared long and hard at me. I looked at them, without emotion.

"Wasn't me. I have brown eyes." They both looked furious, but kept their composure. No point in getting angry with me. I wasn't going to be rattled, and they knew it.

Detective Moretti rubbed his stubbly chin in thought. Both men looked tired and worn out. "I guess you heard about that massive explosion at the Jansen-Simms cottage? It's all over the news."

"No, Annie and I were probably watching Elf when the news was on."

"You're a funny guy," said Moretti with an edge to his voice. "The fucking house blew up. Prusinowski, Edgerton, and English, are splattered all over the fucking Muskokas!"

I stared back at him blankly.

"Have you no emotion? Speak to me."

"It's a North American Indian trait. We don't speak much unless we have something worth saying. We're not big on idle chatter. You white people, you gabble on like parrots."

Moretti was still angry. “You haven’t even asked about Nicholas fucking Jansen-Simms, for Christ sake.”

I stared back. No expression on my face.

“Don’t you even want to hear about what happened to him? You talk to him, Gabrio. I need another infusion of caffeine to keep me awake.” Santoro composed himself by taking a deep breath and letting it out slowly.

“He survived the explosion. Once he realizes what’s happened to him, he’ll wish he was dead, like the others. Second and third degree burns. He’s a mess. No hair at all anywhere on his body. He’s permanently blind and you wouldn’t believe what fire can do to your manhood. For the rest of his life he won’t need to stand to go for a pee. In fact, he will never need a zipper in his jeans, ever again.”

For the first time since entering their office I broke into a huge smile. All my pearly white teeth must have been on display. The hostility in the room disappeared. They were now smiling, too.

“My brother’s the Fire Marshall up there,” said Detective Moretti.

“I know. I did my research.”

“Sam, you scare me sometimes,” he said, looking genuinely worried. “If my partner and I ever really piss you off, do me a favour and give us a chance to say we’re sorry. I don’t ever want a little red dot on my forehead, with my face in your crosshairs. Detective Santoro. Would this be a good time to give Constable Stephens his present?"

"Detective Moretti, I think that would be a first rate idea. Yes, let's do it now. Sam, follow Detective Moretti and me."

I walked with them all the way down to the police parking lot. On the other side of the lot, a K9 vehicle was parked, the officer texting on his cell phone. His dog was going berserk in the back of the vehicle. The handler got out to calm his dog down, without success, and then suddenly flung open the door. The huge dog hurtled across the parking lot as Moretti and Santoro flung themselves into their unmarked car. It was Jansen-Simms' dog. Officers pulling into the parking lot, stayed in their cruisers. Others coming out to get in their cruisers ran back for cover. One officer drew his gun.

"Don't shoot," I screamed at the top of my lungs. "He's my dog."

The German shepherd hit me like an express train. Nobody in my entire adult life had ever put me on my ass. The dog jumped all over me, wagging his tail and chewing playfully at my arm as I struggled to my feet.

Detective Moretti shouted out through the passenger window. "The detective office clubbed together and bought it for you. The pound was reluctant to hand him over, saying he had to have his balls cut off before he could go to anyone. My words, not theirs. I told them the guy he's going to has the biggest balls I've ever seen. Figuratively, I mean. Not literally. *That dog's got the biggest balls in the canine world*, I told them. *They should be together, with all their parts intact.* Once Santoro and I handed over another hundred bucks, he was ours. Well, yours now."

I laughed and smiled at them. "I will pay you for him. I say this because I know a relative who will give this dog the best home he could ever have and love him unconditionally."

"He's yours, Sam. Do what you want with him. We figured you two already knew each other anyway. See you at Callaghan's. It's free breakfast this morning."

They were good. I was impressed. Honourable men. I liked them. I liked them a lot.

"His name's Warrior, by the way. Truthfully, it is. I'm not making it up," called out Detective Santoro.

The K9 officer was still in hysterics as he too pulled out of the police station parking lot on his way to Callaghan's. Warrior jumped in the back of my cruiser and came for breakfast with me, sitting at my feet like the loyal dog I knew he was. I petted him gently and reassured him in the language of my people. His ears pricked-up. He knew.

Seamus Callaghan came out of the kitchen with Jimmie. They both shook my hand and thanked me.

"You, my friend," said Seamus in his broad Gaelic accent, "will eat here free always, anytime of the day or night. You are always welcome. Now, don't stop coming because you're too proud, otherwise I'll be sending Nicole after you. She sends her love by the way and can't wait to thank you in person for all you've done."

"I've done nothing," I said.

"Sam," said Jimmie. "Don't say anything, just listen. The way it's going down, is this. There was a leak of gas from the barbecue tank that seeped unfortunately into the house. An electrical spark ignited the gas mixture and the rest is history. That's what the Fire Marshall's report is going to say. As for the dog. For some reason it got away, swam miraculously from island to island, all the way back to the dock. Can you believe it? Possibly the person who broke into one of the cars, shut him in the SUV. Of course, we'll never really know now, will we. But I know the real truth, so do they," he said looking toward Detectives Moretti and Santoro.

I looked Jimmie in the eye and smiled. "Jimmie, my good friend. You guys have got it all wrong. It's a nice story. I only wish it were true."

The End

Also from Ronald Ady Crouch published by
Books We Love Ltd.

O'Malley's Cottage
Murder On Spithandle Lane

About the Author

Ron was born in Brighton, England and has worked in the U.K. and Canada for over thirty years as a police officer. He has extensive international travel experience while working with the British Merchant Navy as a navigator, where he travelled extensively in the Middle East and throughout Europe.

He is an avid outdoorsman, enjoying wilderness camping throughout the year. With a love of nature, he also paints in watercolors. Ron has always had a passion for writing which started in his early years. He enjoys writing in various genres, both adult and children's fiction. He continues to write from his home in Ontario, Canada.

Author Site
www.ronaldadycrouch.com
Facebook:
https://www.facebook.com/ronadycrouch
Twitter: https://twitter.com/#!/ontariowriter
Shelfari: http://bit.ly/wwFGqd
Watercolour Paintings:
www.etsy.com/shop/roncrouchfineart